THE LADY IS A SPY

A DANGEROUS LADIES OF PARIS ROMANCE

ANNA KLEIN

BONNETPUNK PRESS

Originally published as Maid for the Musketeer in 2019. This edition published 2022

Published by Bonnetpunk Press

[Kindle] ISBN 978-0-473-62362-3

[Softcover] ISBN 978-0-473-62360-9

[Softcover POD] ISBN 978-0-473-62361-6

Cover by GetCovers

ACKNOWLEDGMENTS

I want to thank all the people who were involved in the long editing process for this book: Emma Bryson, for her fantastic and insightful feedback on an early draft of this novel. I'm grateful to to my editing team at Hot Tree Editing. And thank you also to my star proofreader, Amy Hart.

I want to thank the people who read it early and gave me useful and encouraging feedback: Elle, Ellen, Moo, Prema and Sarah. Prema and Moo in particular went above and beyond with their attention to detail and helping me get this as good as possible.

I am, as always, indebted to others in the writing and publishing world for helping me. I want to thank the SPA Girls for their ongoing mentoring support, Jamie for trying risky new things and encouraging me to do the same, and Michelle for being my convention-buddy and constant cheerleader.

I owe thanks to the world of Three Musketeers inspired movies, TV and books that came before me, for giving me inspiration. And thank you to Derek who introduced me to it all.

There are not enough thanks in this world to adequately express my gratitude to my Mum and Dad, to my sister Judit, and to my husband Tigger. Without your practical and emotional support, I wouldn't be able to tell these stories. Thanks so much.

To everyone who helped bring 'Not-Quite-Paris' to life
October 2016 - March 2019

AUTHOR'S NOTE

HISTORY IS MORE WHAT YOU'D CALL A GUIDELINE, THAN ACTUAL RULES...

This novel is not historical fiction, it's more accurately described as historical fanfiction. This book in no way seeks to represent actual historical events.

Like most works of fiction set in the 'heroic musketeer' setting (including Alexandre Dumas's original novels) it borrows historical figures and historical situations, and uses them as fodder for tales of adventure and romance. King Louis XIII, Queen Anne of Austria, and Cardinal Richelieu all existed - but while characters in this book bear their names, they are fictional characters inspired by their real world counterparts.

CHAPTER 1

"Stop! Thief!"

Shouts rang out behind Gregoire as he half climbed, half fell from a second-story window. Grunting, he pulled himself to his feet and set off at a brisk pace. Perhaps he was dazed from the fall—or more likely, he thought with a guilty twist of his gut, his judgement was impaired by the drink—but he didn't see the coachman step out from a narrow alley. Gregoire made to dart around him, but the coachman wasn't having it. He brought his arm up in a rapid movement and struck Gregoire across the face with the butt of a horse whip.

"Dirty thief!" the man snarled, then shouted to his fellows, "I have the scoundrel here!"

Paris spun around Gregoire, and he noted dimly he was on the ground again. Then the world went red in a haze of pain as someone—possibly the coachman—began to kick his ribs and stomach. Gregoire tried to scramble to his feet, but he was overpowered as more men arrived, and he found himself dragged along the cobblestone streets.

"There's been a mistake," he wheezed, only to be punched in the stomach again.

"There's been a mistake all right. Aren't you the new fellow that's been playing cards with the master? Where'd you get the nice coat? Murdered some other rich monsieur for it?"

"You caught him?" Gregoire heard the voice of the youngest son of the Marquis of St Augustine-de-Ile. "*Mon dieu*, Pierre? Is that you?"

"There's been a misunderstanding," Gregoire tried again.

"His pockets were full of your valuables, monsieur," the damned coachman said, handing the coat, its pockets filled with incriminating items, to the marquis.

"I can't believe this. I can't believe this at all." The young nobleman was outraged. "I want him hanged for this."

"Please, no." Gregoire felt something inside him snap. "Please, monsieur, I'm only trying to protect my sister," he begged.

"Well, you should have thought of that before you became a criminal! Take him to the watch. I'll be making sure he is hanged at first opportunity."

His sister's face flashed before his eyes, and he redoubled his efforts to get free, but his broken body didn't respond to his commands, and his struggles seemed to give license to his captors to abuse him once more. Gregoire frantically tried to think of how he could get away, and how he was going to pay for his sister's future, but with a blow to the head, everything descended into blackness, accompanied by angry curses.

GREGOIRE SPENT four days alone in a filthy cell, contemplating his sorry situation. His physical shape was bad, but not dire; he would recover, given time and rest. Or, as his mind frequently reminded him, there was no recovery required for the great eternal rest. Most of his time was taken up thinking about how he had failed his family at every turn. His sister was the last person he could have helped, and now he was going to vanish from her life, and she'd never even learn what became of him. What would happen to her without the resources to make a good marriage? Without a brother, or any family, to look after her?

He spent his nights praying, on his knees in the filthy straw, looking out at the sliver of sky he could see from his cell window. *Lord,* he prayed, *I care not what happens to me. Spare me only so long that I can do right by my sister. Or if I must die, please send her someone to help her.*

He didn't think He listened. But it was all right. It gave Gregoire something to do.

As darkness fell on his fourth day, he resumed his position of prayer, but he had barely bowed his head when the door opened and two men far too well equipped to be city watch entered his cell and grabbed him by the arms.

"You can't kill me!" Gregoire said, fear chilling every inch of his body. "You must let me see a priest first!"

The two men laughed uproariously at this.

"Well, all right," one smirked. "Since you asked so nicely."

"Heaven forfend we stand between a man and his shepherd," the second said. They laughed again.

Strange sort of executioners, but this must be what they call gallows humor.

They came to a heavy wooden door. The men rapped upon it twice, the door opened, and they all but threw Gregoire in. Gregoire landed painfully on his knees on the stone floor, and the door slammed shut behind him. He looked up and realized he was in a chapel.

"This must be a joke," Gregoire said aloud as he stood up.

"No joke, monsieur," a deep, authoritative voice replied

from the far end of the stone vault. Candlelight flickered, bouncing off the figures of ancient gargoyles and holy statues, throwing twisted shadows into relief. A shiver ran down Gregoire's neck. "Come here. It is long past time we talked."

Painfully, Gregoire limped toward the disused altar between uncomfortable-looking pews. Closer, he saw that beside the altar, in a round nook of some kind, was a desk with a man hunched over some papers. As he drew near, the man looked up, and his expression could be nominally termed a smile, though there was no mirth or kindness, only a sort of wolfish baring of teeth and the anticipation of a meal.

The man was unmistakable, even though Gregoire had spent the last seven years in the gutter and not at court. For a moment, Gregoire found himself unable to speak and instead looked to the heavens. Was God laughing at him?

I did, I suppose, ask for a priest ...

"Allow me to introduce myself." The man rose, the red robes of his cardinal's office shining even in the dim candlelight. "I am—"

"Armand Jean du Plessis," Gregoire interrupted. "Richelieu. Traitor."

The other man's eyebrows arched into his broad forehead. "Bold word to be throwing around, Monsieur *de Medici*," he replied. "These days most people call me Cardinal Richelieu, or 'Your Eminence,' but I expect your manners are somewhat rusty, given your current state."

"I don't care what I should call you. You betrayed my grandmother. You destroyed my family—" He took a step forward, but Richelieu held up his hand.

"Sit down, Monsieur de Medici. You can't fight me in this state, and it would embarrass us both if you tried, as well as ruin any chance of us striking a good working relationship. Then you'll go to the gallows tomorrow, and what will become of poor Elise?" Gregoire froze. "Yes, your sister, the one you've been protecting. Hiding from all your family's enemies."

Gregoire stared at the man before him, his sharply defined features thrown into ominous shadow by the play of the candlelight. He looked no less ghoulish or frightening than the gargoyles. Gregoire had met him once before, when he was a young man, when this man was only Armand du Plessis, the clever politician his grandmother had taken to her council.

"You betrayed my family," Gregoire repeated.

"I'm sure it helps you to think that," Cardinal Richelieu replied, eyes boring into Gregoire.

Silence hung between them in the candlelit crypt, and Gregoire's stomach churned. It had nothing to do with the beating he had taken. Gregoire knew who was to blame for his family's fortunes. It was his hubris and an unknown traitor he had failed to find and exact revenge on in all these years. He looked away.

"Monsieur de Medici," the Cardinal continued pleasantly, as though the previous comments had not passed. "I've had my eye on you for a few years. A thief amongst the lower nobility. All your proceeds go to pay for your sister's education. What a devoted brother you are."

"There aren't many prospects for someone of my family," Gregoire said with difficulty.

"Indeed. However, your luck may be about to change. Because I'm willing to give you a job."

Gregoire's head jerked up, anger pouring through him.

"What if I don't want it?" Gregoire replied.

"Then I will perform last rites and say a prayer for you tomorrow morning when you go to the gallows." The cardinal shrugged. "It's neither here nor there for me. However, it matters a great deal for your sister."

"Is that a threat?"

"No, monsieur, do you think I am in the business of bullying the unfortunate?" The cardinal smiled. "On second thoughts, perhaps don't answer that. In any case, I am simply stating that if you die, your sister's options are drastically reduced. You've done a lot of bad things to protect her from reality. Now you are about to die for her. Is anything I ask of you going to be worse?"

"You have a reputation."

"And *you* have very few options. So before you throw your life away on hearsay, I suggest you listen to my proposal. If you don't like it, you can go to the gallows with what remains of your honor and dignity. And if we can find an accord, your sister's future will be assured. Come now, monsieur, will the hangman give you a better offer?" He spread his hands. "I'm a gambling man myself, but those are some long odds."

Gregoire stared at the cardinal for a long moment. Dammit, but he was right. Gregoire lowered himself painfully into the chair opposite the holy-man-turned-spymaster.

"Very well. What would you have me do?"

CHAPTER 2

Charlotte Menard did not know what she waited for in the enormous room with vaulted ceilings, polished marble floors, and windows taller than her, and she rather felt she should have asked the nuns a few more questions. On the other hand, she felt that arguing with women who were giving her a roof over her homeless head—who were, perhaps more importantly, women of God—was churlish.

The chair she sat in was small, just a carved spindly thing that felt at once very expensive and very fragile. Charlotte sat still in her borrowed gown, crisp and clean from the hands of the devoted nuns. There was a large table in front of her. Now, as she eyed the expensive and ornate wallpaper, she was stuck waiting in a room that was in every way the complete opposite of every room she had ever set foot in.

The feeling this was all a strange dream had not left Charlotte. Nothing had seemed real in the past four months since her husband had died. It had been a loveless marriage of practicality, but as a widow, her means were limited and her options even more so.

Her wait ended with a door opening, the sound echoing off the myriad of hard surfaces in the room. Two armed guards in matching red uniforms marched in and parted to make way for a man adorned in crimson robes that swept the pristine marble, a color richer and more resplendent than that of the guards. He strode with purpose across the room to the table, placed a stack of papers onto the already burdened desk, and took his seat. Charlotte dimly noted his chair was a lot bigger than hers and looked a lot more comfortable.

"Madame Menard," he said by way of greeting, looking over the carved desk. His dark eyes bored into Charlotte, and she suddenly realized in whose presence she was.

"Your Eminence," Charlotte said, struggling to stand from that wretchedly uncomfortable chair. "I beg your pardon. I did not realize ..." She hastily curtsied, muscle memory from years of practicing courtly manners mercifully dipping her to the right depth despite her brain having taken its leave of her. Her heart pounded in fear.

The First Minister of France was not a man that people of her station often met. The king's right-hand man, the stately Cardinal Richelieu, was a man spoken of in tones of fear and awe. A powerful man of God and state, he could make people disappear with a gesture. His eyes were everywhere. It was said, but never loudly, that it was in truth *he* who ruled France for King Louis XIII and his wife, Anne of Austria.

"Be seated, madame. I don't wish to waste time with frivolous formalities," the cardinal told her, his face unsmiling but voice cordial. Charlotte sat back down and hid her shaking hands in the folds of her skirt.

"Thank you, Your Eminence."

There were a few beats of silence as the cardinal glanced over the topmost sheet of parchment.

"I trust you are flourishing in the hospitality of Port-

Royal-des-Champs convent?" he asked without looking at her.

"Yes, Your Eminence. I am grateful for their care and hospitality." Seconds ticked by, and the pressure in the room was intolerable. Despite its soaring ceilings, the place felt more closed-in than the cramped apartment where she had lived with her husband.

"I understand you are a widow, Madame Menard? And turned out by your landlord into the streets?"

A chill ran down Charlotte's spine. "Yes. My husband died some four months past."

"My condolences, madame. I will remember him in my prayers tonight."

"He was not a good man," Charlotte said, then felt color rise to her cheeks. Surely, she should not be showing judgement in front of a holy man, even if that holy man was whispered to be a murderer himself. She glanced up at his face. It was unreadable.

"And he left you on your own with no income, in Paris."

"Yes, Your Eminence," Charlotte confirmed reluctantly, looking down. Memories of Gustav's death were less painful than the fear she had felt in the months since. After the momentary relief of realizing she was free of him, there came the mounting panic for her future.

"I understand from the holy sisters that you are in a most terrible of situations with the debts your husband had, which you did not know of. How those he owed came and took everything of value. How your landlord turned you out, cruelly, even though you had paid the rent he asked. How you lost the garden you were living off by making poultices and the like."

"I'm not a witch," Charlotte whispered.

"I never considered that you might be," the cardinal said with a chuckle. He seemed to not notice her fear. "I know the difference between herbs for a toothache and the work of the devil, madame. Merely, I meant without your husband, with no savings, no apparent inclination to seek out family, and now with no hope of an independent industry"—he spread his hands—"what future awaits a widow with no prospect?"

"I don't know, Your Eminence," Charlotte whispered, looking down to hide her tears. She clutched her skirts tight enough to turn her knuckles white. The abject hopelessness the cardinal laid out so easily was what she had avoided thinking of since the relief of her husband's death had passed. Now it was impossible to avoid, hanging in the air between herself and the most powerful man in France.

"Which is why I wanted to offer you an opportunity."

Charlotte's head snapped up. She blinked, uncomprehending. He continued.

"You are in need of a stable position, in a respectable fashion, and for some support while you get back on your feet. You are a young widow. I'm certain, in time, you will attract another husband, but even so, I'm sure you would be loath to be dependent on a man for your support again." There was a knowing look in his eyes that Charlotte could not quite decipher. "And I am in need of some assistance on a delicate matter, and one I believe you will be well suited for."

Charlotte could not shake the sudden impression that he knew more about her life than she had told the nuns, more about her life than he had any sensible reason to know. And what was a cardinal doing telling her about independence? It was the preachers who spent all day long in the pulpits haranguing women to the altar and the marriage bed.

Charlotte had once seen some street graffiti in which the cardinal had been depicted as an enormous red spider with long legs that stretched to all parts of an all-encompassing web. And she suddenly had the sinking realization that she had been pulled into that web.

"What assistance can I render to one such as Your Eminence?" Charlotte asked.

His smile widened, a toothy smile, as if that was exactly the question he had been hoping for. He rose from the desk and walked over to the window. "You know, of course, that France has many enemies. Spain is, at best, a fickle older brother—close but constantly wanting to test his strength against us. England is the eternal thorn in our side, the potential enemy just over the channel. The Protestants from the north, from Germany and Holland, are a perpetual threat. While you know this, I think you scarcely imagine the amount of danger France's most loyal friends thwart every day."

"Your Eminence, I have no aversion to helping, but there is little I can do about England or Spain, if they've made their minds up against France. I grow herbs and make medicinal teas. That will not help anyone win a war."

"You are literate, well spoken, and have impeccable manners. You've been trained, rather well, to be of service to noble women." He turned and swept across the distance between them to stand over her. "And that is precisely what I need you to do. There is a noblewoman visiting here from England. She is in need of a lady's maid, and it would be advantageous to the both of us if you were to take this position. You will be well paid, you will be in a position above reproach, and you will want for none of the necessities of life."

He was very tall from where Charlotte sat. With the rich, red velvet tumbling from his shoulders and sleeves, the sharp lines of his jaw and cheekbones, and an angular dark moustache and beard, Charlotte wanted to say he looked intimidating, but he was captivating more than anything else.

"So the stories are true," Charlotte heard herself whisper. "You are the red spider at the center of the web."

This made him smile even more as he calmly swept back to his desk. He clearly felt she needed no more intimidation. "If you're this good at hearing stories about everyone, then I am doubly pleased this opportunity is available for us both." He steepled his fingers and looked at her over them. "Well, Madame Menard?"

"You want me to be a spy." Her stomach clenched. "To snoop and eavesdrop and betray?" A vivid sensory memory engulfed Charlotte for a second: *lying beneath furniture on a dusty floor, hearing things she should not have.* She leaped to her feet, heart in her throat. "Do you wish me to poison her too? I won't. I can't."

The cardinal waved his hand in a downward motion. It was decisive and utterly irrefutable.

Charlotte sat back down.

"Goodness gracious, no poisoning, not at all. Is that what you think I do?" He looked amused for a moment. Then his face fell back into serious lines. "Sometimes there is a need for extraordinary measures, but rarely, and only in the most ardent protection of France. After all, murder is a sin."

The protection of France. The last time she had done something in the name of protecting France, she'd lost everything she loved.

"Last time I was in a church, I heard lying was a sin too," she all but whispered.

"And you're going to have to watch that rapier wit of yours when you're acting as a lady's maid," was the cardinal's entirely nonchalant reply. "It might be mistaken for cheek, and you might be fired, and I might find myself entirely unable to help. It would be quite a shame." He rose again. "I am pleased we find ourselves both well disposed toward this working relationship."

Charlotte didn't remember agreeing to take the job, but she found herself nodding all the same.

"You will spend the next few days back at the Port-Royal-des-Champs. There you will be instructed in any details that are lacking from your repertoire, the latest fashions and such things, as well as being briefed on some of the altered details of your identity. When your new mistress, the daughter of the Baron of Camoys, comes to select a lady's maid from the fine finishing school, she will love you and select you. Make sure of it. Then there is the matter of communication. Obviously it is best if no one were to learn of any connection between our two selves." He waved his hand at one of the guards, who moved across the floor toward the double doors at the end of the cavernous hall. "Therefore, I have organized an intermediary. He is a member of the king's musketeers. Perhaps you can pretend to be courting or some such; either way, it will not be remarkable to be seen talking to him. You can give him reports on what you find, and he'll bring them to me."

There was a dull echo as the heavy door opened. The cardinal gestured toward the figure that approached, led by one of the Red Guard. Charlotte rose out of her chair to see a tall, muscular man in a swooping blue cloak.

CHAPTER 3

The blue musketeer cloak hung on Gregoire's shoulders with a weight that was disproportionate to its reality. The weight on his shoulders had nothing to do with the fabric and everything to do with the years of expectations and disappointment he had attached to this garment. Once, long ago, it had been the symbol of his hopes and dreams.

Marble floors, vaulted ceilings, embossed wallpaper, a glimmering chandelier ... *Well, well, well, God does reward the faithful,* Gregoire thought as his gaze swept across the room. His lungs emptied of air when his eyes locked on something that was more beautiful than all those ornaments.

Standing beside the cardinal, looking at him in fearful amazement, was Charlotte Menard.

"Charlotte." He almost choked on her name. He felt like a young man again, all gawky limbs and insecurity. "What are you doing here?"

Charlotte's face was stricken and pale as she stared at him.

"Gregoire!" Her strangled tone was an echo of his own. "You're alive."

She flew at him and threw her arms around him with such force that it nearly knocked him off his feet. He grunted in pain, his ribs still tender.

"You're alive," she repeated in wonder, holding him tight enough to hurt.

Gregoire was speechless. His heart pounded in his chest as he was overtaken by the scent of her skin and hair, and for a second, he was back in his childhood home, in a time when his parents were alive and Charlotte, the daughter of the governess, was his best friend and near-constant companion.

A time when he had loved her with all the passion that could fit into his teenaged heart.

Charlotte pulled back to look up into his face. Tears glistened in her eyes as she reached up to take his face in both her hands. "I thought of you every day. I prayed for you every night, since ... since then. When I never heard from you, I was sure you had been killed. But you're alive! And you're a *musketeer*!"

"Charlotte." Her name was all he could manage. His heart beat wildly, and he couldn't think straight. "What are you doing here?"

"I have no choice," she said, looking down.

"I am to take it that the two of you know each other?" Cardinal Richelieu interrupted, his voice calm and measured. "God *does* work in mysterious ways. This will make both your jobs much easier."

Gregoire felt nauseous as he saw the cardinal's gaze settle placidly on Charlotte.

"Yes, Your Eminence," Charlotte said, reluctantly stepping away from Gregoire, releasing him from her arms. "I am grateful to you and will do my best not to disappoint you."

His Charlotte seemed to shrink as she spoke the words,

and her eyes held a thousand unasked questions as she looked at him. He looked her over for signs of violence, for any clue why she was here. But she seemed whole and clean, and her plain clothes revealed nothing of her situation. There was a redness around her eyes that told him she had cried recently. It had always given her away when they were children, even though she liked to pretend she never cried.

"We will skip the introductions in that case," Cardinal Richelieu said, penetrating his reverie. Gregoire let out a ragged breath, trying to surface from the barrage of memories that threatened to drown him. "Madame, if you would return to the convent as discussed. He will make contact when you are on assignment. Ensure you remember his name is Monsieur Guillot. Calling him by any other names you know would be disastrous."

"Yes, Your Eminence," Charlotte said. She looked at Gregoire, relief and happiness and sadness fighting for prominence on her face. "I am so glad you are alive," she told him before reluctantly turning away, curtsying to the cardinal, and walking out of the room the way he had come in, her head held high despite the trembling of her lip as she passed him.

The door shut with a tremendous echo. The cardinal looked Gregoire up and down, inspecting him.

"It would be to the benefit of this mission if you would look happy about your appointment to the musketeers, Monsieur de Medici," the spymaster told Gregoire. "It would, I feel, sell the ruse better."

Gregoire made no response. The cardinal smirked and moved back behind his desk.

"And will you sit?" Richelieu didn't even look up. "Of course you won't. Well, I do like the silent type. I'm to take it you and Madame Menard are formerly acquainted."

"You must have known."

"Oh no, I am quite surprised, really. I don't know *everything* there is to know in France." He carefully turned a parchment over. "Yet."

"Save the mysterious spymaster routine for someone who is easily impressed. I don't want to be here. I will do this one job for you, and I'll do it well, and after that, you'll hold up your end of the bargain."

"Certainly. You will receive enough money for a new life in England, and your younger sister will receive a marriage."

"A good marriage," Gregoire pressed. "To a kind man."

The cardinal looked at him disparagingly. "To a veritable saint; I'll see to it myself. Do you have any further questions or fussing about the assignment, or can I get on with my work?"

Gregoire sighed and tugged unhappily at his cloak. "I don't want to be a musketeer."

"You must be the only boy in France to ever utter those words. I practically have to blackmail soldiers into my guard; everyone desperately wants to wear a blue cloak and be a dashing hero." The cardinal shook his head. "And here you are, throwing a fuss. I've explained it. If you are disguised as Red Guard, then my agent, Madame Menard, is far too easily connected back to me. It won't do. So you are a musketeer."

"I'm stealing the identity of some poor boy you had bumped off en route."

"I had him *rerouted*. He'll be fine. He will have a—" He paused. "A character-building experience."

"I don't like this," Gregoire muttered.

"My advice is to learn to like it," the cardinal replied, sudden and forceful as a thunderclap. "We have an accord. You get a new life in England, and your sister gets a far more advantageous marriage than she could otherwise. You will both be taken care of, regardless of your family's shambles, because I pity the fact you and she were caught up in the foolish actions of those before you."

Rage clouded Gregoire's vision for a second, and his hand went toward his rapier. "Don't you ... don't you dare."

The cardinal didn't even flinch. "Or you will what?" He stood, taller than Gregoire, and looked down at him, meeting his eyes directly. "Or you will what, Gregoire de Medici, son of Michel de Medici, cousin to the traitor Marie? You have suffered injustice. Your parents and their associates made their choices and lost a gamble. Do not blame me for their decisions."

Gregoire was the one to look away, sliding his hands from his weapons.

"My parents were belied. They were not traitors," he said quietly and with conviction.

"Then they are pardoned in heaven," the cardinal said curtly. "Now, if we may return to the present. This is hardly an onerous task and stands to bring you a significant improvement in your circumstances. Were I you, I would be counting my blessings." He sat down. "The good Captain Treville expects you on the stroke of eight at the musketeer barracks a week hence. You have a week to learn your new identity; I trust that is sufficient. See that you are on time. If you are not, I'd hate to see what sort of drunken wastrel your sister might end up married to." The cardinal smiled at him.

Gregoire didn't acknowledge him with a response. Instead, he turned on his heel and stormed out of the cardinal's cavernous hall.

Curse him! Curse him and his arrogance and his reach and his resources. Curse him straight to hell, Gregoire thought viciously. How dare Richelieu threaten his sister. How dare he speak ill of their parents. How dare he use Gregoire's misery for his personal gain! How dare he involve Charlotte in all of this—whatever this was.

God, Charlotte.

What was she doing involved in this? Did she end up in the cardinal's employ after they had lost touch? After he and his whole family were carted to Paris to stand trial for treason, what had happened to her that she would end up here? His Charlotte had never been subtle or conniving. She had been forthright and more likely to hit you than flatter you.

At once, he vowed to himself to find out what hold Richelieu had on her and free her, but he was interrupted midthought by a familiar rush of shame.

His sister. He couldn't risk his sister. He couldn't ever put his family at risk because of his feelings for Charlotte. Not again.

CHAPTER 4

On the toll of eight, Gregoire strode up through the open gates into the training yards of the musketeer barracks. He knocked on the captain's door before the last peal rang out across Paris. A man opened it promptly, and he recognized Captain Treville instantly. Fear flooded him, and for a long moment, as Captain Treville stared at him, Gregoire panicked that the older man recognized him too.

"You must be Gregoire Guillot," the captain said, smiling at him. He was an older man, in his late forties or thereabouts, though it was hard to gauge, as the wear of war was obvious on his face. His hair was thick, and its mahogany shine was heavily dulled by steel gray. His goatee, too, was heavily flecked with gray, and a day or two of unkempt growth made him look even older. Scars wove their way through the lines on his face, marks of a life subject to the elements.

There was, however, a lack of the immovable hardness that Gregoire had seen in older men, particularly those who had lived a hard life. His carriage was proud and strong, but the lines around Treville's eyes and mouth tilted upward, indicating they had an equal share of laughs as well as frowns. When Treville smiled at him, part of Gregoire relaxed, even as another part still whispered urgently, *Does he know? Does he recognize me? Will he arrest me?*

"Sit down, lad. Don't stand on ceremony. You'll be doing enough of that around their majesties." Treville waved at a comfortable chair opposite his work table. All the furniture was well worn, the floor was scuffed, and the walls were papered with maps and lists of assignments. Like the yard, Treville's office exuded a sense of being functional and well used.

"So," Treville said, smiling again and flipping open a small file as Gregoire slowly lowered himself into the large wooden chair. "Gregoire Guillot, the sixth son of the Comte de Guillot's sister."

"That's right, sir," Gregoire lied.

"You never stood a shot at getting any of the family wealth, did you, lad?" Treville said, sympathetic. "It's common enough amongst the lads here. Well, except the heirs that are in hiding or have left their estates to stewards. There's not as many of them as you think, and they don't tend to make good musketeers. What we value in musketeers is a strong sense of duty, even when that duty doesn't fit with what we might want to do personally."

"Yes, sir," Gregoire replied, feeling his throat constrict uncomfortably. He couldn't look at Treville's eyes, and his words stung like lemon juice in a cut. Gregoire knew all about duty. He mostly knew about how to completely fail to live up to it.

He forced himself to pay attention as Treville explained the mundane details of being a musketeer, nodding as Treville talked about rosters, wages, expenses, and equipment. When Treville finished, he leaned back in his chair and grinned.

"I know what you're thinking. You came for honor and glory, and instead you're listening to an old man talk about paperwork. Do you have any questions?"

"Well, it seems a bit late to be asking this, but can you tell me exactly what we—what a musketeer—does, exactly?"

"You're not the first boy to ask me that after signing their name." Treville chuckled. "Largely, we do whatever their majesties need us to do. Sometimes they tell us directly. Sometimes we have to infer from circumstances. Being a musketeer isn't like being in the army or the city watch. It's more than that. It's being ready for any sort of task. At any time. And to do it to the best of your abilities. Sometimes it's standing guard. Sometimes you're chasing traitors across France. Sometimes you're trying to get information out of people who don't want to give it."

Gregoire winced slightly. "How do we find the traitors?"

"There are people who take care of that for the king. More often than not ... well"—Treville's smile turned a little sardonic—"there are those at court who are better equipped to ferret out treason. We are just 'the blunt instruments,' as we're called. Why? Have your heart set on spying, lad?"

"Definitely not, sir," Gregoire answered with complete honesty. No, he had never had his heart set on spying. He was a man of action, which was why his current position galled him.

His answer made Treville smile again. Rising, he led Gregoire out of the office and through the training yards. There were musketeers up and about, some clearly nursing hangovers. Treville walked him through a short underpass to another courtyard where they found a half dozen musketeers warming up.

"Etienne, Monnier, Reynaud," Treville greeted them. "This is Gregoire Guillot, new recruit. For acts of extreme bravery, he has been granted entrance to the musketeers regiment."

Treville clapped Gregoire on the shoulder. "You'll be fine, lad. Reynaud'll look out for you. Make your country proud."

With a nod to his men, Treville left. Gregoire was on his own with his new company.

The three men staring at him looked several years older than he was. Reynaud was the tallest; he had blond hair he wore long. It was tied back in a ponytail with a blue ribbon that matched the color of the musketeer cloak. He had a thin, blond goatee and eyes that seemed to sit undecidedly between green and blue. He would have been striking even without the burn scar down the right side of his face, a line as thick as a thumb where the skin was bubbled and warped.

Monnier, to his left, was incredibly wiry and shorter than Reynaud. His dark hair hung in a curtain around his face, and he was deeply tanned. He had dark eyes under thick lashes and a smiling mouth surrounded by a well-trimmed beard.

The third man, Etienne, was different again. His hair was a lighter brown, wavy, and sat at his shoulders. He had a full goatee and several thin, fading lines near his eyes.

"So, Guillot, you're the new man," Reynaud said genially, stepping forward. "Been to Paris much?"

"Not often," Gregoire lied. "Big place. Smells bad." This got a peal of laughter from Monnier and Etienne. Reynaud grinned.

"Well, nothing wrong with your nose then, Guillot; good to know. Are you sick of it already and want to go back to the countryside?"

"Haven't been here long enough to tell. Suppose I should see what the job's like. Besides," Gregoire added, "the farm smells pretty bad too, and there's no good beer for miles around."

"If it's beer you want, Paris is definitely the right place for you, Guillot. On our first day off, we'll take you around, show you the sights and see how our Paris vintage sits with your country stomach."

"I look forward to throwing up in your fine gutters, gentlemen," Gregoire replied.

"Not as solemn as you look, Guillot," Reynaud said as the three men laughed in response. "Well then, let's show you the barracks."

The musketeers' barracks were cramped and far more spartan than Gregoire had expected. They looked out over the training yard through one set of windows and over a busy Paris street through the other.

"It's not much, but it comes paid for with the job, so you don't need to find board elsewhere. And it gets cleaned every day, so you just need to look out for your own equipment."

"And," Etienne jumped in, speaking for the first time since Gregoire met him, "there's a cheap little inn across the way, so if you find yourself a lass and you spend the night with her instead of us, we can signal you from here when it's time to leave your *cher amour* and jump back into your uniform." His grin was lazy and suggestive, and Gregoire got the impression this was a system of his own devising.

"Got a sweetheart back home, Guillot?" Monnier asked.

Gregoire inadvertently thought of Charlotte.

"No," he said.

"Never mind," Etienne said. "Paris has many beautiful women, and they love a man in a blue cloak."

"I'm not here for women," Gregoire said. "I'm here to serve France."

This unexpectedly set the three men off again into peals of uproarious laughter.

"A month," Monnier said, pulling a coin from his pocket and slapping it down on the windowsill. "He'll be lovelorn by his first inspection."

"Nay, a week," Reynaud chimed in, throwing his own coin

on top of Etienne's. "He'll be head over heels for a lass by this time next week."

"You're fools, the both of you," Etienne said with a knowing smile. He added a coin to the small pile. "He's already got his heart set on someone, I bet you."

"Do I get to bet?" Gregoire asked, slightly disgruntled. They laughed again. Reynaud swept the coins into a small clay pot and put it on his desk. "It's my heart, surely I get a say."

"Ah, but *mon ami,* that's the beauty and the tragedy of love," Monnier said. "You *don't* get a say."

CHAPTER 5

The following week Charlotte spent at the convent was not what she expected. The nuns she dealt with were not the kind, dreamy nuns she had encountered as a child, the ones who had radiated unshakeable serenity. No, these sisters were doing the Lord's work, and they were doing it with vigor and ruthless efficiency.

"Pay attention, madame," one shouted at her, slamming a hand down on the desk where Charlotte was working. "How do you expect to be able to send coded messages if you cannot decipher a simple code? You will not have the document at hand at all times. You will learn it."

It seems I've been vastly misled about the church, Charlotte thought to herself as she lay in a room that was barely more than a cell, exhausted after a long day of ciphers and learning to pick locks. At least the branch of it that ran under Cardinal Richelieu's command was very different.

I wonder if Jesus would approve of lock picking.

She never got a chance to pose her philosophical rejoinder to any of the sisters. Upon completing what she supposed must be the most basic course in spy craft imaginable, she was then inducted in a whirlwind fashion into being a lady's maid. The cardinal's assessment had been correct—though Charlotte never stopped wondering just how he knew so much about her. She was already well versed in most of the skills required, thanks to her mother's diligent teaching, and here she acquitted herself well with the nuns.

She preferred the exhausting days of spy craft to the slightly more leisurely days of lady's maiding. When she went to her cell to sleep, she wasn't tired enough to drift off immediately, and instead she found her thoughts returning to Gregoire.

Happiness had burned like the sun in her chest when she realized he was still alive. She thought he had died after he and his family had been taken away by the musketeers, implicated in Maria de Medici's failed coup for the French throne. She remembered vividly the day that musketeers had arrived to search the house and interrogate them all. That was Charlotte's first experience with the "heroic" musketeers. Gregoire had told her about them for years, of their heroism, their daring, how they saved France twice a day. But all Charlotte saw them do was interrogate everyone in the house, including her mother. Including her. Then the musketeers took Gregoire and his family away. Eight years ago, Gregoire had ceased to exist.

Charlotte had hoped for a long time he was still alive. She looked for him in the faces of strangers. She wanted to know if he was all right.

She had given up all hope of ever seeing him and learned to live with the ache of missing him and the guilt of knowing her part in his disappearance. Then there he was. Alive. A musketeer. Just like he had always wanted.

Was he truly a musketeer? How could he bear it after

what happened to his family? Or was it a ruse like her own position? Was he being manipulated by Richelieu same as she? Perhaps that was where he had been all these years, trapped in the spider's web.

All the feelings she had kept locked away had broken free when she saw him. The thrill she felt as a child at seeing her best friend had hit her with the force of a punch. Her chest ached with affection and guilt. She couldn't wait to see him again. Yet at the same time, she couldn't fathom how she would talk to him when she had to.

THE WEEK WAS DONE; her time with the nuns was up, and it was time for Charlotte to go on her mission. She was still a little puzzled how this was going to work exactly. The abbess had arranged it that she would be one of several maids that the Lady Abigail could choose from.

"And what do we tell the cardinal if she chooses someone that isn't me?" Charlotte asked, trying not to sound too hopeful. "Am I free to go?"

"She's going to choose you. Just be your most charming and polite self, and you're a shoo-in. The other candidates are just going to be terrible." The abbess smiled widely, obviously enjoying herself. Charlotte thought it must be a sin for a nun to be so happy.

"Why don't you just tell her I'm her maid, so we don't have to do this peculiar charade?"

"Because of how people think, dear girl. People like having choice, or the illusion of choice. If we tell her you're her maid, she won't like it. If she thinks she chooses you, she'll be that much more invested in you already. You'll be a representation of her excellent judgement. It'll make your job much easier."

"How do you know this? Is this in the Bible?" Charlotte asked, mystified.

The abbess laughed. "No, it's from a lifetime of watching people and how they behave, my girl. You'll see. As a spiritual figure, you get to observe human nature in its many forms. And the biggest thing you learn is, it's infinitely predictable."

"I don't think I like that. I don't think I ever want to be predictable," Charlotte mused, half to herself.

The abbess smiled again, this time kindly. She reached out and took Charlotte's hand in hers.

"Then listen to me. People, for the most part, in most situations, for most of their lives, are ruled by fear. Sometimes it's rational. Most of the time it's not. Fear can be good for you—it's trying to protect you from emotional harm, from risk, from injuring yourself. Fear is designed to keep you alive. But it's far from a perfect system. And a lot of the time, you'll feel fear even when you should just go on and do whatever it is anyway. If you want to be unpredictable, then here is my best advice for you, Charlotte Menard: act fearlessly."

Charlotte looked away uncomfortably. "I'm not sure I'm brave enough to do that. I'm not so invested in the dream of being unpredictable to start fighting the Red Guard in the street."

"Fearlessness isn't about violence. Fear is about risk, and risk can take many forms. Showing mercy instead of harshness. Choosing to love instead of turning away. Speaking instead of staying silent." The abbess patted her hand. "Fear is how the world controls people. If you want to be unpredictable, you will need to master your fear."

"With all due respect, holy mother, I don't think that's it at all," Charlotte said after a long pause. "Taking stupid risks has only ever brought me problems and sorrow."

"Dear girl, I don't know your story, but let me ask you

something. When you agreed to this job, what were you feeling? Was it rebellious fire and patriotic zeal?"

Charlotte didn't say anything. The abbess smiled kindly again and rose.

"Well, the lady will be here in less than an hour. You should go prepare while I set the stage."

"You should have had a career in theatre, holy mother," Charlotte said.

The old woman winked. "Who says I didn't?" Then she strode from the room.

LADY ABIGAIL, daughter of the Baron of Camoys, was a woman of average height with thick, shining blonde hair piled into elaborate twists and pinned with pearls. Her eyes were the clearest blue and sparkled out of her heart-shaped face. Charlotte couldn't imagine anyone who looked less like a national security risk than this doll of a young woman.

"This is Charlotte, recently widowed, fallen on hard times, very skilled already. Her mother was a governess," the abbess was saying.

Charlotte looked up and met Lady Abigail's blue eyes before offering a shy smile and looking down again.

"A widow," Lady Abigail said in heavily accented French. "How awful for one so young. Was your husband in the army?"

"The city watch, your ladyship," Charlotte said, looking up again. "He was killed in a disturbance of the peace." *Never mind that he was the one disturbing the peace.*

"How awful," Lady Abigail murmured. Charlotte could feel the abbess's eyes on her. She needed to look sad. She needed to think of something to make her cry. She thought of Gustav's death. For several long seconds nothing happened. *Sadness,* she screamed at her brain. *Sadness. Be sad.*

She thought of when she saw Gregoire's face a few days ago, which led to memories of seeing him and his family being taken away without even a chance to say goodbye. The world went blurry in front of her, and she quickly looked down, several tears spilling over her cheeks. She started to speak, but her words caught in her throat.

"He is with the Lord now. We must all make our way in the world as best we can."

"And the holy mother said your mother was a servant?" the lady pressed.

"A skilled governess, your ladyship. I was training to follow in her footsteps, but when I married and moved to Paris, our plans changed."

"Oh, you poor dear. And what have you to learn here then?"

"She came to us initially intending to take vows, your ladyship," the abbess interjected. "But after prayer and contemplation, we decided it would be best for her to go back into service."

Charlotte bravely met the ladyship's eyes and smiled, trying to look radiant despite the tear tracks on her face. "I feel I still have life and love left in me. I hope perhaps one day I might fall in love again."

Lady Abigail's eyes were wide. "I will pray for your late husband when I am next at church, madame, and for your own healing."

"Your ladyship is too kind," Charlotte murmured and curtsied. Lady Abigail finished her inspection of the other candidates quickly and left the room with the abbess. Charlotte's shoulders sagged with relief. It was out of her hands now.

The discussion that took place between the abbess and

Lady Abigail was audible in the room where Charlotte was waiting, and she was horrified to hear that the abbess was attempting to talk Abigail out from choosing Charlotte. Lady Abigail grew insistent that she would take no one but Charlotte, and she would have her that afternoon, not next week like the abbess suggested. With a convincing sigh of reluctance, the abbess agreed, and the deal was done.

Not long after, the abbess came in, practically skipping, unbearably spry for an old woman.

"Well done, girl, well done. You have a gift for this. She has chosen you."

"I didn't expect you to drive such a hard bargain," Charlotte said. “I honestly thought you were going to talk her out of it.”

"And now she’s deeply invested in you. See? Fearlessness is the key to unpredictability." Her smile faded, and she looked hard at Charlotte. “Are you ready for this?”

“I don’t have much of a choice.”

“There’s always a choice,” the abbess replied, voice hard and flat, her dark eyes boring into hers.

“And you’ll report me to the cardinal if I say no, I expect.” Charlotte looked down. Conflicting thoughts warred through her. In the end, this hardly seemed a terrible fate. The daughter of the Baron of Camoys seemed nice, and Charlotte thought they could get along, and she hardly looked like a spy or criminal. Maybe it was good that Charlotte was her assigned minder; she would not be harsh or unkind or too suspicious of her. There was work and a roof over her head and something to do with her days. And if the prospect of facing Gregoire rankled her, she would cope. Plus, it didn’t sound like the cardinal would display interest in her.

“I’m ready. But I think there’s been a mistake. That girl doesn’t look like she’s dangerous.”

"And you, my dear, don't look like a spy. Do you see how this works?"

"I think he's wrong about her," Charlotte said.

The abbess looked nonplussed. "Then this should be very easy for you. Pack your things. It's time for you to join your new mistress."

CHAPTER 6

The journey to the palace from the convent was a quick one, and she was shown to Lady Abigail's quarters in the wing reserved for visiting foreign nobles. Charlotte hoped very much to never have to navigate the palace passages by herself; she feared she might never be seen alive again.

When she was announced into Lady Abigail's apartment, she found her new mistress curled up in a chaise lounge with a book.

"Oh, Madame Lefort!" Lady Abigail said, twisting around and jutting her chin over the ornately carved back of the chaise. "You are here already!" Throwing aside the thin volume, she rushed over to take Charlotte's hands. Here, in the large room with just the two of them, she seemed even smaller than at the convent, her frame slight and her shining blonde hair unbound around her shoulders. "I am so pleased you are here. The holy mother was not certain they would be able to spare you until next week. I had to insist. I hope you do not mind. I am going mad here with only my hag of a housekeeper and John, the servant." She sighed. "It's lonely here in France. Everyone is suspicious of me because I am English, and I swear my housekeeper is spying on me for my mother. It will be so nice having a lady's maid again. Let me show you your quarters!"

She swept away, leaving Charlotte to trail behind her, unable to get a word in edgewise. Charlotte's room was a small chamber in front of Abigail's. No one would be able to get through to Abigail without passing through her room, a standard arrangement at court. It had a window that looked out over the gardens, a bed with clean sheets, a small bureau and armoire, and a desk. Charlotte drew in a breath. It smelled like fresh herbs—not like the pungent odor of a working apothecary, nor like the sweat of women in close confines of the convent. It felt light and clean.

"It will be enough, I hope. My chambers here are not as grand as at home. I had them freshen the sheets, and look." She held up a small journal. On the front inside page, it said, *To Charlotte, from Lady Abigail.* "A gift. The nuns said you like to read and write."

"My lady, this is too much. I am just a servant," Charlotte stammered. This was not what she had expected. "I do not expect any gifts or considerations. I am here to look after my lady."

Abigail's heart-shaped face lit up. "I know. My mother warned me not to spoil my servants. I just wanted us to be off on the right foot."

"I hope I will ..." Charlotte trailed off and looked around the room prepared with kindness. "I hope I will be able to repay my ladyship's compassion."

Abigail's face lit up again with a smile.

"I am not a demanding mistress, I don't think, and I certainly have no intention of beating you, but that's said with the hope you won't steal from me or spit in my food or do anything else horrid I've heard stories of," Abigail said.

"What I need from you is simple. I need someone who can be my friend at court. You've never been to court. You don't know how dreadful it can be with all the gossip and the sniping and rumors. And I'm English. You know how you French look at the English. As if we're about to produce a battalion from under our skirts. I need you to do my hair and dress me, carry things for me, and just don't let me be alone in that den of vipers." Abigail shuddered, her entire slight body quivering with the dread of it. "And if you can do that, then we shall be splendid friends, and we'll look after each other. Do you understand, Madame Lefort?"

Charlotte dipped into a curtsy. "Of course, my lady. I understand perfectly. I will not let you be alone in court."

"And you will not let me be betrayed?"

"Of course not, your ladyship," Charlotte said, curtsying again, the words of the lie bitter on her tongue.

Abigail went to stand in the casement, looking out over the garden paths. "My mother warned me against Paris, you know. But I'm Catholic in my heart of hearts, and Protestant England is too dangerous for one such as me, who cleaves to the mother church." She kissed the rosary she wore around her neck and turned her blue eyes onto Charlotte. "You cannot imagine how terrible it is to be caught between your home and your faith. The home of your body and the home of your soul. I pray every day that when King James passes to the keeping of his protestant Lord, that his successor will be kinder to us."

"I will pray for that as well, my lady," Charlotte replied. It seemed like what she was expected to say. Abigail appeared satisfied.

"And you, madame ... may I call you Charlotte? Charlotte, are you a godly woman?"

"Of course, my lady. I am in all my thoughts and actions mindful of the Church." Charlotte was quite pleased with herself. That, at least, was true, even if it wasn't in the sense that Abigail would interpret it.

"Oh, stop that, Charlotte. I don't need an echo. I need you to be a person, at least when we are alone. Tell me of your heart."

Abigail's expression was imploring, and Charlotte wasn't sure what to say. Her own life and feelings danced around her head, and she tried to remember what her identity was, what of her own life she had been allowed to keep, and what the spy nuns had expunged. Who was Charlotte Lefort? Was her heart so different from Charlotte Menard?

"I feel alone, my lady. The death of my husband set me adrift, and I feel I haven't found my path." Charlotte looked down. The death of her husband certainly had an impact on her life, but in the heart of Charlotte Menard, her feet hadn't been on her right path since they took Gregoire away.

"Then we shall find a path together, you and I," Abigail said with a shining smile.

They were interrupted by a knock at the door, a court messenger delivering a message on creamy parchment, elaborately sealed with wax and ribbons. As Lady Abigail broke it open and read the contents, she paled and threw the message on the floor. Charlotte resisted the urge to pick it up immediately.

"I've been invited a *diplomatic dinner* to receive *the Duke of Buckingham.* Oh, this is awful. It's tonight. We have hardly any time to get ready. Come, Charlotte."

Abigail swept into her room, and Charlotte followed, pausing to push the invitation under a chair with a swish of her skirts, making a mental note to retrieve it later.

"What does King Louis mean by this? It is well known that he cannot stand the sight of the Duke of Buckingham. So is this invitation a slight? Oh," Lady Abigail lamented, wringing her hands slightly and throwing herself down on her bed while Charlotte unlaced Abigail's finest gown and the housekeeper ran out the door to fetch Abigail's cleanest underdresses from the palace laundry. "Oh, Charlotte, why must I be English? Will I forever be seen as English? What 'comforting presence of home' can I give someone like Buckingham? We are nothing alike. There are gulfs between our stations. I am pious, he is not, and his reputation is dreadful."

Charlotte made comforting noises where she could, though her own mind was in a riot. She wasn't entirely sure what her role was in these sorts of proceedings, but she knew that it was probably expected by the cardinal that she find out as much as she could about the duke and Abigail's connection. It would have helped if she had any idea who the Duke of Buckingham was. He was English. The king didn't like him. He had a reputation.

Yes, clearly I am an excellent choice for a spy, being as well versed in international diplomacy as I am ..., she thought wryly to herself.

"My lady, forgive me," she said, interjecting in a pause in Abigail's sighs. "Who is the Duke of Buckingham?"

"Of course, you wouldn't know," Abigail said. "Absolutely everyone knows who he is in England. Even the common folk know about George Villiers, the Duke of Buckingham. He's King James's best friend, you see. He gets to do all kinds of special things and get away with positively *anything*. He's got a vile reputation for debauchery, and no one does a thing about it because he's the Duke of Buckingham. A great many people love him because they think he's fun, but I think he's ill-mannered and devoid of all piety. If I want to have anything to do with him, it is simply to save his soul."

As the housekeeper came back in with the laundered underdresses, Abigail stood to allow her ladies to dress her.

"The Duke of Buckingham is the last person I wish to be associated with, and so soon after my arrival!" Lady Abigail said as Charlotte slipped the soft cotton dress over Abigail's head. "I have not even been properly at court yet, apart from my formal announcement. I have no friends to defend me at this dinner."

"My lady, you will make friends soon enough. You are kind and agreeable. They will look past your Englishness in time," Charlotte said. "Perhaps this is a good opportunity to make it clear you are not at all like this awful duke, and that will make the king favorable toward you."

Abigail sighed and gave her a kind smile but was lost to her own thoughts as Charlotte finished dressing her and fixing her hair. Looking resplendent, Abigail self-consciously smoothed her skirt down and looked to Charlotte.

"You must hurry to dress. We do not want to be late. What? Why do you look surprised?" Abigail said at the stunned look on Charlotte's face. "What use are you to me here? Oh, you won't be allowed in the dining hall, but you can't be too far away. What if I need you? You'll be with all the other maids and manservants."

"Of course, my lady," Charlotte said and wrangled herself into her best clothes. A diplomatic banquet was a vastly more formal duty than she had expected when she was hired that morning.

"And you must tell me anything good you find out from them too," Abigail added as an afterthought.

Charlotte Menard, professional gossip, she thought to herself.

When they arrived at the banquet chambers, Charlotte realized she needn't worry herself about having no idea what to do. The palace staff were well versed in directing inept nobles and confused servants and had the entire process running like a well-oiled machine. As they arrived, Abigail was directed to one area to be announced, while Charlotte was steered toward a sparse room filled with others of her station seated at tables. Their clothes varied in their levels of opulence; clearly some had wealthier, or more generous, employers than others. Sitting apart at a table talking quietly to themselves in English were what Charlotte surmised to be Buckingham's retinue's servants, while everyone else chattered uproariously in French.

"Are you English?" one of them demanded of her when she walked in. "You're here with the English girl, aren't you?"

"No, monsieur, I'm as French as the Seine," Charlotte replied. "I was taken on only this morning."

"You owe me money then, Dubois!" a woman called. "Told you no one that pretty could be English! Sit yourself down, mademoiselle. Let's get to know you then, now that we know you're not English."

Charlotte allowed herself to be pulled into a seat, but her eyes lingered for a second on the table of the English servants, from whose faces she knew they had understood enough of what was said to know they were insulted.

"First time at one of these big palace to-dos, *cherie*?" the older woman who pulled Charlotte into a seat asked. "Don't fret yourself. We mostly just sit here and eat and play cards and talk until one of our lords or ladies calls for us or it's time to go home. We don't have to worry about the politics or the fancy talk. And your lady is quite safe in there. They've got musketeers doing security. They don't drag the Red Guard in for this."

"Musketeers?" Charlotte's heart leaped. Was Gregoire here? Would she see him again?

"Of course," the woman said and started shuffling cards. "Now, do you know the rules for playing English hangman?"

CHAPTER 7

"Next man to complain about this assignment will get a flogging," Reynaud snapped at his men as they prepared for the upcoming diplomatic dinner.

"All I said was, I don't see the point of us spending our time getting prettied up for Buckingham," Monnier repeated. "The king already knows we sometimes have mud on our boots, and there's no point in looking good for Buckingham since he doesn't look at anyone unless he means to fight them or bed them. And if he wants to fight us, then I can do that in dirty boots as well as clean."

"What if he wants to bed you, Monnier?" Etienne asked. "Then won't you be glad you have a clean shirt and trimmed whiskers?"

"I'm far from the prettiest creature in that room; I don't need to worry about that," Monnier replied. "I have a sweetheart waiting for me at the end of the night, and I tell you what, she's a damn sight better looking than Buckingham. What's the matter, Guillot? We haven't hurt your feelings, have we? If you're a lover of men, that's nothing to us. We're just mocking Buckingham, is all."

"No, I am definitely a lover of women," said Gregoire, whose thoughts had unexpectedly turned to Charlotte during the ribaldry. "They, however, do not love me so much. If this Buckingham lavishes his attentions on me, I may be a fool to refuse."

The entire company laughed uproariously, and even Reynaud—sick to death of their complaining as he was—cracked a smile.

"All right, enough of that," Reynaud said. "Our goal is to not be graced with any of Buckingham's attentions. Guillot, you should be aware, he does like to pick at the musketeers because he likes any excuse for a fight. But you just give him that deadpan look you have most of the time, and I promise we'll find you a sweeter armful than that pillock of an ambassador. Smarten up, lads; it's time." Reynaud turned to Gregoire. "This isn't how it's normally done. We'd normally have a formal introduction to the king first, but somehow most of the lads have other, urgent assignments tonight." He rolled his eyes. "You're versed in how to behave around a monarch, Guillot?"

Gregoire nodded. Reynaud looked satisfied. Gregoire tried not to remember that once, a long time ago, he'd been the eldest son of a high-ranking family. He had been raised with the expectation that his adult life would daily involve the king.

"Gentlemen," Reynaud commanded, "we're going to court."

The walk to the palace didn't take long, though the locale did change considerably. The small businesses and residential buildings that crammed in and leaned on each other around the barracks gave way to much grander buildings, and the streets became cobbled instead of being simply mud. Gregoire followed his companions as they walked through the streets of Paris, not saying anything even as they exchanged banter and jokes, reminding each other of barely concealed faux pas at previous banquets.

Reynaud led them through a small gate where the old guard on duty recognized them and tipped his hat to the company as it filed past. His eyes lingered on Gregoire, but he made no protest. They walked through a side entrance, where servants rushed to put an extra layer of polish on their boots, and a tiny old woman in the dress of a housekeeper looked them over.

"He's new, is he? Everything is still clean," she said about Gregoire. Her eyes were still bright and alert. "Comb your hair, boy." She thrust a bone brush at him. "His Majesty will die of shock if he sees your hair in a rat's nest like that."

"Don't worry, she does that to all of us," Etienne whispered as Gregoire awkwardly brushed his hair. His new colleagues sniggered and nudged each other with suppressed mirth. "I think it's her way of establishing authority. We can wear a blade in the company of the king, but she can make us brush our hair when she's half our size and built of twigs."

Gregoire made a grumpy noise. When the housekeeper was satisfied with Gregoire's hair, Reynaud led them down corridors that got progressively more impressive as they walked. Soon, the galleries were as splendid as the cardinal's had been, and he suspected they must be getting close to the seat of power.

An uncomfortable feeling sat inside Gregoire's stomach at seeing these rituals and watching the men interact with each other. He frowned as he tried to place it. Was he simply nervous about meeting the king? Yes, there was some of that, but it wasn't it. He didn't feel like an outsider; the men were doing a better job of making him feel welcome than he would have ever attributed to the musketeers. He felt like a fraud, but he knew that already. He knew this cloak was nothing but a fancy noose around his neck, and if these men found out who he really was, they wouldn't be so welcoming. He was looking forward to leaving it all behind.

His stomach twisted. He wished it wasn't like this. He wished all this friendliness was real.

Envy.

That's what it was. He was envious of their familiar rituals and easiness. He was envious that they had things they did every time they went to a certain place, that they had familiar people, familiar jokes, a routine. A home. He hadn't had a home for eight years, no routine, no familiarity, and his only family was a sister he kept in hiding who barely knew who he was anymore.

"Buck up, Guillot, it's an introduction to the king, not your execution," Monnier told him with a wide grin.

And just like that, with the word "execution," all of Gregoire's wistfulness vanished and was replaced by his own familiar ritual—seething hatred for the past. Hatred for his family's fate. Hatred toward the musketeers. Toward France. Toward the king.

"Unless you really screw it up," Monnier added. "Then can I have your shirt? I'm tired of having to visit the seamstress to get mine mended. My sweetheart is getting jealous."

"Sweetheart?" Etienne asked. "You mean your favorite prostitute, and I think she'll be more angry about the money you're not spending on her."

"I wouldn't let anyone hear you say that, Etienne. Claudine is much more frightening than she looks."

"Oooh, Monnier's prostitute is going to come get me. I'll sleep with one eye open." Etienne sidestepped Monnier's kick.

Reynaud pinched the bridge of his nose and held up his hand to halt their progress. "All right. Enough. You all know the drill. From the top." He pointed at Monnier.

"No one leaves His Majesty unattended," Monnier replied, with the air of one who has recited this often.

"No one leaves Her Majesty unattended," continued Etienne with the same bored tone.

"No one leaves Buckingham unwatched," another musketeer, whose name Gregoire had forgotten, said as Reynaud pointed to him.

"No one leaves the cardinal unwatched," continued a tall musketeer with a Scottish accent, and everyone smirked a little.

"And no one drinks, no matter how annoying Buckingham gets," finished Reynaud. "Honestly, men, he's the ambassador from England, and we are going to behave, even if he doesn't."

"I don't understand why the English king keeps him around," Monnier complained.

"Obviously he doesn't," the Scottish musketeer replied. "He constantly fobs him off onto us. I think it should be taken as a declaration of war."

"A terrible dinner guest is not a declaration of war," Reynaud said, his patience wearing thin. "It's time to work, lads."

For all their banter, Gregoire noted, the musketeers knew when it was time for business. They quieted down, checked their equipment, and marched after Reynaud into the banquet hall. The places were set, and the entire table was laden with sparkling gold and glassware. Reynaud positioned them around the room. Gregoire, as the newest recruit, was given a quiet position, not near any doors and not near anyone desperately important. Reynaud was to be positioned by their majesties. Monnier was right next to Buckingham—almost certainly for his cheek.

For the agonizingly long first fifteen minutes, they stood at attention in a room empty of all but a glittering dinner table. Then, at last, they stood through the announcements and arrivals. The Duke of Buckingham was unmistakable. Even though Gregoire had never met him, he would have recognized him even without the chamberlain's announcement. Buckingham swept in with resplendent clothing and well-coiffed and sculpted facial hair. His face was set in a lazy smile as if everything amused him.

"I do so love visiting France," he said loudly to no one in particular as he was seated. His French was, Gregoire had to admit, good, if heavily accented. "The meals here are to die for, and the company even better." He leaned back in his seat and surveyed the guests and the table, for all the world as if he were a king himself. His eyes lingered on a Spanish noblewoman, announced to be a visiting friend of Queen Anne. "And you, my dear, are new. We simply must get acquainted"— he paused as the chamberlain fixed him with a glare that ought to have struck him dead—"after their royal majesties have arrived, *bien sur*." He winked and then motioned magnanimously at the chamberlain to continue. The look of deep offence on the man's face seemed to amuse Buckingham further. Gregoire saw Etienne roll his eyes ever so slightly.

As their majesties entered, Gregoire looked for the first time at the king who had been the source of so much of his personal misery.

King Louis looked young. Gregoire knew he was a year or two older than him, but he looked much younger. His whole demeanor radiated inexperience, like a garment that had arrived newly made and had never been worn out of doors.

It was evident that the king was there under duress. He slouched inside his fashionable garments, and his face was a thundercloud with no pains taken to conceal it. He looked nothing like how Gregoire had imagined. There was no worldly arrogance, no obvious cunning. Was it in favor of this youth that Gregoire's family's fortunes had fallen?

Queen Anne's hold on the king's hand was white-knuckled, as if she, by sheer force of will, was keeping him from bolting from the room. As they sat, Buckingham fixed the king with a taunting smile. It reminded Gregoire of the smile that his older cousins had smiled at him right before beating him up or getting him into trouble. He caught Reynaud's eye across the room. The older musketeer, standing at the king's back, quirked his eyebrow slightly at Gregoire and then returned to fixing Buckingham with a dead-eyed stare that seemingly dared him to start something.

The lads were right about the dinner. Gregoire quickly learned why the night was so painful for his compatriots and the deep loathing they all had for the English ambassador. Standing stony faced while one person cleverly verbally berated another was chafing. Even though Gregoire had, less than an hour before, burned with hatred at the abstract of King Louis, the sheer one-sided nature of the repartee galled him. Gregoire never liked bullies, and it was hard to watch.

"So, Lady Abigail, was it?" Someone new had caught Buckingham's eye. Gregoire started. *Lady Abigail.* He'd noticed her briefly when she first arrived. It was Charlotte's new mistress, their target, and now the object of the smooth-talking Englishman's attention. King Louis had been left to eat his dinner, looking like he was on the verge of calling his musketeers to turn the duke into shish kebab for the next course.

"Yes, Your Grace," Charlotte's blonde mistress replied, barely raising her eyes.

"You were not in Paris when I was last here."

"Very lately arrived, Your Grace."

"Is it not a magnificent city? Not at all like London, certainly, but it has its own unique charm."

"I have found the French court magnificently welcoming and am grateful for the forbearance of His Majesty King Louis in welcoming me here," Abigail replied meekly. "His kindness is great."

That, Gregoire noted, seemed to soothe some of the king's ruffled feathers. His queen looked grateful. Lady Abigail was making friends.

"I have been to Paris many times," Buckingham boasted, swirling a large glass of wine in his hand and taking a drink as he leaned over the table. "I would be delighted to give you a tour of the highlights."

"Your Lordship does me great honor," Abigail said in hesitant tones. "It would be very remiss of me to refuse."

"Ah, well, there's code for *'I don't want to go but can't think of a polite way to get out'* that I've heard a hundred times. What the hell, I'll take it. I'm sure I can change your mind about me by the end of the tour. What, have these boring Frenchman been in your ear about me already?"

"Oh, but even the gutter rats have heard of you, Duke Buckingham," an unfamiliar male voice interjected. Gregoire saw that the baroness's sudden savior was a young man seated in a far corner. Lady Abigail's shoulders slumped in relief, though she didn't turn. "Can't be blaming us for any opinions the fine lady might have about you. You make it your singular mission that everyone you walk past talks about it for the next three weeks. And do you know what I think of that?" The young man leaned forward. "I think it's *boring.*"

"Be quiet, Orleans," the king snapped. "That man is the ambassador of England. We must be civil."

The younger man put his hands in the air. "We must be civil? And being civil means letting him get away with bullying your guests? Strange civility." He shrugged and went back to his meal.

Buckingham arched an eyebrow at the king. "Is he anyone I ought to challenge to a duel for his cheek?"

"He is Gaston de Bourbon, Duke of Orleans," the king replied tightly. "He is my brother."

"In that case, I will refrain. Not much of a challenge then, is it?" Buckingham threw a glance at the Duke of Orleans to see if he reacted, but the man might as well have been deaf. "Still, he makes a good point. Perhaps my manners have been lacking." His eyes roamed the room. Gregoire tensed as the duke's eyes landed on him. "I don't believe I've even had a chance to meet your new musketeer."

Gregoire glanced uncertainly at his new friends. He could see Reynaud's jaw tighten and Monnier's eyes dart around the room frantically. Etienne mouthed the words "Be careful" ever so subtly.

"Who? Oh, yes," the king said, glancing at Gregoire. "Quite a heroic man, new on the musketeers."

"Is he?" Buckingham drawled. His plate was empty, and he was in the process of filling his wine glass again. "And what's your story, musketeer? What heroic deeds have you done to earn yourself the plum role of standing and watching me eat?"

Gregoire didn't reply.

"Well then, a mute? Or have you instituted a policy of cutting tongues out, Louis?"

"Your Majesty," Gregoire said, looking Buckingham. "You call him *Your Majesty*."

His musketeer friends were shaking their heads slightly.

"Not a mute then, an etiquette expert. You like them multitalented?"

Gregoire knew what was happening. Buckingham was fishing for anyone whose skin he could get under. But he never did respond well to teasing.

"Since you've proved you're not a mute, why don't you regale us, musketeer, about what heroic deeds you've done?"

The king waved his hand. "Answer him, musketeer. He'll pester us both all night otherwise."

Buckingham grinned.

"Well, Your Grace," Gregoire said, a rush of aggression clouding his judgement. "I think that was standing here listening to you talk without knocking your teeth in. Then again," he added, still deadpan, "perhaps that's not heroism; that's just excellent self-control. Heroism might be, in fact, knocking your teeth in. But, out of respect for their majesties' appetites and for the cooks who made the meal, it seems a wiser choice to leave your teeth where they are, no matter how much you go looking for that punch to the mouth."

Silence descended on the room. Louis stared agape at Gregoire. Queen Anne hid her mouth behind a napkin but couldn't hide the smile from her eyes.

"Your Majesty, I beg your pardon. I will have him removed at once," Reynaud said, stepping forward from his post and grabbing Gregoire by the shoulder.

"Must we?" Louis asked, disappointed, then shook his head. "I mean, yes, yes, of course, we must. Very badly done, musketeer. Very disappointed. Tomorrow you will get what you deserve for talking like that to Buckingham."

"From both of us," Buckingham added as Reynaud grabbed Gregoire by the shoulder and shoved him toward the door. Reynaud's face was set in hard lines that invited no argument, and Gregoire let himself be manhandled out the door. Behind him was a flurry of whispers. He swallowed hard.

"Is the impertinent thug going to be dismissed?" Buckingham drawled as the door swung shut. "Do tell me it's a record, a musketeer being fired on his first day."

Then the heavy door cut off the duke's words. Reynaud spun Gregoire around to face him.

"*Mon dieu,* Guillot," Reynaud's breath rasped out. "What the hell did you think you were doing? We warned you that Buckingham was going to get under your skin. If you can't follow instructions like 'keep your mouth shut,' how can I trust you to follow instructions on the field?"

Gregoire looked down, his adrenaline ebbing. "He was making fun of the king," he said. "It wasn't fair."

"It doesn't matter what's fair. The orders were to keep your mouth shut no matter what spewed forth from the mouth of that gutter-crawling bilge rat ambassador!"

"He was picking on the king," Gregoire repeated. He finally found the courage to look up into Reynaud's eyes. "And we're supposed to protect the king. The king couldn't say anything because he's the king, and if he mouths off, it'll start a war. So I said it for him. And if it costs me this commission, that's fine. If the only bullet I ever take for the king is what was said back there, that's fine. I did my duty."

Reynaud rolled his eyes. "Spoken like a true musketeer. All idealism and idiocy."

"I am happy to accept whatever punishment you and the king sees fit."

"All right. You stay out here for the rest of the night. Now I'm going to yell at you just long enough for it to sound like I'm actually mad, and then you can go sit in the servant's dining hall and enjoy a better night than the rest of us. I think the worst part about all this is that I have to go back. It's hardly a punishment to miss the rest of the dinner." He took a deep breath. "Right. Try not to laugh."

Reynaud launched into an impressive verbal tirade, insulting everything about Gregoire's ability to listen, follow instructions, shut his mouth, and comprehend the French language. He stopped just shy of asking what moron his mother had chosen for his father. After he stopped, Gregoire blinked and said in an undertone, "Sir, I hope I never cross you enough to receive one of these in earnest."

Reynaud smiled thinly. "Don't be so sure some of it wasn't in earnest. Servants' dining is through there. The king will probably have something to say to you as well. And, Guillot," Reynaud added with his hand on the door, "Buckingham knows you're an easy mark now. Watch yourself."

He disappeared back inside. Gregoire strode in the direction of the servants' dining but stopped short. In a darkened corridor devoid of sniggering palace guards, he sank onto the stone floor and held his head in his hands.

What had he done in there? Stuck his neck out for the king, when all he had to do was keep his mouth shut? It was hard to imagine an easier set of orders. All he had to do was let a king he hated be verbally eviscerated, and he had messed it up. Though, truth be told, Gregoire had trouble reconciling the mental image of the king he'd had for years with the young man in the banquet room. It had been like watching someone pick on a younger cousin.

It *had* been watching someone pick on his younger cousin, now that he thought of it. Not that the king knew, or would have cared if he did, that Gregoire was his older cousin. Their family connection had not bought them clemency; in fact, it had damned them. They were de Medicis, not de Bourbons, and when Marie's uprising failed and the traitors were cut like canker from the flesh of France, his family had been cut with it. He had to remember that. The whole reason he was here was to give his sister a future. To escape to England.

He had to focus. He couldn't be distracted.

"Gregoire?" Charlotte's voice sounded in the darkness. "What are you doing out here?"

CHAPTER 8

For a second, Charlotte thought she'd made a mistake. The musketeer who looked up at her with a harrowed, gaunt face couldn't possibly be Gregoire. Then recognition dawned in his eyes and a smile that was unchanged by years and circumstance spread across his face. It was a smile he had just for her, and it set her heart racing.

"Lottie!" He scrambled to his feet. Charlotte's breath caught in her throat. Emotions hit her as hard as they had when she first saw him in Richelieu's office, but this time, they were alone.

For the first time in eight years, they were alone together, and Charlotte's heart was rent by joy, grief, and an overwhelming force that was old childish adoration turning into adult emotion.

"Aren't you going to tell me not to call you that?" Gregoire asked as she did nothing but stare at him.

"Don't call me that," she whispered, latching onto an old argument as a life preserver in her internal storm. How many times had they had this squabble? "It's babyish. I'm not a baby."

"No, you're not." The way he looked at her was like no look he had ever given her before. Like he was seeing someone wondrous, someone extraordinary.

The next moment Charlotte was in his arms in a tight embrace. She didn't remember if he had run to her or she to him or if they had both moved at once; all she knew was that she was holding the person who had been the dearest to her in all the world, save for her mother.

"I never thought I'd see you again," Charlotte said. Gregoire held her tighter. "They took you away."

"I know."

"Your parents? Elise?"

"Elise is safe. My parents ..." She felt a shudder run through his body. "Dead."

Cold guilt gripped Charlotte. She pulled away from him, looking up into his face, though only for a moment. The pain there was raw, even after all these years.

"Why?" she asked.

"They were deemed to be traitors because of our name. Because of our family. As if my parents would betray their country on the whim of a sneaky old woman!" His lips were pale with anger, even as he spoke in a harsh undertone. "As if they would betray their king, no matter how young he was. We were loyal."

"But if they *were* traitors—" Charlotte ventured and immediately bit off the thought at the flare of anger in Gregoire's eyes.

"They weren't, and anyone that says otherwise is a liar." His hands tightened into fists, and Charlotte took a step back. She had never seen Gregoire so angry. Nothing in their childhood had elicited such violence from him, not his disagreements about his future with his parents or fights with his cousins. This was a man's rage, not a boy's anger.

Charlotte's heart thudded in her chest.

"I'm sorry," she whispered. She *was* sorry. Sorry for more than she could ever tell him. Sorry for what she had overheard and what it had cost him, his family, and her. Guilt and knowledge sat like lead within her.

He shook his head and, with visible effort, released some of the tension from his shoulders.

"I'm not a traitor, and I'm tired of being looked at like one."

From nearby there was a muffled burst of laughter, and they both froze.

"It's from the banquet hall," Gregoire said after a tense moment. "Buckingham probably said something hilarious."

"We should stop talking about this here," Charlotte said. Gregoire nodded. "We're not very good at being spies, are we?"

Gregoire snorted, a mannerism unchanged by years. "I don't know about you, but it turns out I'm not much good at anything. I wasn't good at being the eldest son of a comte, and I haven't been good at ... anything since." He looked away. "What happened to you? After ..." He swallowed. "After we were arrested."

Charlotte winced. She vividly remembered the days after the arrest of Gregoire and his family. They had been among some of the worst in her life. Of course, she wasn't the one whose parents were killed.

"Everyone was devastated. Do you remember Madame Bisset, the cook? She cried so much she had to be sedated. And Francois Gagnon, one of the footmen? He got into a fight with the musketeers they left behind. He put two of them in the mud before they managed to beat him down."

"Madame Bisset always liked something to cry over," Gregoire said. He looked faintly comforted. "And, *mon dieu,* I would have loved to see Francois beating the snot out of some musketeers! But, Lottie, I want to know what happened to you."

Charlotte sighed. It was easier to talk about the cook's hysterics or the fact that the house had nearly mutinied against the musketeers en masse than to think about herself in those dark days. "I tried to go after you."

"You what?" That warm smile lit his face again. "Of course you did. I never should have expected anything less."

"I didn't get far. One village over on the post carriage before one of the groundskeeper lads caught up on horseback and hauled me back." And then there was hell to pay when she arrived home, her pockets full of stolen money and her dressed in boy's clothes. "Maman was incandescent with rage. I didn't get a chance to try again."

"Oh, Lottie." The warm affection in his voice nearly split her heart in two. This trip down memory lane reminded her keenly that her life was one in two acts: Before and After. For the first time since the end of Before, she could see clearly everything she had lost. That he had lost. But how could she ever compare her loss to his?

At least Gregoire was still alive, she reminded herself. For years she had wondered if she had killed her best friend. Now she knew she had not.

"We went to live with my aunt for a while, before Maman found a new position. But it wasn't as good. She had to work as a maid, not a governess. Hard to get work when your former employers can't give you a reference. She still wanted me to become a governess or a maid to a high-born lady. It wore on her that I resisted at every turn. I shouldn't have. I know that now."

"But you always wanted something more," Gregoire said. "You had even bigger dreams than I did."

"I was foolish. And in the end, I realized that. I worked for a country lady for several years. She married a Spanish man and wanted me to move with her. I didn't want to leave France. But I couldn't force my mother to support me. One of the footmen had gone off to Paris and had a job with the city watch. He came back to visit and told us about his life here, how good it was." Charlotte twisted the fabric of her skirt in her hands. She found she didn't want to tell him. She didn't want to tell him about Gustav and the mercenary, practical choice she had to make.

"Did you come to Paris to get a job on the city watch? That's the Lottie I know."

Charlotte's stomach sank at the twinkle in Gregoire's eyes.

"I wasn't the Lottie you knew by then. He wanted a wife. He asked me." She took a deep breath. "I needed security. I said yes. It was necessary," she added, as if she could explain it, "in my position."

"You're married?"

Charlotte couldn't entirely read the layers of meaning in those two short words. Was she imagining horror and disappointment?

You know he loved you, one part of her whispered.

We were stupid children. It wasn't real love, she told herself firmly.

"Widowed, actually. He died four months ago. He had debts. I had nothing, which is why I'm here." There it was, the sad and pathetic story of Charlotte Menard over the last eight years. Over the years, she thought she had made peace with the life she had grown up to, but somehow telling it to Gregoire made her feel terribly lacking. If her childhood self could see her now, she would be very disappointed. She imagined Gregoire was too.

"I'm sorry about your husband," Gregoire said stiffly.

"May God rest his soul." The reply was automatic, a safe reply she practiced and repeated so she wouldn't accidentally come out with the truth to well-meaning strangers: *Don't worry, I'm not.*

The silence lay heavy between them, laden with secrets and years passed apart. For Charlotte, her stomach was cold with guilt.

"At least I didn't have to marry that stupid girl," Gregoire said with an awkward laugh. Charlotte laughed too, the memory unexpected. "Mademoiselle Froo-Froo de Ooh-la-la, as you liked to call her. You put a toad in her bed."

"You can't prove it was me." Charlotte smiled at the memory.

"Are you suggesting there were others on the household staff who were petty enough to? Was it Madame Bisset, do you think?"

"She was horrid to the servants. And I stand by the fact that a girl who can't handle a frog wasn't good enough for you, Gregoire. You needed a girl who ..." Charlotte trailed off, blushing.

"A girl who could hold frogs without screaming?" Gregoire suggested. "A girl who could climb trees, who never cried if she scraped her knees, who could run faster than me? A girl who couldn't abide ribbons and never cared about the state of her dress so long as she could go get herself into trouble?"

"Something like that." Charlotte's mouth was dry. It had seemed so straightforward when they were children, but now they were adults. "I was jealous. She was taking my friend away."

"You know I didn't want to marry her. You were right; I wanted someone with frogs and a taste for adventure."

Charlotte realized they were standing very close together now, drawn together by the intimacy of the past, by memories of shared happiness, clustering like two people over the last embers of a fire. She looked up at Gregoire, into her friend's familiar eyes in the landscape of a troubled man's face.

"I'm not her anymore," Charlotte forced herself to say. His brows creased, a small line of confusion drawn across the bridge of his nose. "No frogs or adventure here."

The way he was looking at her ... She wanted him to look at her like that. And she couldn't let him look at her like that. There were so many things she wanted to say to him, but she had just gotten him back. She was sad, and he was making her feel better, and for just a few minutes, everything felt like they were back to Before.

"Charlotte," Gregoire whispered, reaching out with one hand and brushing his thumb over her jawline. She tilted her head up and leaned forward, not entirely sure what she was doing, but she saw he was leaning closer.

A kiss. A kiss she thought she would never get. A kiss she had coveted. She held her breath.

"Guillot!" came an indignant, regal demand from behind them. "Is this what passes for punishment amongst the musketeers these days?"

CHAPTER 9

As Reynaud led the musketeers back to the barracks, Gregoire listened in silence while his new colleagues alternated between venting their frustrations about the duke and teasing him about being caught tête-à-tête by the king with a pretty lady's maid while exiled from the banquet.

"What's the matter, Guillot? Nothing to say all of a sudden?" Monnier demanded as they left the cobbled streets of the well-to-do palace precinct and went into the muddier lanes that led to the barracks.

"Guillot is practicing keeping his mouth shut for the next dinner," Reynaud cut in before Gregoire could even think of responding.

"Don't mind Reynaud," Monnier told him in an undertone. "He's just angry because he wishes he could have said it."

The sun was barely over the horizon when Reynaud woke Gregoire and sent him to meet Captain Treville to discuss what he had done. Gregoire trudged up the stairs to the captain's office, burning with humiliation that less than twenty-four hours after his arrival, he was being sent for discipline. Reynaud dispassionately recounted his offence to Treville, who fixed him with a piercing look.

"You disobeyed an order. What do you have to say for yourself?"

"I was defending the king," Gregoire replied. "I'll endeavor to keep the urge in check in the future."

"You're to spend the next three mornings polishing equipment in the armory," Treville said after a long moment. "Don't let me hear about disobeying orders, Guillot. I'm certain you can find your way to your task?"

"Yes, sir," Gregoire said and left. As he walked down the stairs, he was certain he could hear them laughing.

It was slow, hard work, and it gave Gregoire plenty of time to fume to himself about the unfairness of it all. He was protecting the king. It was his job, wasn't it?

No, came another part of his mind. *You're only a fraud. You don't have to protect anyone, except Elise.*

Gregoire clenched his teeth and scrubbed harder.

"He's not truly angry, you know." Monnier's voice snapped Gregoire out of his reverie. "If Treville were angry, you'd be on stable duty." The other musketeer sat down next to Gregoire and picked up a polishing cloth. "This is what he makes us do when he has to give a punishment but doesn't really want to. The equipment needs polishing anyway. It's not really something we get out of doing."

Gregoire grunted.

"I hope you're not thinking of running home just yet. We haven't been drinking!" Monnier laughed. "Hey, Guillot, it's fine. Not one of us hasn't made an ass of ourselves in our first week. Ask Reynaud about the Lady of the Seine when he's drunk."

"I think it's just nerves," Gregoire offered after a few minutes. He was going to have to start being friendly. Just because he felt like a fraud, didn't mean he had to advertise that fact. "I never thought I'd end up here. I'm just a country bumpkin."

"Not so much a bumpkin. We all saw you nearly kiss that pretty maid!" Monnier grinned. "Anyway, everyone feels that way on their first day. First week. Hell, it took me most of my first year. But you're not alone here, Guillot. We're your extra pair of eyes and ears. You're not looking after their majesties. We all are. And it's not just a trite saying. We look after each other too. Besides, last night isn't anything to worry about. I think the king likes you."

GREGOIRE'S BODY ached from the labor by the time the lunch bell tolled. To his enormous surprise and Monnier's delight, it turned out the wiry musketeer had been correct. Captain Treville had received word that Reynaud, "the new fellow," and the others were invited to spar with the king after lunch.

The king was waiting for them in a private courtyard deep inside the palace, dressed in pristine dueling clothes, swishing a rapier around with abandon. Gregoire suddenly wondered if "dying for France" included being skewered by the king in a practice duel.

"Afternoon, gentlemen!" the king cried, handing his rapier off to a nearby servant who, Gregoire was reassured to see, did not seem to be in fear of his life. "So, you're the new man. Gregoire Guillot! Wonderful. What an outstanding man you are. I told Reynaud that you absolutely must not be dismissed. I don't care how bad form it's supposed to be; that Buckingham had that coming and worse besides. Armand would be so angry if I said something like that, but you! How I wish you *would* knock Buckingham's teeth in, but I suppose neither Treville or Armand would let that go. What a pity. Maybe I'll have the cooks bake stones into his pie, and he can break his teeth on them." The king contemplated this merry thought for a moment. "Anyway, I will duel you first as a reward. Warm up, lads!"

"The real problem," Reynaud muttered in an undertone as Gregoire and the others began to warm up, "is not so much that the king doesn't like Buckingham being mouthed off to, it's that it encourages him to do the same sort of thing."

"He's the king. Can't he do whatever he wants?" Gregoire replied. Reynaud sighed in a way that made Gregoire feel exceptionally naive.

Gregoire wasn't sure how dueling with the king would go. He wasn't sure if he should deliberately lose, no matter how terrible the king was, or if he should just do his best to stay alive. Thankfully, his morning's labor meant he wasn't in excellent form and Louis was better than what his wild swinging when they arrived had indicated. Reynaud gently coached the king from the sidelines, and Gregoire found himself losing without needing to play at it.

Several hours passed as the men took turns dueling each other and the king. Louis won a good number of the bouts; whether his skill was truly prodigious or if the musketeers subtly ensured they lost a reasonable amount, it was hard to tell. As they all paused to take refreshment under the hot sun, Louis stripped off his gloves and pointed at Gregoire.

"Guillot, come walk with me." He rose from where he had been resting, sliding his rapier back into its sheath. He saw Gregoire hesitating. "Come on!" he repeated imperiously.

Gregoire sheathed his own weapon and drew off his fencing mask and gloves, quickly mopping the sweat from his face. He strode over to catch up with the king, who began leading him down a set of gravel paths through the rose gardens.

"You're very lucky, you know," the king said as they walked.

"Your Majesty?"

"I mean, that you can do this sort of thing." Louis waved his arm around nonspecifically.

"Keep Your Majesty company, you mean?" Gregoire asked, confused.

Louis sighed. "You can be a musketeer. You can leave your family's house and go make your fortune. You can travel abroad. Open a tavern. Kiss pretty women in hallways."

Gregoire stayed silent for a long moment. He knew perfectly well the feeling the king was describing. He knew the tone of resentment that permeated Louis's voice, and he knew how it felt to have his heart strain against the confines of his life.

"I am sure that if Your Majesty wished—"

"Wished to do any of those, it could be arranged?" the king filled in the end of Gregoire's sentence, then snorted derisively. "It would be nothing but playacting. I am a king. I have always been a king. It is all I ever will be. And it is a great privilege, do not mistake me. France is as my own body to me. I am it, it is me, and I am not ignorant of my tremendous blessings in this world." Louis stopped as they came out of the maze of roses to a little clearing with a large fountain in it. He gazed thoughtfully at the fountain for a long moment and then looked at Gregoire. His face seemed younger than ever. "But the tremendous sacrifice that it comes with is that my outcome was predestined. In the great plurality of the world, this is all I will ever be, with never a chance to try anything else."

He sat down on a marble bench beside the fountain and dipped his hand into its sparkling blue waters. Some exotic fish darted away from his hand. Louis looked up at Gregoire, who had remained standing, unable to say a single word.

Every word the king uttered had resonated with him. It was everything he had known as a young adult growing up. The weight of expectation, the ache of predestination. He had wished so hard and so often to be free of it. His fondest hope, his daily prayer had been that he wasn't the heir to a great family, that he was an everyman, free to make his own destiny, free to marry whom he loved.

When it had come true, it had been nothing like he imagined. As a young man, he believed that it had been punishment for his ungratefulness. That his wishing it and praying for it had brought about his family's downfall. In truth, he had not shaken that belief. He had asked for it, and God had granted it, and it was folly to believe there would be no price to pay for the privilege.

Yet this was not a thing he could say to the king. The king would never know what it was like to have that wish fulfilled —if his power ever fell, he would be too dead to feel the guilt in the aftermath.

The king mercifully mistook his silence.

"I do not expect you to understand, Guillot. You are what, the sixth son? You had every option in the world ahead of you. A world of potential adventures, potential friends, potential ..." Louis trailed off again. "Anne is—I mean, the queen, she is a wonderful wife. She has been my friend for a very long time, since we were both but children." Louis shook his head. "I just wish I had the chance to fall in love. Have you ever been in love, Guillot?"

Gregoire cleared his throat. "Once, my lord."

"What was it like?"

"It was terrible, Your Majesty," Gregoire said honestly.

"You are lying, Guillot, to spare my feelings. I have read many poets on this matter; they can't all be wrong. Tell me about her."

Of all the topics for the king to pick, he picked this one?

"I was in love with a girl I knew growing up." Gregoire hesitated. "We weren't able to be together. Eventually we had to go our separate ways. It wasn't much fun, Your Majesty."

"Really, Guillot. No wonder you're not a poet. That's not a great romance. Was there at least a passionate parting? Did she profess her undying love for you as she was carried away?"

"She didn't know I loved her. I don't know if she loved me. I don't think she did. We were only young. Overall, Your Majesty, being in love was painful and confusing. It made me want things I couldn't have and be angry at someone for things they couldn't help."

The king sighed. "Well, if you do fall in love again, tell me, won't you? Sometimes I feel like I can live through other people." He dragged his hand through the water again, making a half-hearted attempt to catch one of the colorful fish. "What about that girl you nearly kissed last night? The lady's maid? I mean. All right, yes, she's a servant, but lady's maids are very good servants and quite educated and well mannered. It's not below you."

"Oh," Gregoire replied, startled. "That was a mistake. I'm not sure I should be looking for a courtship. I am anxious to do my duty for Your Majesty."

Louis squinted at him. "You are very proper, aren't you? Do you have any fun?"

Was the king telling him he was boring? What did one do when the king of France told him he was boring? Gregoire stared at the king, slightly open mouthed, and then blushed.

"No. I'm pretty terrible at having fun. I've been told I'm too serious."

"We can't have that. I'll inform Reynaud you need to start being instructed on fun." The king hopped to his feet and stretched. "We ought to return. Someone will be missing me or fussing or something." He paused for a moment and looked back to Gregoire, considering something. "Look, Guillot, I hope you understand everything I said here is ..."

"Between us and God, Your Majesty."

The king looked relieved. "I love Anne, you understand. She's everything a man could hope for in a wife."

"If I may speak freely, Your Majesty?"

"Oh, do."

"I can only imagine what a lifetime of duty would feel like. Though I do not experience it myself, or never in the extreme that Your Majesty does, I have seen it in those around me. And duty does not make a man inhuman. It doesn't make a man stop wanting things. A man's devotion to his duty is made all the more commendable the more he has to sacrifice in order to keep it. Your majesty has given up more than any of us to duty. Wanting the experience of other things makes Your Majesty a human man, not worse at it."

Louis smiled, a slow smile spreading across his face like a sunbeam.

"That's quite the speech, Guillot. I take back what I said. I think you could very well be a poet. There's only one thing I don't understand." Louis bit his lip. "Why do men like you so desperately seek duty to follow, when men that have it, such as I, dream of divesting it?"

"I cannot say, Your Majesty. That's well beyond my meagre philosophizing."

"But what brought you to duty, Guillot? Why don't you buy a commission on a ship and sail freely? Why don't you run a farm or travel or have many children? Why do you instead come to serve?"

The truth burned in Gregoire's gut. This deception would lead him to his freedom. This duty was self-serving, selfish, and not at all what he had been raised for. Gregoire bowed his head. He tried to think of something his father said, something from one of the many lectures about his duty as first-born son to the family, to the crown, to the land. Nothing came at him; nothing had stayed with him from the many times his father had screamed at him.

"I want to make someone proud," he said at last, a vague answer that seemed to confuse the king, but it did not matter. The king was already walking away, distracted by the next thing.

Who would be proud of him if he succeeded? Not Elise; she should never know anything about his deceptions.

Charlotte? She was another person he'd let down. Not just another person, she was as important to him as his own family. Gregoire's gut churned as that thought crossed his mind.

No, she had been *more* important, hadn't she. Important enough that he'd wished all of it away. Important enough that he had wished and prayed for his family obligation to vanish. He had held her higher than he ought to have, and because of his fervent prayers, his mother and father were dead and his family in ruins. All because he had loved Charlotte as a boy. Now every time he looked at her, he was reminded of his childhood.

His childhood. His loving maman with her kind eyes and soft skirts and her violet perfume. His maman who loved him so dearly, who had herself taught him how to read and they shared books together. She was the one who had taught him to be kind to his sister, who had told him, "When I am not around, you must show her the same love I do. She is your sister. She will have less power. You must be her power for her." His maman whom he had argued with so much over his marriage. Even the day before they were all arrested, he had shouted unkindly at her. She had cried. It was the first time he had seen her cry, and it broke his heart, and he had agreed to the marriage, just to make her stop.

After they were arrested, she cried almost constantly. His heart twisted.

It might not be Charlotte's fault that seeing her face broke his heart into hundreds of pieces all over again and reminded him of all that he had lost, but it didn't change the fact that was what happened.

And he'd let her down too. The truth was, he had never been in a position to give her what she deserved. Even now, free from the bonds that had tied him then, he couldn't. He was a disgrace, a fraud, a criminal.

The last good thing I can do for my family is to do this job and secure my sister's happiness. And the last good thing I can do for Charlotte is to vanish again.

CHAPTER 10

The Parisian spring was in full bloom before long. Charlotte and her mistress maintained what became a comfortable routine of church every morning, a walk through Paris, and then engagements at court, interspersed with clandestine meetings with Gregoire. The espionage itself appeared fruitless. Lady Abigail did nothing of note. Even when she could not escape a day's outing with the Duke of Buckingham, Charlotte was in attendance for the whole of it, and nothing passed except the slow siphoning of life from her mistress.

The short meetings with Gregoire were the highlights of her days, though neither of them seemed willing to repeat the closeness of that evening in the palace corridors. Even the guilt she had to deal with after each meeting was worth it. Every moment in his company was a short trip to the past, when they were each other's worlds and life had not made things hard and complicated. She at once looked forward to and dreaded the day the assignment was complete and they would have no reason to see each other anymore.

Two weeks after the dinner at the palace, Charlotte met

Gregoire outside the church where Abigail was taking confession and they strode along the crowded streets of Paris in the morning.

"I've told her I'm running low on certain threads and need to pick them up before we return to the palace," Charlotte explained. She was glad to be out of the church. Her skin felt overwarm, and the incense and choir singing made her already aching head pound harder. "She's quite relieved I'm going while she is in confession. She loathes shopping for needlework supplies."

"The two of you have that in common," Gregoire said with a smile, and Charlotte laughed.

"Yes. Alas, I am to pretend a love of it." Charlotte made a face. "But if it is the most distasteful thing I do for this job, then I'm going to count my victories."

"Speaking of which. Anything?" Charlotte shook her head. Gregoire cursed. "What does he mean by this? Setting us up on a job with no end?"

"I don't know. I watch her closely. I look through her things whenever I can. I'm even learning English so I can try to read her writing. It's a *terrible* language."

"Is she doing anything suspicious?"

"Gregoire, I swear to you, she is a boring young noble woman. She chatters and fusses and goes to confession, and most of all, she worries about being accepted in France." Charlotte threw her hands in the air, nearly losing her basket in the process. "She's so pious it almost puts my teeth on edge. There is nothing."

"Then what are we to do?" He turned away from her, frustration seething from him.

"That's an excellent question for you to ask *him* when you next meet." She sighed. Her vision swam briefly. She blinked to clear her eyes. "I should be grateful. It could be so much worse. I am well looked after. My mistress is kind. I am in higher circles than I could have dreamed. The work is not hard. There is only ..."

"The indignity of feeling like a puppet?"

"Yes," Charlotte said. "I would not be here if I had any other options. And I know you wouldn't either." She reached out and touched the edge of the blue cloak with her fingers. "I know how much you wanted this. The Gregoire I know would never betray it."

Gregoire looked at her, a tortured expression on his face.

"And you?" Charlotte asked. "How did you end up here? You never talk about what happened ... after."

Gregoire shook his head.

"Well. My mistake. Pardon me, monsieur. I had become confused. I forgot you were not whom I remember." Gregoire gave her a pained look. "Don't give me that tortured by a thousand agonies expression, 'Guillot.' You have heard of all my humiliations in the last eight years, and you have told me nothing of yourself. What have you done that is so bad? Or is this that noble boy's pride?"

"Charlotte, what is the matter with you?" Gregoire asked. Charlotte wasn't sure she could answer him. She did not know where this burst of anger came from. Was it the guilt she held or the blinding headache? She held a hand to her head.

"Charlotte?" Gregoire's voice sounded distant. He was holding her. Had they been playing tag?

"It's so hot. It must nearly be time for the summer festival. Will we go together again?" she asked and then sneezed a half dozen times in rapid succession.

"Good God, Charlotte, what is the matter with you? You're burning up!"

"I think I've caught some malady," Charlotte said. She truly had a fever; she couldn't deny it. She shut her eyes and swallowed the nausea down.

"I'm taking you back." Gregoire's voice came from a great distance. "Or should I get a doctor? Dammit, Charlotte, tell me you haven't been poisoned!"

Guilt was its own sort of poison, Charlotte thought. She looked up into Gregoire's face, so full of concern, his eyes intense and worried. Perhaps it was the fever talking, but some part of her soul still clung to his. *Gregoire and I are meant to be together,* she thought, then shook her head. Childish thoughts brought on by the fever.

"No. I think I'm sick. It happens to me sometimes during the spring." She steadied herself on Gregoire. She held Gregoire's arm as they made their way back toward the Baroness Abigail's quarters. Fever pounded in Charlotte's head.

"I am glad to see you," Charlotte found herself saying. "I am glad to see you again. At all."

For a long moment, Gregoire said nothing, only looked at her. He reached out with one hand and touched it to her warm cheek.

"Lottie," Gregoire said quietly to her as they walked. "Lottie. All I meant before was that I didn't want to ruin our precious time together by talking about my awful past. I can't bear the thought of you being ashamed of me."

"I could never be." And that was the truth.

"My dear Charlotte!" Abigail exclaimed on finding them outside of church. "What has happened? Have you gotten yourself in trouble with the law, or is this handsome musketeer come courting you again?" There was a delighted look on her face. "I clearly have the best lady's maid in all of Paris, if you are so sought after! A musketeer!" A mischievous light lit her eyes.

"Madame, she is not well. She nearly swooned in the streets. I believe she is feverish."

"A spring malady is all, my lady. I might need some rest," Charlotte explained, then sneezed again.

"Of course, my dear Charlotte. Monsieur musketeer, if you would be so good as to help me get her back to the rooms?"

Charlotte was half asleep as Gregoire carried her, Abigail keeping pace alongside them. She stole a look at his face, his clear blue eyes that spoke of the pain he couldn't bring himself to put into words. She wondered if he could see the pain in hers. Having Gregoire around was nothing but dancing on a knife's edge. Things could never be the same between them, no matter how much she pretended in stolen moments forced on them by circumstance.

She whispered a prayer in her heart for Gregoire's mother and father. Executed. *No matter how he sometimes makes me feel, no matter what we had in the past, I must keep my distance. He can't ever know what role I played in his family's downfall.*

He can't ever know what role I played in his parents' death.

THE NEXT MORNING, the worst of Charlotte's fever had abated, but she was still wretchedly ill, sneezing and her nose running. She suffered through accompanying her mistress to her regular confession, but after a spectacular sneezing fit inside the old church, Abigail dragged her back to her rooms and forbade her to attend her that afternoon.

"Charlotte, you are unwell. You must stay here. There is nothing so important happening at the queen's salon that requires you to be there." Her mistress patted Charlotte on the arm. "I'll have the housekeeper bring you up some hot honey drink, and you have my leave to go to the apothecary to get some medicine for the grippe. Otherwise, I insist you stay abed and tend only to your duties here in the apartments."

Charlotte nodded and sneezed. "Thank you, my lady."

"My poor dear," Abigail said. "You look a fright. I shall miss your pleasant company, and it is ever so good to know I have someone there watching my back. The women are more vicious than any group of thugs I have ever met."

Once she was dressed, Abigail departed, accompanied by the dour manservant, and the housekeeper left her with a honey drink before departing to do whatever it was she did the rest of her time, leaving Charlotte alone in the apartments. It was peculiar to be alone again. She had spent so much time alone when she was married to Gustav, when he was at work, and then again afterward, when he had died, she had been alone in the darkness working by candlelight. Being at court she was constantly surrounded by people. She preferred it that way. That said, she thought, sinking into her bed fully dressed and with a pounding headache, she was glad she did not have to be at court smiling today. She felt patently awful.

She had not been lying in bed more than five minutes before she opened her eyes again and sat up. This was the first time she had been alone in the apartment. What better time to search it? She bit her lip and looked around guiltily, as if someone could have heard the thought. Her heart was racing already. *When did I start thinking like this?* she wondered as she swung her legs over the edge and got up. Tiptoeing for no reason whatsoever, she fetched a variety of cleaning implements from where they were stored and looked at the apartments, wondering where to begin. The cleaning implements would help disguise what she was up to, and it would look good in the eyes of whoever walked in that she was so industrious even while sick.

Those nuns were a terrible influence on me, she told herself as she dragged a broom and a bucket filled with cleaning solution to Abigail's apartment. She had been here plenty of times before; she and the housekeeper regularly cleaned and maintained it, and it was where she helped Abigail dress for the day and settle into bed. She quickly made the bed, doing a more thorough job of searching it than before, with no luck. She checked the bedside tables, but they contained little other than medicinal bottles and a Bible. A scrub of the floors revealed no hidden trapdoors, and the window casements were sound. She checked behind the portraits as she dusted them—a hell of a job. She had to rest for ten minutes after another sneezing fit, and then she rifled through the desk carefully. There was a locked drawer in the desk, which she didn't have the key for. She made a mental note to go back to it, though she wondered if anyone would really leave secret documents in any place so obvious. The armoire too was filled with only clothes and hatboxes, and the hatboxes only contained hats.

Charlotte was carefully repackaging the hats when she noticed something about Abigail's church hat. She had seen it often enough; she wore it to confession. It was a large, somber thing. But now, looking at it up close, there was something imperceptibly odd about it. Her heart rate increased, and her fingers trembled as she turned the hat over in her hands. There, underneath the ribbon, there was something. She unwound the ribbon, which came readily away, unclasped it, and pulled the top of the hat away, revealing a smaller one beneath it ... and plenty of room within it for things such as ...

Letters.

Letters like the one that came tumbling out.

Charlotte felt cold all over. Had Richelieu been right after all?

Nonsense, she's your friend. She wouldn't be a spy. It's probably just something sentimental. Something precious. Something that might look bad, but isn't, her brain rationalized. She didn't want to find this. She wished she had just slept and not gone looking. Because if Abigail was a spy, then Charlotte wasn't merely a lady's maid keeping an eye on no one. Then Charlotte herself was a spy, and she might have to make decisions she didn't want to.

With trembling fingers, she unfolded the letters. They were not in French or even English. Charlotte's English lessons were coming along well enough that she knew she'd be able to recognize it if she saw it. Instead, these pages were in another language altogether.

They were in Spanish.

There was no reason for Abigail to be writing or receiving Spanish letters. There was no reason for Abigail to know Spanish at all.

Charlotte dimly realized her hunch had been right. The only time Abigail wasn't with anyone was at confession. Perhaps she went to confession, took her hat off, removed the letters, and placed them somewhere in the confessional booth for another agent to find.

She mechanically folded up the letters and replaced them in the hat, clasping the false dome over it and setting it back in the box. Her mind a million miles away, Charlotte finished cleaning the apartments and was lying in bed with a grippe tincture by the time Abigail returned.

"Charlotte, my dear maid! Did you do all this work while sick?"

Charlotte looked at her smiling mistress's face and felt none of the warmth, only a hollow resentment and distrust. She coughed weakly. "I wanted the place to be fresh for you, my lady," she said, the lie springing easily from her lips. "I did not want you to return to a sick house."

"You are too good to be believed," Abigail told her. "You

are to rest, do you hear me? For the rest of the night. The hag will help me to bed."

"But, my lady," Charlotte said, feigning protest weakly. The coughing spasm that followed was partly real but partly exaggerated. Charlotte had practiced that afternoon.

"I managed before you came, and I will manage now. I think you will stay here tomorrow afternoon too after church. I will not have you carried off by the reaper and leaving me bereft of my only true friend in Paris!"

Charlotte let herself be convinced to bed, and as she lay there, feverish, she knew exactly what she was going to do tomorrow afternoon. Copy the letters, arrange a date with Gregoire, and deliver the secret letters to the cardinal.

CHAPTER 11

Charlotte found her presence requested at the convent. Abigail, as a devout soul, did not impede her paying back for her charity with good works, though she made Charlotte promise she would not be absent for more than a few hours. Upon her arrival, Charlotte was shown to where she was to read Bible passages to the poor and illiterate. She was only half surprised to find the room occupied by Cardinal Richelieu.

"Your Eminence, is there a particular favorite passage you wish me to read?" Charlotte found herself asking. To her surprise, the cardinal looked amused at her quip.

"I am glad you asked, Madame Menard. What I wish for you to read are the letters in the possession of a certain merchant. The letters you recovered were very interesting. We were able to discover that the destination for Lady Abigail's confession hat deliveries is to this merchant. Another operative indicates there's certain papers in his possession we need to recover urgently. Tonight he will be dealing with an unexpected fire at one of his warehouses across Paris. His offices will be deserted."

The cardinal gazed expectantly at Charlotte.

"And what am I meant to do with this information?" Charlotte asked, confused.

"Madame Menard, coyness does not become you. I obviously expect you to go there, break into his offices, and find me the papers."

"Your eminence must have people more capable of doing that than I."

"I have many capable people, indeed, and yet I am asking you and your musketeer to do this. It should not be hard. There are no guards; it is not risky. It is simply breaking and removing. It's hardly a step above what you've been doing for me so far." The cardinal looked down at her. "Do you have any further objections to offer? Please make it quick."

"What if I don't want to do it?" Charlotte asked. Her nerves hummed at the thought, at the risk, at the potential for trouble.

"Ah." The cardinal nodded sagely. "In that event, you will need to find a way to convince yourself before you arrive at the door with the lockpicks."

"Your Eminence must be a world of comfort in the confessional," Charlotte said before she could stop herself. To her surprise, the cardinal laughed.

"Try it and see, Madame Menard. I would love to hear all about your sins."

Charlotte felt herself blush and looked away. She'd sooner take damnation in hell than tell Cardinal Richelieu anything further about herself. He laughed at her reaction but not unkindly.

"If your conscience does bother you, think of it this way. You are doing your duty to France, and the king of France is appointed by God. God will forgive you your trespasses against mortal authority in the service of the protection of His chosen regent."

"I'm afraid of being shot, Your Eminence," Charlotte informed him.

"In the event that you are, Madame Menard, then the Lord Almighty will be able to thank you for your service even faster than we dreamed, and you will take your place in Heaven with all the other saved souls." He crossed himself and murmured amen, even as something humorous glittered in his eye.

Charlotte looked at him for a long moment. "Are you as terrible as they say?" she asked, unable to contain her curiosity.

"I am," the cardinal said, with no shame or self-recrimination in his voice, as easily as though he admitted to no more than his own name. "And worse, besides. But I don't have to be. Don't look so surprised. You have not earned my ire. I can afford to trade a few jests in idleness. Don't mistake it for weakness, madame."

"I won't," she told him quite honestly.

"The abbess will furnish you with the thief's tools. Good luck, Madame Menard. I will pray for your soul." With a slightly mocking nod, the cardinal turned and swept away, his crimson train trailing after him.

"Very well," Charlotte said to herself. "Accomplished today: given a mission to break into a Paris merchant's office by a cardinal, who is also planning arson. Exchanged pleasantries; was mildly threatened. Next, pick up lockpicks from some nuns. Tonight, robbery. The sooner this is all over, the better." Despite her flippant words, Charlotte felt a rush of excitement at the thought of some harmless robbery. She pushed that feeling away. She'd kept her reckless tendencies locked away since they had brought her nothing but trouble. She couldn't afford to start giving them license now.

It was nice to see the nuns again, even if the abbess insisted on conducting their conversation in English and reproached Charlotte for her lack of practice. "It's a beastly language, it's true, but it's a lot nicer since we invaded them six hundred years ago!" she chirped. "Keep practicing, madame. You'll never know when you'll overhear something that will save your life."

Even after refreshing her lock picking skills, Charlotte still felt greatly unprepared as she dressed in her darkest, plainest clothes for the mission. With her hair tucked up under a cap, she strode along beside Gregoire in the dark streets of Paris.

Paris felt like a different city at night. Under the veil of darkness, its beauty was no longer visible to the naked eye, and all that remained was what was directly in the pools of light from windows and torches. It was Paris in tableau, with smells and noise and a certain rawness that only came when people felt hidden. She had always hated Paris at night when she lived with Gustav in a less-than-salubrious neighborhood. She was glad that Gregoire was walking with her now.

His blue cloak drew curious stares, but the citizens of Paris even at night viewed it with respect, and they were not bothered. The roar of the night-veiled city quieted slightly as Gregoire and Charlotte passed before returning to full volume as soon as they were out of the puddles of light.

Gregoire led them through the streets, and eventually they reached a much quieter neighborhood. There were no taverns here; it was all closed establishments belonging to bankers and other paper pushers.

"Here," Gregoire said. "I'll wait here. You go in. I won't move until you return. Are you going to be all right?" Charlotte nodded. Gregoire still looked concerned. "Do you want me to go instead?"

This made Charlotte smile. "No. It'll be far worse if you're caught. Besides, you haven't had nuns teach you how to pick locks. This won't take long, I hope."

She turned to go.

"Charlotte," Gregoire called after her. She turned, and he was right there, his face suddenly so close to hers. Concern and other feelings flickered through his eyes. In the low light, his eyes glowed as a pinprick of light. "Stay safe," he said finally, his familiar breath on her face. He lightly touched her cheek, and Charlotte felt her legs wobble.

"I will," she whispered back.

She turned away and walked quickly toward the building that was her target. The outer door gave way easily under the lockpicks, and she quietly tiptoed her way past the offices on the first floor and up the stairs. The door at the top of the stairs was a more complicated beast. Charlotte knelt on the ground with the picks in her hands, barely breathing as she slid the slender metal tools into the lock and worked the mechanics. Sweat trickled down the back of her neck and time seemed to stretch. The lock was not giving way. Panic threatened her. She forced herself to continue, slowly, switching tools one at a time until finally, she heard a click and felt the mechanical resistance yield.

She breathed a sigh of relief.

"Very good work," a woman's voice said from behind her. "No sudden movements please. I have a flintlock loaded and pointed at your back. I was just about to step in, actually. Didn't think you would get the lock, but clearly I had too little faith in you. Well done. You may stand, by the way."

Charlotte rose shakily to her feet. She started to turn to see who her captor was.

"Let's not waste time with that on the stairs. You worked so hard to unlock the door. Why don't you open it, and we'll go inside. Much less chance of getting caught. Go on."

Charlotte complied. The woman with the gun was

blocking her only exit, so the only way to go was forward. Charlotte opened the door and stepped into the apartment, and she heard the woman follow her and shut the door behind them.

"Who are you?" Charlotte asked.

"An operative, same as you, though it's extremely unlikely we work for the same person." The woman walked past Charlotte, continuing to point a flintlock at her as she did so. She was tall and seemed even more so with her hair elegantly piled high. Her large gold dress and her makeup seemed more reminiscent of a court function than breaking into a house in lower Paris. The flintlock pistol, however, was neither delicate nor ladylike, and Charlotte felt it was prudent to keep still.

The woman sauntered over to the desk and, with her free hand, began to rummage through the drawers. "You're new with those picks, aren't you? Most experienced people would have known to go for the wider angle pick straight off. You weren't bad; you were methodical, and that's as good as anything in the field. Kept your cool too." She pulled papers from the desk and began to look through them, still talking. "So what does Richelieu want from here? I didn't think this man was big enough to attract His Eminence's attention."

"I'm not—I don't know who you're talking about. I'm just a thief. I have many children at home. I've been paid to come here," Charlotte lied desperately.

"Paid or not, there's better thieving to be had in the shop downstairs. You're not an opportunist." The woman looked up from the papers, an amused smile playing on her too-wide red lips. "You're a widow, one of many he's found and brought into the fold. Your husband died, you have no means of livelihood, so you're in a plum position somewhere in Paris, all for a few reports now and then. A few favors. A few jobs." She smiled even wider at whatever the expression was on Charlotte's face. "Richelieu and his widows; I'll say one thing for that wretched rat, unlike every other man on God's green earth, he's figured out that women are just as smart as men and completely overlooked." She shook her head.

"What do you want?" Charlotte asked desperately. She considered the door behind her.

"Don't bother running for the door. You haven't got what you want yet. I'm here for a few things of my own. And since I bumped into you, I thought it might be nice if we had a nice chat. Just us girls." She smiled again. Wicked. That was the only word Charlotte had to describe her smile. It was as though everything she did was a sin that she enjoyed very much.

"Are you going to shoot me?"

"Only if you do something stupid," the woman in gold replied calmly. She looked up again and jerked her head impatiently. "Well, come on, we don't have all night. He's got a false bottom on most of his drawers. What you're looking for is probably in there."

"How do you know?" Charlotte asked as she went over to join the woman in searching the desk.

"His cabinet maker was in trouble with his wife, so I did some marriage counselling in the form of a nice necklace, and the cabinet maker was ready to part with some secrets." The woman tucked some letters into a pocket hidden in a drape of her dress while Charlotte fumbled with the false bottom of the drawers. One held potent apothecary concoctions that were clearly poison. The other held pictures of naked women. The third held the letters she was looking for. She looked up to see that the woman in gold was prowling the room.

"Have you got those naked women pictures there?" the woman asked. "I'll take them."

"What for?" Charlotte asked incredulously, handing them

over. Stashing the letters on her person, she replaced everything as she'd found it.

"Women who take their clothes off for drawings and paintings know a lot of secrets," the woman in gold replied. The pictures disappeared into her gown. "And they can very often be convinced to share."

"You aren't afraid they will corrupt you?"

The woman in gold arched an eyebrow at her that plainly suggested she thought Charlotte was mad. "We're in the middle of breaking and entering, I've already admitted I'm a spy, and I threatened you with a gun. How much more corrupted do you suppose I can be?" She waved the gun toward the door.

"You don't lay with men for money," Charlotte said as she moved slowly onto the landing.

"Of course I don't," the woman in gold said as she pulled the door behind them, replaced the lock, and snaked her arm through Charlotte's to prevent her from getting away. "I lay with men for *far* more valuable things than just money." And she laughed, a sound so rich and wicked that Charlotte didn't know what to think.

"You are deliciously new, aren't you?" the woman in gold said, shaking her head in amusement. "Well, all the more reason you should hear from someone experienced."

"Why do you think I want to hear from you? Why should I trust you?" Charlotte asked, feeling dismayed as the woman firmly steered her down a short set of steps into the building's cellar.

"You're in over your head, poppet, and you need to know how to protect yourself in this business. As to why you should trust me, well, I haven't lied to you once this entire conversation."

"You think I work for someone you don't like. You might kill me for that."

"You're so paranoid. How gorgeous. But stop it now. It's tiresome." For a few heart-stopping moments, Charlotte thought the woman might murder her in the dark room, but soon they were climbing up again, out into an alley behind the row of houses. "We're going to have this conversation; you might as well put up with it."

"I am so desperately sick and tired of people using that line on me," Charlotte said waspishly as she let the woman all but drag her out of the alleyway and onto a different Parisian street. Now more than two entire rows of houses stood between her and Gregoire. He would never know she was no longer in the building he saw her walk into.

"In that case," the woman in gold said, laughing again, continuing to hustle Charlotte along. "Trust me, sweetpea, it's going to be of benefit to you, since it doesn't sound like you'd like to remain under our mutual scarlet-clad friend's incense-stained thumb for long. If it helps, think of it like this: I could have killed you by now, and I haven't, so your odds are looking pretty good."

"I would just like to get a say in any part of what I do with my life."

"Such is the plaintive sigh of every mother's daughter cursed to walk as a woman in this world." The woman in gold stopped outside a nondescript building and opened the door with a key. Leading Charlotte up the stairs, the woman opened the second door with a golden key and pushed Charlotte inside.

Charlotte couldn't refrain from gasping. The interior of the nondescript apartment was unexpectedly plush. Rich fabrics were draped from the rafters, and all of the furnishings were soft, resplendent, and expensive.

"Make yourself at home," the woman in gold said gaily, gesturing to the apartment as she locked the door and hid the key inside one of the pockets of her voluminous dress. "There's drinks in the cabinet; choose anything you like."

Charlotte glanced around the apartment again and perched on the edge of a velvet chair next to a dining table. The woman bustled around, finding cups and plates and laid out a small set of confectionary in front of her. "Any preference for drink?" she asked, standing in front of an enormous glass-fronted cabinet. Charlotte shook her head. "Something expensive then. To celebrate."

"Celebrate what?"

"A job well done, both of us, and our serendipitous meeting." Bringing the alcohol over, she poured them each a glass. "To women," she said, raising her glass in toast. "May those fools one day realize what they've overlooked."

Charlotte toasted silently and noted that the woman had an elaborate black tattoo on the underside of her wrist. "What do I call you?" she finally asked.

"Clarisse will do," the woman replied. "And you?" Charlotte opened her mouth and paused. Clarisse smiled widely. "Oh, well done."

"What should I tell you?"

"I strongly suggest a lie," Clarisse replied, helping herself to chocolates.

"Call me the widow, then, if there are so many of us. How do I know this isn't poisoned?"

"You don't. But you're welcome to drink anything from the cabinet. It's unlikely I poisoned everything in the alcohol cupboard in the event of suspicious guests. Else, here." She switched their glasses. "Better?"

"I've never been more paranoid in my life than since I ended up here," Charlotte confessed.

"Good. It'll keep you alive. Now listen, I have advice for you. And before you question my motivations, I'll lay them out for you. It's a cutthroat profession, and I'd like to at least be working with fellow professionals, not poor women scared witless by circumstances they can't control. I happen to like being a spy. And I have no love for Richelieu. If I can help you be a better operative, you'll improve the game overall and possibly be clever enough to escape his nasty clutches. Else I'll help you find a way to slip away. Maybe you'll owe me one. That's always nice."

She sliced up some fruit and laid it out in front of her. Charlotte gave in and reached out for a handful of fruit slices.

"So, first rule, you need to bank up enough information to protect yourself. You never let your employer have everything. You never rely on your employer to be there to save you. Most of the time, as long as there is no way to link you back to them, they'll cut you loose. Now believe it or not, the cardinal is slightly better than most. He's got some vague soft spot for the women he presses into his service, but I would never count on it. From my estimation, he won't hang you out to dry for no reason, but he's hard as nails when it comes down to it, and he won't save you if it involves risking anything he really cares about. And anyway, for all I know, you aren't even working for him, so just take my advice and make sure it's worth your employer's while to save you."

"How do I get out of this life?" Charlotte asked. "I didn't want to be here. Things just happened around me."

"You make yourself powerful," the woman calling herself Clarisse replied. "You make it so that you're not in a position where they can use money or threats over you. You cut yourself off from anyone you love so they can't be used against you. That's how you break free."

Cut yourself off from anyone you love. Charlotte couldn't help but think of Gregoire. She didn't love him—no, truly, she didn't, she insisted internally. But he was a weakness.

Some part of her would always yearn for him, if not the man he was today, then the boy he used to be in their youth.

The woman watched her face carefully.

"I wouldn't plan on getting out. It's a long game, getting out, now that you're in. Depending on how much like a lame duck you can act, you might be able to convince your boss to release you whenever your current job finishes, but if your boss has half a brain, they'll see you're playing it. No, play the long game. You're in it now. Get all the information you can. Get what you can for it. Don't get caught."

Charlotte pushed her chair back from the table. "Thank you for the advice. But seeing as I don't trust you, I don't think this conversation is going to be very productive."

"But I haven't even told you all the things you ought to learn." Clarisse looked up at her, smiling brilliantly. "Practice your lock picking; that's a good one. Learn more languages than anyone can reasonably expect you to know. Learn to sew so you can tailor your clothes to work for you. Learn to shoot a gun. Learn to run—learn to run faster than any man you know. Learn to change your appearance in less than a minute."

Charlotte walked over to the window while Clarisse talked. All these things sounded so tempting to her, more than she would ever admit out loud. To be able to vanish. To be able to understand things she shouldn't. To be able to fight. To be able to have the upper hand in situations where nobody would expect her to.

She looked back over her shoulder. Clarisse was puttering around the apartment. The letters she had stolen from the merchant had reappeared, and she was sliding them into an ornate box on the bedside and spraying the pillows with perfume. She hummed slightly and acted as though she had forgotten Charlotte existed.

"But isn't it lonely?" Charlotte asked. "Not having loved

ones, not having anyone close, not having anyone you can trust?"

Clarisse paused in what she was doing and looked at her with something like kindness. "Are we not always lonely?" she asked. There was no tone of wicked delight in her voice now. "Us women, I mean. We exist to alleviate the loneliness of others. To mollify men and children. Everyone uses us. In this business, they are just more explicit about it." She turned back to leafing through the collection of naked drawings. "There will be people you trust and people you care about. But how much can you care about them, really, if you expose them to the dangers of this business?"

She selected two of the drawings while Charlotte thought about her response and tucked them into the mirror.

"There is someone I'd like to trust."

"You'd like to trust. Ah, that's a ringing endorsement already."

"He's someone I'm ... having to work with."

"Your handler? Definitely don't trust him."

Charlotte bristled. "You don't understand what our relationship is."

"I think it's you that doesn't understand." Clarisse turned her back on Charlotte as she began stripping back the bed and spraying the sheets with perfume. "He's been promised something too. Do you think he's there out of charity?"

Charlotte blinked, tears of disappointment and rage unexpectedly filling her eyes. When she cleared them, she saw the woman who called herself Clarisse sashaying across the floor to her. "Here," she said kindly, handing her a drawing of a naked woman. "On the back is where to find her and my sign, so that she knows you come recommended. She can help you with some of those skills I said. But for now ..."

There was the sound of a carriage and horses. Charlotte

looked out the window and saw several people disembarking from a coach.

"You have guests," she started and looked up. The woman in gold was pulling a hook and a rope out from somewhere in her skirts and moving quickly toward the window at the other side of the apartment. "Where are you going?"

"I'm leaving, and I suggest you do too. It really won't do for either of us to be found here." She threw open the casement, dug the hook in, and swung her leg over the edge of the window.

"What are you doing?" Charlotte asked in a panic. "Is this not your home?"

"Of course not," came a calm reply as the woman used the rope to make her way down the side of the building and landed in the alleyway. "Why on earth would I take you to my home?"

CHAPTER 12

"Hurry up. Up and over," Clarisse called. "Leave the rope when you're done."

Charlotte found she had no choice. The voices were in the stairwell now, and with a quick prayer to a God she hoped would listen to her, she followed the other spy's example. Exiting a second-story apartment via a rope ladder wasn't as easy as Clarisse had made it look, and by the time she had landed in the muddy alleyway, her palms had several raw patches on them, but she had no time in which to think of it. The arrivals had entered the apartment and would any second notice the rope out the window as well as all the disturbances. Charlotte looked around, finding no sign of the woman in gold, and cursed. How could a woman in such a large gold dress vanish so entirely? But rather than dwell on it, she ran down the alleyway as fast as she could.

Before she had time to wonder about being lost, the alley let out into one of Paris's arterial streets, and she realized where she was, not a two-minute walk from where she had left Gregoire. Checking her pocket to make sure the letters were there—suddenly, she didn't have a single doubt the woman in gold would have pickpocketed them off her if it suited her—she made her way on trembling legs to Gregoire, who was there, as she left him, face impassive, waiting patiently.

"Gregoire, I need you to come visit a woman of the night with me," Charlotte said. She'd debated a dozen variations on how to ask such a strange request of a man, even one she trusted more than any other, and in the end opted for plain speech. She should have perhaps, she realized with dim regret, waited until he didn't have a mouthful of ale.

"Charlotte, are you trying to kill me?" Gregoire wheezed, after hacking up what must have been most of his lungs, while glancing about the busy tavern suspiciously. "What on earth do you need to see a woman of the night about?"

"Spy things, I think. And how to shoot a gun." She smiled a little nervously. Gregoire looked at her with the same expression he had the time she had suggested staging a haunting to frighten the superstitious stable master. She had been angry that he beat the stable boys. Gregoire was aghast when she suggested they pretend to be the stable master's dead mother to put the fear of God in him.

But she'd talked him around. And Charlotte was sure she could talk him around on this too.

"This is her." She slid the postcard-sized painting face-down across the table to him. He flipped it over for a half second before he clapped his hand over the small painting.

"Charlotte! Where did you get that?" he hissed at her. "Her looks are not the issue here. Did you think if she was pretty enough I'd suddenly have no problem with you meeting strange women of ill repute to learn spy craft and shooting?" He paused for a moment. "Is that rat cardinal getting you to do this? Because he didn't have time to say two words to me when I gave him the letters this morning. I wanted answers about that woman you met last night. If he's sending you to—"

"No, it has nothing to do with the cardinal." She yanked the picture back. "The woman gave me this ... woman of the night's details. She said the woman could teach me things. Make me better at ... spying."

"And you're just going to go do what this strange woman tells you to do? After she threatened you with a gun? Charlotte, why?"

Charlotte remembered how she'd felt the previous night, after she'd returned to the palace. She'd joined Lady Abigail and several of the queen's ladies in their late-night salon, working on her needlework, until Lady Abigail wished to return to her apartment. There, after her lady was undressed and settled in to sleep, Charlotte lay in her own bed and felt disconnected from the sedate leisure of courtly service.

She could not fall asleep as her body hummed with excitement. Picking the lock, the standoff with the gun, the witty repartee, the escape out the window—it woke something in her that had long lain dormant, a desire for adventure she thought had died when Gregoire vanished. Awake now was the Charlotte who liked to sneak, to climb, to challenge, to defy—the servant girl with scabby knees and tattered dresses and no desire to know her place.

And when she heard Clarisse's advice in her head: *Practice lock picking. Know more languages. Tailor your clothes. Learn to shoot a gun. Run faster than any man you know. Change your appearance in less than a minute.*

She yearned to learn it all. It filled her not with fear but excitement. She still had no desire at all to remain in the spy business, and despite Clarisse's stark predictions, she was confident she would be free just as soon as she uncovered what Lady Abigail was up to. But these skills were more useful than just in spy craft. With skills like that ... she might never be helpless or dependent again.

"Charlotte?" Gregoire's voice called her back to the present.

"She said she could teach me things. Things that would help keep me safe. Please, Gregoire."

"Fine," he relented, and picked up his hat. "But only because I know if I don't go with you you'll just go alone."

"At least I'm not asking you to help me pretend to be someone's dead mother this time," Charlotte said as she followed him out of the tavern.

A laugh burst out of Gregoire. "You're right." He grinned at the memory. "The veil caught fire and we nearly burned the stable down. That still has to be your worst idea to date."

Not by a long shot. Charlotte felt cold guilt pierce her stomach. For a second, she could smell the dust under the settee where she hid, pressed against the ground, wishing she were deaf. *Not my worst idea by far.*

"It worked though," Charlotte said, forcing herself to sound cheerful as they exited the tavern and walked into the streets. "He was convinced the devil himself was after him, and he never laid a violent hand on anyone again."

In the light from a window they passed, she could see the smile on his face. Charlotte's heart thumped. In these moments, she could see the old Gregoire. He looked at her out of the corner of his eye, and they both burst out laughing at the memory.

When they arrived at the address and rang the bell, they were greeted by a tall, thin man with features so delicate they looked as though they had been daubed on by a master painter. His opulent silk frock coat was a brilliant shade of red, glowing like hot coals under the lights. He looked at them expectantly.

Charlotte thrust the picture forward.

"*Bonsoir*. We'd like to see this woman, please."

The man looked down at the picture, and then his gaze roved over Charlotte and Gregoire.

"Madame Sabine. Is she expecting you?" He flipped open the large book he was carrying and drew his finger down the lines of a ledger.

"No," Charlotte admitted. She felt quite foolish. She was a lady of the *night*. It was night time. She had engagements.

"When might she be free?" Gregoire inquired. The expression on his face was so serious, one might think he was asking to see a diplomat. "We need only a short time—fifteen minutes at most."

"Really." The man raised one sculpted eyebrow slowly. "Most men, monsieur, would not be quite so ... open with that fact."

Charlotte bit the insides of her cheeks as Gregoire turned the color of the man's frock coat.

"As your luck would have it, Madame Sabine will conclude her present engagement shortly and has some time afterward. I am sure she will take pity on you. Please be seated." He snapped his book shut and waved them inside with a long-fingered hand. The door locked behind them, he smirked at them and disappeared through an inner door.

Charlotte and Gregoire sat on a scarlet sofa so plush they nearly sank into it. Charlotte could think of no topic of conversation appropriate for what she presumed was the antechamber of a bawdy house.

As they sat in silence, the ceiling above them began to creak, erratically at first, then hitting a rhythmic stride. Gregoire cleared his throat and gazed at the wall, apparently absorbed in the embossed wallpaper.

I've come with Gregoire to visit a prostitute. She clutched her skirts tightly. *We are listening to people have sex above us.* Now she too was red, staring straight ahead, barely breathing. *We're adults. I'm a widow for heaven's sake, not a blushing bride. I know about the realities of carnal relations.* She just wished she did not have to be so aware of carnal relations with Gregoire so close by. She was keenly aware of him beside her, his body carefully not touching hers, held in rigid tension, as they were serenaded by the increasingly vigorous creaks.

Then the ... noise started.

Charlotte guessed it must be some kind of expression of pleasure, though it reminded her of nothing so much as ...

"Nostradamus." Gregoire said from beside her in a strangled voice. "Nostradamus, the cook's favorite goose."

"Yes!" Charlotte cried. "That's *exactly* what it sounds like."

Upstairs, the lovers continued making their moan-honks of pleasure. Charlotte made the mistake of catching Gregoire's eye, and they were both lost to mirth, the tension gone, the absurdity of the situation making it safe for Charlotte to lean on Gregoire for support as they both shook with laughter. Suddenly it did not seem threatening to feel his thigh against hers as the sofa conspired to pile them onto each other, feel his breath on her neck as he stifled his laughter in her shoulder.

"Can you imagine if that's the Duke of Buckingham up there?" Gregoire half gasped.

"No, that's worse than you reminding me of Cook's goose!"

There was a soft cough. They froze and looked up to find a striking woman wearing a long silk robe standing in the room with them. Though more clothed, she was easily recognizable as the woman from the painting.

"You are the two young walk-ins Raphael told me about." It was not a question. A friendly, flattering smile played on her painted lips. She took a step toward them, the robe fluttering slightly to reveal a glimpse of expertly tailored undergarments. "I am Madame Sabine. What is your pleasure?"

Charlotte scrambled to her feet, Gregoire close behind her.

"I've come to ask about lessons," Charlotte said.

"Lessons?" Madame Sabine asked. "Is your lover not satisfied with your natural gifts?"

Gregoire made indecipherable noises of indignation. Charlotte willed the ground to swallow her up, not in the least because she suddenly had an image in her head of her dressed as the woman, with Gregoire peeling off her robe. The thought left her feeling far too warm. She wordlessly handed the small painting to Madame Sabine with its back facing up, Clarisse's "signature" clearly visible.

"Oh, I see," Madame Sabine's expression relaxed, and her come-hither swagger vanished. She suddenly looked rather businesslike. "Lessons in women's survival skills. Happy to oblige. You can pay?" Charlotte nodded. "And what would you like to learn?"

"Everything I can. Running. Disguises. Lock picking. Shooting." The words tumbled out of her. "So I can look after myself in a pinch."

"Well, then." Sabine smiled kindly. "Who am I to deny an eager student?"

CHAPTER 13

Gregoire stood in front of Richelieu's desk in the decrepit stone church where he insisted on meeting.

"I hope you know what you're doing. Charlotte was very nearly captured during the last little errand of yours," Gregoire told him.

"Was she? Well, I trust Madame Menard had the mental wherewithal to escape." The cardinal ever so slightly stressed the words "Madame Menard," and Gregoire felt himself flush angrily. His use of Charlotte's first name had not gone unnoticed.

"There was another woman on the same target. Madame Menard said she was a professional." Gregoire quickly repeated to the cardinal what Charlotte had told him, in short, hard sentences, the broad strokes of the encounter. Richelieu listened, his face revealing nothing but a degree of concentration that seemed frightening to Gregoire, as if he were trying to pull more information from his words than he had intended to put there.

"Is that all?" he asked at the end of his recount. Gregoire

nodded. Richelieu snorted and shook his head. "Interfering harlot. You'll need to inform Madame Menard that she is to avoid any association with that woman in the future if they encounter each other in the field. She is dangerous, ruthless, and most definitely not acting in the best interests of France."

"What was she doing?"

"It does not concern you what she was doing," the cardinal replied smoothly. "Suffice to say she acts in the interests of England, not France, and that she has been in business a long time, and Madame Menard best be more circumspect else she might find herself in a position she cannot extricate herself from; then we are all at a disadvantage and France imperiled."

"Not to mention Madame Menard."

"I expect she'd be dead or framed for treason by this point in the hypothetical crisis." Cardinal Richelieu made some marks on one of his many sheets of paper and looked up. "I didn't set her up to encounter the Rose. She handled it well. I was merely offering a warning. Now, the reason I have called you here is to tell you that we have discovered that the letters Lady Abigail was smuggling were being delivered to a rather talented forger. He can be found in a small shop, of sorts, across the road from the Dirty Eel tavern. Do you know where that is?" Gregoire nodded. "Excellent. You and Madame Menard are to discover what you can about the involvement of the forger, preferably what he is doing with the letters and for whom. I look forward to your report." He returned to annotating his papers in his own peculiar coded shorthand. When Gregoire did not move to leave, the cardinal sighed. "Was there some further point I can enlighten you on?" he asked, not looking up.

There were all manner of things Gregoire wanted to demand from the infuriating schemer, but he was, as always, appearing entirely reasonable. His blasé attitude to Charlotte's safety irritated Gregoire. The man seemed to have no regard for the danger he was putting Charlotte in.

"You know, it's just as bad for you if Charlotte dies. You really ought to be more careful with her."

"Madame Menard is a capable woman."

"But this ... Rose is a professional. You just said."

"From my intelligence on the activities of the Rose, and our investigations into the matter of Lady Abigail, the Rose and Madame Menard are not at cross purposes," the cardinal said, not looking up, his tone as patient as though speaking to a child. "If my information changes, rest assured I will look to protecting my investments."

"I won't have to worry about this Rose woman in England, will I?"

"In England?" the cardinal asked, finally lifting his head. He sounded mildly exasperated.

"Yes. When I go. You remember our agreement, don't you, or do you plan to weasel out of it?"

"My, my, someone has his breeches on too tight this afternoon. I am grateful we have no coals in here; I fear you'd put my feet to them. No, Monsieur de Medici," the cardinal said with an exaggerated sigh of patience, "I do not intend to renege. I am surprised you still want to leave though."

"What do you mean?" Gregoire asked.

"Only that my understanding had been that ... well, that you have tender feelings for dear Charlotte."

Gregoire hated the way he said her name, deliberately provocative, too sensual and intimate. His heart pounded at the insinuation. "You're falling for our cover story. I have no feelings for Madame Menard. My wishes stand."

"Really," the cardinal said, amusement lighting his eyes. "I told you once I was a gambling man, didn't I, Monsieur de Medici?" Gregoire nodded. "Let me propose a wager then. High stakes. In your favor, by all accounts."

"Go on," Gregoire said after a pregnant pause.

"Let us bet upon your desires at the end of this investigation. I wager you will no longer want to leave for a new life in England."

"Easily done. I have nothing here, not once my sister is taken care of. What do I get if you're wrong?"

The cardinal leaned back in his chair, eyes narrowed, concentration playing over his face as if measuring probabilities. "I wager Charlotte's freedom. If you still wish to leave to England, I will release Charlotte from any further obligation to me. She will be a free woman to do as she pleases, provided for with all the necessities of life." He smiled slowly. "What do you say?"

Gregoire swallowed. He did not like the look of confidence in his eyes. "You think you know me, do you?"

"I know people better than most any creature alive," Richelieu replied. "And if I am right and you do not wish to leave France, what do I get? What will you give me?"

"Well, you will certainly save yourself the money on transport fares and the new life, won't you? Isn't that enough?"

"Why don't we say that if I am right and you wish to remain in France, you'll owe me a favor. I do not see why you should mind. After all, you plan to leave. Do we have a deal?"

Gregoire wasn't so certain now. Something inside him wanted him to stay. Perhaps it was nostalgia, perhaps it was the pointless resurgence of his childhood crush, but either way, it would not do. He pushed it away. He would get his new life in England. Nothing would sway him, and his parting gift to Charlotte would be freedom from the cardinal's clutches.

"Deal," Gregoire answered.

The cardinal smiled. Despite being in a church, Gregoire felt as though he'd just made a deal with the devil.

CHAPTER 14

"The cardinal has reason to believe the letters Abigail was moving around were being passed to a forger," Gregoire told Charlotte as soon as he was able to meet with her in the palace. "I have to go and meet with the forger he suspects the letters were delivered to and find out what he's doing with them."

"By yourself?" Charlotte asked, surprised. "I hardly think that sounds safe. Are you sure I'm not meant to assist? Or perhaps the musketeers?"

Gregoire huffed impatiently. Of course she'd guess that it was a fool's errand to go by himself. But no. His meeting with the cardinal reminded him how little Charlotte's life was valued by the players in this game. Next time she might get into a situation with someone more cutthroat than this "Rose". Lessons in "survival" or not, he didn't want her facing a situation where she might be captured, hurt, or killed.

Guilt nagged at him. Was it right to treat her this way? She always prided herself on being indomitable when they were young.

This isn't games as a child, he reminded himself. *This is life or death. And I have to get Charlotte out of this mess.*

"He didn't think you'd be necessary for this," Gregoire lied. "It's in the underworld of Paris, and I already have some contacts there." He turned his face away from her.

"I see," Charlotte said dubiously, clearly waiting for an elaboration that Gregoire chose not to offer. "When?"

"Tomorrow. I have the day off."

"Well, if you let me help, I'm sure we'd be back in time for whatever it is that musketeers do. I presume it involves women and alcohol."

Gregoire tried to keep his face blank. "I need neither. I will let you know how I go with the forger."

He strode off before Charlotte could protest.

THE NEXT MORNING, Gregoire emerged from the barracks earlier than his fellows, who were using the day off to sleep in past dawn. There was no one on the streets outside, save for an elderly woman walking along slowly with a cane and a large basket, her hood pulled up over face. Gregoire nodded politely to her and went on his way, away from the direction of the palace, toward where the streets grew more cramped, the houses ricketier, and the smells in the air far worse. He passed through two markets, and in the second, he hid his coin purse well inside his clothes. There were pickpockets in the crowd.

He mentally reviewed his plan. Visit the forger. Pay him to spill the beans, and if that didn't work, he'd just beat him up. Forgers didn't tend to be bruisers of their own accord. Gregoire knew he would have to be fast, before the forger's backup arrived. He still knew how to escape the lower city.

He adjusted his dark cloak and prepared to step away when a voice spoke up beside him.

"Are you sure you don't need any help?" Gregoire's hand went straight to his dagger. Beside him was the old woman from outside the barracks. A moment later, he recognized her. "Charlotte! What the hell are you doing here?"

"What does it look like?" she retorted.

"Like you're acting like you're a child again. This isn't the summer festival. Following me here can get you in serious trouble."

"Not taking help will definitely get you in serious trouble," she replied. "You need someone to watch your back. What do you say in the musketeers? All for one and one for all?"

"You're not a musketeer," he said out of the corner of his mouth, trying to pretend he didn't know her. "And I don't want to have to save you."

"I don't want to have to save you either, but on the whole, I'd rather save you if I had to than not!" She took a deep breath. "So, what's the plan?"

"I go in. I see if he'll talk. If he doesn't, I beat him until he does or until he's unconscious and I can search the premises."

"That's a terrible plan," Charlotte replied after a moment.

"Do you have a better idea?"

"Yes."

"Well, I don't want to hear it. Stay here." He strode off into the crowd. He could see from his peripheral vision that Charlotte followed him regardless, and he whirled in a temper. "Dammit, Charlotte, we're not children. You can't just follow me!"

"I'm sorry if I don't want you to be killed!" she snapped. In a softer voice, she added, "I only just found you."

"I wish you hadn't," he said before he thought about the words. Charlotte didn't reply. "Wait, I didn't mean it the way it sounded."

"No, you did. Go on then. I'll wait here." She sat down on a low wall around the edge of the ramshackle square where the lower city market was.

"They'll rob you blind here," he said.

"If you can look after yourself, then so can I. Besides, what do you know about all this?"

Gregoire cast his eyes over the teeming crowds of poor and thieves. "Me? I used to work here. As a thief."

Charlotte's eyes widened with surprise. Gregoire tried not to feel bitter and turned away, losing himself in the crowd. The forger was a few streets away yet, deeper into unsavory territory. Charlotte would be safe enough at the market, if not slightly poorer for the visit.

He turned a corner into a long, cramped street. The sign for the Dirty Eel, one of Paris's least salubrious taverns, creaked in the wind. Just across the way was the shop of the forger. He paused in front of one of the doors, adjusted his plain tunic, and hammered on the door.

"So, what exactly is the work that you need me to do?" the forger asked. He was a young Frenchman with wild, disheveled hair and alcohol on his breath. Either he had started drinking early, hadn't stopped from last night, or drank all the time. He looked like he might have been handsome in the right light and in the right clothes, but the lines already on his face were hard, and there was a slightly unfocused look in his eyes. The cramped room that Gregoire sat in stank of solvent and paints. Canvases leaned against the wall in various states of incompletion. "Do you have a lady you want me to paint a picture of?"

Gregoire cleared his throat. "I heard you're not exactly in

the business of originals. I have some special work that needs doing."

"Heard that, did you?" The forger eyed Gregoire suspiciously. "You're a bit too clean to be my usual sort of customer. Don't know if I like the look of you."

"I'm clean because I'm doing a job," Gregoire said. It was true enough; even he could sell this lie. "Heiress scam. Need some help with some penmanship, if you mark me."

"Penmanship is such a bore of a job." He sighed, fidgeting. "Let's see then, if you're an honest thief."

Gregoire nodded. He knew what he was asking for. This part, as much as anything, was why he didn't want Charlotte along on this mission. He stood, pulled his tunic out of the way, and slid his belt down just enough to give the forger a look at his left hip bone.

The forger leaned over his small desk to look right up close at the two brands side by side on Gregoire's hip. One was the mark of belonging to the criminal underworld of Paris. This one was old, a dark scar that had long ceased to pain him. Next to it was a newer one, barely two months old, and hiding this from his fellow musketeers had been a challenge. It was the brand of a condemned man. A criminal marked for execution.

"Looks the business," the forger said and leaned back in his seat. "You got money?"

"I do," Gregoire replied, "but I want to see some proof first. That you're as good as they say. Let's see some of these forgeries you've done."

The forger gave a wheezing, unhealthy laugh.

"No," he drawled. "That doesn't sound like something I want to do. I don't give references. I'm a criminal, aren't I? If you're so skittish then, let's see what you want me to copy and I'll do you a sample. How's that? Fairer than fair." He fumbled around the desk for an ink pen that was the most expensive looking thing in the room and reached a hand out expectantly. "What do you want me to copy?"

Gregoire pulled out a letter, the only one he had, a letter from Treville.

The forger squinted at it.

"I want to forge a letter of commission into the musketeers," Gregoire said. "To fool the heiress."

"Seems a lot of effort. How would the heiress know what Treville's hand is?"

"Her uncle is a musketeer. I just need it to hold up long enough."

"It's sort of a stupid plan," the forger muttered, still studying the letter.

"I'm not paying you to think," Gregoire snapped. "Just do a line or two, come on." He threw a coin at him. This proved to be sufficient motivation, and the forger, still muttering blearily to himself, loaded his pen with ink and began to scratch at a blank piece of parchment. Gregoire walked around the room while he worked, looking for anything that would give him a clue as to where the letters he wanted were. His ruse for getting in had worked, but it hadn't gotten results.

"If you're bored, I got some sketches and paintings in the corner you can entertain yourself with. Got an heiress scam of my own going." Gregoire walked over and felt his blood go cold. The sketches he could see were nudes, all of ladies of marriageable age.

"A scam? How do you get them to pose all undressed?" Gregoire asked, feigning interest.

A rasp of a giggle sounded from the forger. "Pose as an artist. Go to the finishing schools and convents and things, promise pretty portraits for their families and suitors. And then I embellish. Good money in it, the family usually pays for it to disappear, and then I make extra selling it to folk that like respectable young ladies in compromising positions."

Gregoire stared at the sketch in his hand. He realized his hand was shaking. It wasn't his sister, but it could well have been, if they had any spare money. He could even imagine his sister wanting a portrait as a surprise for him, or to help with the getting of a suitor. She could have been taken in by something like this.

And then people would look at it and think it was her.

His fist connected with the side of the forger's face before he even really realized what he was doing. The expensive pen went flying, splattering them both and the room with ink.

"What the hell was that for?" the forger shouted as Gregoire hauled him and hit him twice more before a pistol ball hit the wall next to him with an almighty bang. Both the forger and Gregoire froze.

"Thank God you're here, boss," the forger wheezed, blood pouring from his nose. A big, burly fellow with two smaller ones were standing blocking Gregoire's only exit. Two of them were pointing flintlocks. The big man smiled.

"I see we've found you in the midst of artistic differences, Jean."

Gregoire had a feeling this was going to go badly. He couldn't fight his way out, and as he was learning more and more, his bluff skills were questionable at best. This was perhaps why he'd done poorly as a thief.

"Gentlemen," he started, "there's been a misunderstanding."

CHAPTER 15

Gregoire started to rise. The forger leaped on him and delivered a series of blows that left Gregoire stunned and bleeding. He lay woozily on the floor as he saw boots close in around him.

Charlotte, he thought. She was the only person who knew where he was. What if she left him on his own as he'd asked?

No, he knew Charlotte. He *really* knew Charlotte. And never once in her life had Charlotte Menard stayed away when he'd told her to. She'll come for me, he told himself. I just have to try and stay alive until then.

Gregoire found himself tied to a chair and being interrogated in short order.

"So who really sent you?" said the large ringleader, who somewhat ironically went by the name of Lepetit.

"I told you," Gregoire said, spitting blood on the floor. "I came to get some help for a job. Then I took offense at some of his work. Like you said, artistic differences."

"Pigswill," Lepetit snarled. "What kind of con man are you, getting all sympathetic for some marks?"

"The kind that only steals money, not virtue," Gregoire

replied. The three bruisers laughed, while the forger made a raspy noise and blood bubbled from his nose. "We all have lines in the sand."

"Us real con men don't. Anyway, Stowaway here reckons he's seen you. Reckons you used to run with Luc La Pied."

"Got caught a month or two back, the fellow I'm thinking of," the red-haired bruiser commented, squinting.

"So I reckon you escaped the noose by promising to bag some others." Lepetit leaned in, his breath foul on Gregoire's face. "Cut some kind of a deal, Monsieur Virtue?"

There was a knock at the door. Everyone froze. Lepetit was too experienced to move his eyes from Gregoire. "Stowaway, get the door, would you? If it's someone coming to rescue our guest ... shoot them."

"No one even knows I'm here!" Gregoire insisted and copped a punch to the gut. Goddamnit, if that was Charlotte ...

No one said a word as they heard the door open and Stowaway grunt, "We're closed."

"Oh good," a high-pitched female voice trilled. "Everyone's free for a drink then! Is he here? That divine artist? He wanted me to come this morning."

Gregoire shot a look at the forger whose face was both confused and immensely interested. He frantically wiped the blood from his nose and ran his fingers through his hair. "Yes, yes, of course, bring her in!"

Gregoire tried to keep his face blank as Stowaway returned to the room, bringing Charlotte with him, but not as he had seen her before. The front of her dress was much lower than when he'd last seen her, the top loosely laced, giving him—and every other man in the room—a very tantalizing glimpse of her smooth, creamy bosom. Her hair was loosely tied up with wisps framing her face as if she'd only just rolled out of bed and if she were quite willing to simply roll back into it at the slightest opportunity. Her hips moved exaggeratedly, a confident, rolling sashay that he had last seen on Madame Sabine. It was a walk that invited everyone to contemplate what those hips might do if they were not preoccupied with walking. She smiled, her lips reddened with some cosmetic, and she brandished a bottle of liquor. Gregoire, and every man in the room, swallowed hard.

She was doing a really good job of being seductive. Gregoire shifted uncomfortably in his seat, forgetting the vast bodily pain he was in for the moment as his blood flow began to make a beeline for one particular area. That Madame Sabine had taught her a lot. It was even working on him.

"There you are," Charlotte said, looking at the artist lazily from under her lashes. "I hope you haven't forgotten me. I came as soon as I could." She sighed. "This man is a genius," she told Lepetit. "And he promised to paint me. Though ... I was under the impression we'd be alone." Her gaze was very suggestive. "Still, my husband is away on campaign for the king, the glorious fool, and I am always looking for more ... friends." She brandished the bottle of brandy again. "Shall we drink? To new friends and to art?"

She hadn't even glanced at Gregoire.

"Yes, yes, of course I remember," the forger said after a moment. "My dear, you came. I was afraid you'd leave me bereft. This is just some business. Can't you take him away?" he demanded from Lepetit.

"And let him escape? No, he can just sit there and watch us have a good time. At least here we can keep an eye on him." Lepetit grinned at Charlotte. "We're happy to be your friends, *cherie*."

"How wonderful. Are there any glasses, or will we drink from the bottle?" Charlotte demanded as she made a space for herself to sit down, shoving aside a pile of papers. The forger hurried over and sat himself beside her, his eyes openly roving her body. Gregoire was ready to pull those eyes from his head.

"You, my dear, are going to be a masterpiece. Look at you, just look at you. After we've all become acquainted, we'll go somewhere where you can ... sit ... for your portrait." His hands slid around Charlotte's waist, and his eyes glanced downward, drinking in the swell of her breasts. Gregoire bit down a growl. "Get some glasses from the kitchen," the forger barked at Lepetit's nameless redheaded bruiser.

"I'm not a maid," he sneered, but Lepetit cuffed him around the head, and he climbed downstairs, complaining.

"So what business are you in, handsome?" Charlotte asked Lepetit.

The big man grinned. "Bit of this and that. You know how it goes." As Lepetit began to talk up his life of thuggery and petty crime, Gregoire tried working on the bonds that held him. He had no idea what Charlotte's plan was, but he hoped it involved him getting untied and both of them getting out of there before she had to strip for the forger.

That was a mental image that made Gregoire feel hot all over. *With rage,* he told himself. *I'm angry for Charlotte's honor.* But again, the uncomfortable state of his trousers told him that the idea of Charlotte taking her garments off one by one, unlacing her dress, and standing there in a soft cotton chemise before untying the bow that held the necklace of the chemise taut, the fabric slipping over one shoulder, then the next, until it lay puddled on the floor at her feet, and there was only the flimsiest cotton between him and all of her unclothed before him ...

Gregoire swallowed hard and shook his head, trying to chase the image away. *No, no, no, no. This is wrong. You can't think of her like that. You can't think like that.* He shifted in his seat, feeling heat in his cheeks—and other places—and was grateful that Charlotte's attention was taken up by the four criminals and none of it was spared for the criminal who should have been the least aroused by her antics.

"To art! And new friends!" Charlotte toasted, the brandy doled out in the glasses. She knocked hers back, followed by the men.

"That's strong, *cherie,*" the forger said.

"It's barely more than milk," Charlotte protested and poured them all another round, and then a third.

"Tastes a bit strange," Lepetit said after the third large glass of brandy. His face was going red.

"Does it? They told me it was genuine French cognac. They better not have given me English muck. Have another. Let's be sure."

The fourth glass went down the gullets of the entire party. Gregoire noticed that Charlotte was now swaying. He looked at her imploringly, wondering what the hell her plan was and if it involved becoming so incapacitated by drink that she stood the risk of being taken advantage of.

Lepetit noticed his look and misinterpreted it. "Want a drink, do you?" he asked. He stood up, a fifth full glass of cognac in hand, and staggered over to Gregoire. "Want this, do you?" He waved it under Gregoire's nose before laughing and knocking it back himself. "Too bad!"

A peculiar look went over Lepetit's face in that moment. A curious, queasy sort of rumbling came from his guts, and suddenly there was a foul stench in the room. Lepetit cried a curse word and ran from the room. The forger and the two bruisers looked confused, an expression that soon gave way to discomfort, then panic, and moments later they too departed at speed. From the street, Gregoire could hear the sounds of retching and other things. Charlotte leapt up from her seat and tottered over to Gregoire, pulling out a knife to cut his bonds with.

"What did you put in the drink?" Gregoire asked. "Are you about to get sick too?"

"No," Charlotte said. "I took a load of charcoal before I turned up. It absorbed most of the emetics and laxatives, but I am quite drunk, unfortunately. I didn't think it would take that much to have an effect. It's just herbs. Madame Sabine told me how to do that. They'll be fine in a day." She smiled, and it wasn't the come-hither smile she had shown Lepetit and the other miscreants. It was the real Charlotte, sweet and slightly uncertain. "Let's get what we need and get out of here."

Gregoire was already up and out of his seat. He seized the drawings and paintings of the young heiresses and threw them in the fireplace before dumping some of the cognac over them and lighting them on fire. The scurrilous images began to blacken and burn, and then he turned his attention to the forger's desk. Charlotte gripped the edge of it to keep standing.

Gregoire didn't waste time trying to identify the papers they were looking for. He wasn't sure how long the thugs would be distracted by their digestive distress, and Charlotte was in no state to be handling a fight, so he piled all the papers he could find into Charlotte's basket and wrapped Charlotte herself in the black cloak she had arrived in.

"Did you get it?" she asked, looking green around the gills.

"Of course," Gregoire lied, pulling books off the shelf and clearing a cache of documents behind them. "And if not, we'll come back and serve them another Charlotte Menard special cocktail. Hold this." He pushed the basket into her hand and, with one arm around her, helped hustle her out the front.

Outside, a small crowd had gathered to jeer at the distress of the forger, Lepetit, and his bruisers, so no one noticed when they slipped out the door and down the narrow way they had originally come. Gregoire moved as fast as Charlotte could, aware that with most of the danger past, she was losing the edge of the adrenaline.

"A moment," she cried as they walked through the market square, which was now in the process of being packed up, and she pulled away from him to stagger aside and started vomiting herself. Gregoire felt guilt gnawing at him with each heaving retch, knowing if he hadn't been so proud and so reckless, she would not be so sick.

He helped her up. She was pale and shaking. "I'm sorry," she whispered.

"Don't worry at all about being sorry. You just try to stay on your feet, Lottie," Gregoire said. "I'll get you back home."

"No. Can't. Abigail thinks I've gone to visit my mother in the country for the day, and she can't see me this drunk!"

"We'll tell her you're ill!" Gregoire insisted, but she only shook her head. He sighed.

"All right. I have another idea."

CHAPTER 16

It took them the better part of an hour to make their way across Paris to the inn favored by the musketeers, across from the barracks. Gregoire paid for a room and then helped Charlotte up the stairs and into a room that surprised Gregoire with its salubriousness. It was whitewashed, airy, clean, and even had some flowers.

"I guess this is where Etienne takes the ladies he really likes," Gregoire muttered as he helped Charlotte to the bed.

"What?" she asked somewhat feebly.

"Never mind." He didn't think Charlotte would appreciate knowing he had brought her to the musketeers' favorite inn for seductive liaisons with women.

After demanding hot water from downstairs, to the confusion of the kitchen staff who normally fielded requests for alcohol of various strengths, Gregoire made up a tea for her from the herbs in her basket to her specific instructions. He sat on a small chair across the room as she slowly drank it, and he was relieved to see some color return to her face and some of the tension drain from her shoulders.

"How do you feel?" Gregoire asked.

"A little better. I feel stupid for not anticipating the effects of the alcohol." Her lip twisted. "I'm not cut out for this."

"You're more cut out for it than I," Gregoire said.

"You're too honorable for this," Charlotte said. "You never think of people's other motivations. You think everyone is as honest and as at face value as you."

"I am not honest, and I am not honorable," Gregoire replied harshly. "I told you. I was a thief. There's nothing honorable about being a thief. And I'm not honorable now, am I, pretending to be someone I'm not, under a false commission to the musketeers."

"You scared me half to death, wandering in there on your own. Then I saw the big fellows go in." Charlotte fixed him with a baleful look, made more heart-wrenching by the thin sheen of sweat across her brow. "From now on, we do this together or not at all, am I clear?"

"*I* scared *you*!" Gregoire retorted. "And how do you think I felt when you come in with ... with your hair all like that and your, your, your, um, dress ..." He waved his hand vaguely. "I was tied to a chair! What was I meant to do if they decided to take advantage?"

"What was I meant to do if they killed you?"

"Rather that! Rather that than what you did with poisoning yourself, the flirting, and just throwing yourself into danger like that."

"You'd rather die than have me pretend to flirt with some men?" Charlotte repeated, aghast. "Exactly who do you think you are to be declaring that? What right do you have to be deciding anything about my flirtations?"

Gregoire flooded with shame. When she put it like that, it did sound rather horribly possessive. She was right; he had no reason to be upset about her flirtations. It was not her fault how attracted to her he was, and it was only the lowliest of men who would blame a woman for it.

"You're right. I'm sorry. I just ... I just felt stupid that I couldn't protect you."

"No, you couldn't, which is why I was doing that thing with my hair and my dress and with the flirting, because you didn't let me help, so I had to come and save you. No, you can't protect me. You haven't protected me in years. I have to protect me. I've always had to protect me. I don't need you to protect me, Gregoire. I need you to work with me, so we can get this done and I can get a respectable job, and you can ... do whatever it is you want to do. Don't go falling on your sword for my sake, monsieur. It'll just make a mess I have to clean up." She threw herself back on the bed and pulled her cloak over her.

Gregoire opened his mouth but nothing came out. He was caught between indignation, anger, and embarrassment.

"You're drunk," he said at last. "Sleep it off."

He left the room, pulling the door gently shut behind him. Even in his anger, he couldn't fathom slamming it and hurting her head. In the tavern below, he sank into a seat with a large ale in front of him and buried his face in his hands.

He couldn't protect Charlotte. She was right. She was always better at getting herself into and out of trouble than he was. As a child, the only thing he had on her was age and longer legs. She was smarter than he was. It bothered him less as a child, because as an older boy, he always had interesting things to teach her that they never taught the girls. But now with that glint of intelligence in her eyes, she saw through people and things. It was hard to imagine her settling back into the life of a servant.

"Getting started early, are you, Guillot?" Gregoire looked up upon hearing Etienne's voice. "You took off so early, I thought you were ditching us in favor of someone pretty with soft skin and big eyes."

Etienne, Reynaud, and Monnier sat themselves at Gregoire's table, each with a drink in hand.

"We were hurt! Wounded! It's your first day off, and we made you bold promises about finding you fine Parisian lasses to warm your country hearth," Monnier said with a grin. "Unless the servant is telling the truth and you already had your way with one and we are completely redundant."

Damned gossips, Gregoire thought.

"I was accompanying Madame Lefort to her coach; she was intending to visit her mother in the country. Unfortunately, she had eaten something that disagreed with her and became quite ill. Rather than vex her lady with her illness, I brought her here to rest." Gregoire looked at them. "It was the only place I could think of. I'm still new to Paris."

His three companions' expressions changed from bawdy humor to genuine concern.

"Poor Madame Lefort," Reynaud said with sympathy. "You're a good man, Guillot. Why don't we check how she is feeling later today, and we can escort her back home when she is ready?"

"Does this mean you're not interested in fine Parisian women? Because if so, that means you're in love, and you have to tell us who wins the bet," Monnier reminded them.

"I am not in love with Madame Lefort," Gregoire replied hotly. "Stop laughing. I am not. She is pleasant enough and kind, but she is too ... too stubborn. I can't figure out what she means half the time, and the other half of the time I get it wrong. She is implacable, and I am all flat-footed and bumbling in her presence." He picked up his beer and downed it.

"*Mon ami*, you are jesting or a fool. That is not Madame Lefort; that is women. They render us into idiots by their mere presence," Monnier told him.

"Oh no, my stupid friend, it is you who are the fool,"

Etienne replied with a lazy smile and a knowing wink at Gregoire. "You do not know how to listen. When you truly listen to a woman, her moods and desires are plain."

"You're both wrong," Reynaud said, slamming his empty tankard on the table. "There's no such thing as love. There's only temporary attraction and bodily comfort. It's when we believe there's such a thing as love that we get confused. No, love, if it exists, it is fleeting and will always end in pain and tragedy."

"Come off it, Reynaud," Monnier complained and launched into a detailed analysis of love that was as long as it was unrealistic, as Etienne countered with his own experiences, and Reynaud pretended to laugh, except when he looked sadly into the distance.

HOURS LATER, Gregoire once again ascended the stairs and let himself into the room where Charlotte slept. The room was lit by the dim orange light of a fading sun, casting long shadows across the walls and floors. Her cloak, that she had used as a blanket, was half slid off her, and Gregoire could see the pilfered papers clutched closely to her chest.

She seemed to be dreaming, her head moving slightly from side to side, her eyelids fluttering, and making indistinct murmurs that had the sound of speech, but there were no words that Gregoire could make out. Her face was red, but Gregoire could not tell if that was simply the glow of the setting sun or if she was ill.

The matter was resolved; he would wake her and ask if she was ill. As he stepped close to her and touched her arm, she seemed to relax.

“Gregoire,” she sighed, curling around the papers in her arms.

"Charlotte?" he asked uncertainly, brushing her hair off her face. She sighed again and murmured. Gregoire's heart pounded. What was she dreaming? Was she having a nightmare about him. "Charlotte? Charlotte!" he said again, more urgently, gently shaking her shoulder. "Charlotte, wake up."

Her eyes snapped open, and she scrambled to a sitting position, papers still clutched against her.

"What's happened?" She was breathless and disoriented.

"I wanted to see if you were feeling better." Gregoire awkwardly pulled his hand away. Charlotte was looking at him strangely. "You've been asleep most of the day."

Only then did she seem to notice the long shadows and fading light. She rubbed her face with a hand. Gregoire fetched a flagon of water from the small table and offered it.

"My only complaint is a headache and the fact I feel ravenous," she said, taking the water and drinking deeply. There was something distant about her manner, and Gregoire wondered if he did the wrong thing. Should he have let her sleep?

"You were agitated as you slept," he explained. "I thought there was something wrong."

"You were watching me sleep?" Charlotte turned red, and Gregoire could not determine if it was anger or a blush.

"No! I wanted to make sure you were all right, and you were fitful. I didn't know if you were sick. You seemed upset."

"It was only a bad dream." She hunted about for her shoes and slipped them on her feet. "Now that I am recovered, I think it's safe for me to return to the palace. Here are the papers to pass along." Charlotte handed him the rumpled stack of stolen papers and began to fasten her cloak. Gregoire was mystified at her haste.

"Charlotte, I can't take these, not right now. The other musketeers are downstairs, and they will wonder about them." At seeing the incomprehension on her face, Gregoire pressed on. "My fellow musketeers. I told them you were ill. They're concerned."

"Oh, so your friends think I'm some sort of drunk or harlot now, do they?" Charlotte cut him off. "Tell me their plan for this evening wasn't to find you someone to warm your bed."

Gregoire's faint guilty flush was enough for Charlotte.

"Don't let me occupy this valuable real estate then." She wiped what was left of the red off her mouth with her cloak. "There. Much better. They will hopefully not confuse me for some bar doxie."

"Why are you so angry?" Gregoire demanded. "What have I done wrong? What was my crime in coming to see if you were all right and waking you when I was worried? I don't care if you're in this bed or not." As he said those words, he was suddenly very much aware of how much of a lie it was, but not in the way she thought. He became uncomfortably aware that there was nobody he wanted more in his bed than Charlotte, and the realization was like a vice around his chest.

"Well, whenever you're done with your friends' choice of Parisian wenches, feel free to get on with the job we're supposed to be doing." She looked close to tears.

"I don't want Parisian wenches, Charlotte!" Gregoire couldn't understand what was happening. He couldn't understand how she was acting. He couldn't even understand how he was feeling. He only knew that his whole being was filled with so much emotion he could no longer ignore or deny it. "Charlotte, I don't want any wenches. You're the only woman I want." Gregoire's brain realized too late the words that were coming out of his mouth, but it was too late to take them back. There was nothing to do but go on. "You're the only woman I've ever loved."

Charlotte froze in the act of reaching for the door. She turned slowly.

"What?" she whispered, her face unreadable to Gregoire.

It was out there now. There was no use pretending to himself or her that he didn't love her. That he never stopped loving her; his feelings had only lain dormant as plants in the winter. Not dead, not gone. Just waiting for the right conditions.

He cleared his throat. "I said I love you."

CHAPTER 17

"I love you," he repeated, his eyes on hers. Even as a blush spread across his cheeks, he lifted his head high and imbued each word with so much passion it made her knees tremble. "Only you."

Charlotte could not breathe. There was too much swirling around her in her mind and in her heart. Her thoughts were in chaos.

"I have to go," she said. She could barely force the words out. "I will be missed."

Without another glance at him, she picked up the papers and rushed out the door, down the stairs, and out the back way into the street. The cool evening air hit her face. She breathed in deeply, refilling her lungs, and all but ran through the streets, back towards the palace. Away from Gregoire.

She hardly saw the other pedestrians, narrowly missed barging into the side of a cart, and half tripped over an errant goose in her haste. Her mind was a whirlwind, and her heart ... she had no words to describe the state of her heart.

While she had slept that afternoon, her dreams had been

muddled by the alcohol, adrenaline, and the unfamiliar noises around her. First she dreamed of following a figure in a black cloak around the streets of Paris at night, always on the verge of losing them until she was closing in, and then she realized it had been a distraction and something else had been tracking her from behind. Then it shifted, the urban dreamscape replaced by the forests on the estate of Gregoire's former family home. She was running through the trees toward the house, but when she arrived, she could find no one she recognized until she entered a wholly unfamiliar room where the cardinal waited for her. He demanded she betray Gregoire, and Charlotte refused but could not escape the room. As she ran from one door to another, Richelieu was always beside her demanding she betray him, as she once did his family.

When she finally wrenched open a door and left the cardinal and his smug accusations behind, she was in one of the gardens at the palace. Gregoire was there, and he pulled her into his arms and kissed her, running his hand through her hair. He was warm against her, his kisses soft, and she wanted them to go somewhere more private than the garden, only she couldn't find the words or the will to break away. All she heard was his voice murmuring her name.

Only seconds later, she awoke to find him watching her, and she was full of feelings she had, until then, ignored. Feelings that had been laid bare by her unguarded mind in sleep, and they were too raw to bear in his company. She wanted to escape, to be away from him, worried she had given away her feelings in her sleep.

Then he was talking about being taken out by musketeer friends, to meet women. Unexpectedly, the idea of him with another woman was confusing too. It made her angry. It hit her like a tidal wave of jealousy, that dwarfed the girlish hurt she had felt as a child when she had learned he was to marry a young noble lady and he was out of her reach forever. She did not understand her jealousy then, but she understood it well enough now. She did not want him finding a lover, urged on by his friends who would have no trouble finding volunteers for the task.

And then he said he loved her.

Charlotte finally stopped running as she reached the roads surrounding the palace. Gasping for air, she leaned against a tall railing surrounding the outer palace gardens. What was she doing, running back here? Did she genuinely imagine she could go back inside, wait on Abigail all evening, read pilfered papers after her lady had gone to sleep, and pretend that Gregoire had not told her that he loved her?

More importantly, how could she pretend that she did not feel the same? Charlotte knew she was a fast runner, but she could not outrun herself. She could not outrun her feelings. Her chest was tight with the emotion; the tension of not acknowledging it was restricting her breathing.

I love Gregoire.

Her breathe escaped in a rush, and she sighed, tilting her head up to the sky, letting the feeling crash through her like a tidal wave. She loved him, and she had left him standing there without any explanation.

What would he be doing now, she wondered. Would he have gone with his friends to bury himself in the warm arms that abounded in Paris's night life?

No. He wouldn't. If he said he loved her, he meant it. And if he meant it, he would not dishonor her like that. How could she have even accused him?

"I'm in the wrong place," Charlotte said aloud, eliciting curious glances from several passersby. She turned on her heel and ran back the way she came, all the way to the inn.

Stepping inside the bright, busy taproom, she couldn't see a single musketeer. She definitely couldn't see Gregoire.

Maybe she was wrong? Maybe he had gone carousing after all?

"Madame?" The woman who spoke was the one who had brought her water upstairs earlier. "The gentleman is still upstairs, if that's who you're looking for."

"Thank you." She stopped short of asking if he was alone. She couldn't imagine what the staff thought of their comings and goings that day, but then she had her hands full trying to manage her own thoughts and feelings. She was going to have to let the staff think and speculate as they wished.

Upstairs, she tapped on the door.

"Gregoire, it's me. Please let me in." She paused. "I'm sorry."

"Charlotte?" Gregoire sounded disbelieving. "Come in."

Charlotte stepped back inside the room. The sun had truly set in the time she had been sprinting around Paris in her confusion, and through the window she could see orange fading to a cool blue, then the deep blue of night across the sky. Gregoire stood up from where he had been seated on the edge of the bed and simply looked at her.

"I am sorry I left," Charlotte said. The door closed behind her. They were alone. "I didn't understand what I was feeling."

"I thought you were supposed to be the clever one," he said, but without blame or rancor.

"It's hard to see the things you are closest to." Charlotte took a step toward him. He looked like someone waiting to be struck.

"I am sorry for this morning," Gregoire said. "For not trusting you to be able to take care of yourself. For acting like I had any right to make decisions on your behalf. I was arrogant and foolish. I care for you exactly as you are."

Charlotte's heart thudded at the apology. He looked truly contrite, wringing his poor hat in his hands. His face was tired, or perhaps that was simply the shadows. She felt her chest grow tight again with the vice of too many feelings and no way to express them.

"Would you kiss me?" she asked. His eyes widened. She took a step closer.

"Gladly," he whispered.

They stood looking at one another. Gregoire frozen. Charlotte breathless. She closed the last step and pressed her mouth to his. It was nothing like the dream. The dream was a hollow fantasy, and this was real. The kiss was soft, and it sent shivers running down her spine. Everything in her sighed with the rightness of the feel of his lips, the taste of his mouth, the warmth of his breath. Gregoire's kiss reminded her of a warm fire on a winter's night, a touch of a clean chemise in the summer, the smell of a kitchen, and, more importantly, wood smoke and summer night flowers of a clandestine trip to the festival. Gregoire's kiss felt like home.

She was folded in his arms, caressed by his lips, and at long last she truly let herself acknowledge the feelings that had been growing in her since their reunion.

"I love you too," she told him.

CHAPTER 18

It was fully dark when they were settled in the room again. Gregoire had gone out to inform Lady Abigail that Charlotte was delayed at her mother's and would return mid-morning the next day. His musketeer friends had already long gone ahead to other watering holes, to find their own amusement; there was no need to worry about them. Now it was only the two of them, Charlotte reflected, alone in the small room, with the outside world not searching for them.

"What did you do before you ended up here, working for ... Lady Abigail?" Gregoire asked, lighting some of the candles in the room.

Charlotte looked away from him and down at her hands. "I was married," she reminded him.

She no longer wore her marriage ring. She remembered the day she had sold it to pay for some of her late husband's debts. She had felt only relief.

"I forget you lived a whole life between now and when we were children," he replied, sitting down opposite her, unwrapping the parcels of food he had fetched for them—

bread, cheese, and some small meat. None of the delicacies that the woman in gold had offered, but a greater feast nevertheless, for it was from Gregoire's hands. Charlotte looked up from the food to see him gazing at her intently.

"I forget too sometimes."

"Was he a good man, your husband?" Gregoire asked. Charlotte paused with the small cheese knife in her hand. She tried not to think of Gustav anymore. "How did he die?"

Charlotte pushed her stool backward and stood up, dropping the knife on the table. She walked to the edge of the candlelight, her arms wrapped around herself.

"He was killed. He was in the city watch, but he was just a thug in uniform."

"Did he hurt you?" Gregoire all but growled.

"No. That is to say, he did not beat me. He was just neglectful and selfish."

"I'm sorry. I should not have asked."

"I don't want to remember him," she told him. She didn't want to return to a place in her mind where Gustav was. She didn't want to remember his death. She didn't want to remember his life. Not here, like this.

She turned to look at Gregoire. He sat behind the table, his soft face framed by the gentle glow of the candlelight. Then her vision blurred with tears. Charlotte felt her heart breaking inside her chest, and she didn't know why.

No, that was a lie. She could lie to others, but it was harder to lie to herself. Her heart was breaking because nothing would be the same as it used to be. She could never undo what she had done.

"Charlotte ... Lottie. Please."

Charlotte looked up. He was standing so close to her, looking so stricken by her tears.

"You look just like you did when I fell out of that tree," she said.

"I'd never seen you cry. Usually, if you fell, you just laughed and got back up. I was afraid you were hurt. Really hurt. You were holding your head." He stepped closer. "I thought I'd lost you."

Was he talking about that afternoon when she had fallen out of the tall tree and hit her head on a tree root? Or was he talking about something more?

"I was afraid you would think I was weak if I cried, which made me cry even more," she told him. "And that you'd never take me on adventures again."

"You were so proud, for a little girl. I knew noble girls who didn't have so much pride."

"Is that what you think? That I'm proud?" Charlotte asked. He was right, to a point. She had been implacable as a girl, iron-willed and without fear. Gregoire as a boy had loved that about her. Did Gregoire the adult feel differently? "That common little girls have nothing to be proud of?"

"No! There you go again, being angry at me for no reason! For God's sake, Charlotte, you don't have to ... you don't have to be anyone with me. You have to be someone for Abigail, for Richelieu, for all the people we have to trick, but you don't have to be so guarded around me. I'm not your enemy." He put his hands on her arms, sliding them up and down against the fabric of her dress.

"You don't understand." Charlotte took a shuddering breath. "Maybe I'm still like that proud little girl, even though I have nothing to be proud of."

"Don't talk about yourself like that! Don't," he repeated softly as he pulled her close to him, his arms finding their way around her.

For a moment, Charlotte forgot the last eight years, and she was lost in memory. There was none of the adult complication. She was not standing in a cramped room in a Paris inn, lit by cheap tapers. She had never picked a lock or been married or been anything other than an adventurous little girl who was good at her letters. She let herself believe for a moment that she was young and had hurt herself and her best friend was hugging it better.

"Gregoire," she heard herself whispering as she leaned against his chest. She could hear his heart beating—familiar, comforting, exactly as it was all those years ago. "Some things don't change. Like your heart. Like my pride."

She pulled back from the embrace and looked up at him. "He wasn't a good man," she said with difficulty. "I married badly. I thought I loved him for a bit, but all I really was, was scared." Charlotte took a deep, shuddering breath. It felt both good and terrible to say the words aloud. "I only married him because I was scared. Nothing was certain after they took you all away and the household was dissolved. Maman found work, but it was never as good. They were never as happy to have her dependent come on board as well. I did work, but it was lesser work than my mother wanted for me, so when I was sixteen, she thought it might be best if I went and tried to get my own place somewhere."

She became acutely aware that she was still lying against Gregoire's chest. His heart was beating fast. His body may have been still, he might have been silent, it might have been perfectly safe and secure in that dark apartment, but his heart was racing as though they were in danger. She tilted her head back from his chest to look up at his face. He was staring straight ahead, lost in his own thoughts.

"Gregoire?"

At the sound of his name, he glanced down, a quick jerk of his head. Charlotte's eyes met his, and he leaned toward her, his lips parting slightly before he pressed his mouth against hers again.

"I'm sorry things became so hard for you," he said, stepping back from her. "We never meant ... Obviously we didn't mean ... I didn't mean to let you down, Charlotte."

Charlotte struggled for words. She deserved every bad thing that happened to her. Gregoire feeling guilty for the problems in her life, that she had caused, that she had caused him ... it wasn't right.

"Don't even think of it. You had far bigger problems. Your family was in danger. Your life was in danger. What could you have done?"

It was the wrong thing to say. He didn't reply, only turned away from her. The silence settled between them. Charlotte thought they looked very foolish, standing there like a tableau at the end of the scene in a play, her half holding out her arms for him, and him turned away, his head lowered.

"I wished," he said in a broken voice barely above a whisper. Charlotte had to strain to hear him. "I wished for so long that I could be with you. All of my responsibility, I would nightly wish and pray away. I did not want my family name or honor. Nor the lands, nor the wealth, nor any of what came with being a Medici, a cousin to the king. All I wanted was to be a musketeer and to marry you."

Charlotte did not move nor make a sound. Gregoire's pain was palpable from across the room. The wounds were years old and years deep, bleeding into his words freshly. Years had not healed them or even begun to knit them closed. Charlotte thought, he must scratch them into himself afresh every day.

"It was my fault, everything that happened. I wished it and prayed for it, and I got it."

"Gregoire, no," Charlotte started.

Gregoire turned to look at her. "*It was my fault.* God punished me for my hubris. Be careful what you ask for, because you might just get it." He sank back into his chair, his face in his hands. "I'm afraid to think of us together. I'm afraid that if I give in to this, to the feelings laying siege on my heart, that God, or the devil, will finally spring the end of their trap. I don't deserve to get what I want. Not after what it cost."

"Gregoire," Charlotte whispered, her heart breaking in her chest, guilt rising in her throat and almost drowning her. "Gregoire, you didn't cause what happened. I am not an instrument of divine penalty."

Gregoire did not respond. Her confession danced on the tip of her tongue, and her conscience taunted her.

"Everything that happened, it was not your fault," she assured him again, pressing her feelings down. "There were traitors, and your family fell into their path. The Queen Mother's plots were not instigated by God because you wished to live a life different than the one allotted."

Gregoire did not move. Charlotte watched him, wracked with the emotional pain of the past that he tethered himself so tightly to. She rose.

"I cannot bear to cause you such pain, Gregoire. I cannot be with you if you see me only existing as divine castigation for your thoughts."

She gathered her cloak, eyes blurry with tears, and unlatched the door.

"No, Charlotte, please wait." Gregoire was now standing next to her. "You are all that remains of my life. Even my sister is distant from me. I hardly know her. You do not cause me pain. I cause myself pain because of my thoughts."

"But I am the prompter of these thoughts. Gregoire, I can't ... I can't stay. I can't be your anything, not if I know that when you look at me, it cuts into you. I won't let you use me to punish yourself. That is the problem. You cannot let me close to you because every time you look at me you are filled with guilt!" She stepped close to him, pushing away her own guilt.

"We were children, Gregoire, and adults far more powerful than us ruined our lives with their treachery and schemes. You asked about my marriage. Let me tell you. My marriage was hollow and cold. I married for economic security, and he did not love me, and in the end, he did not care for me. We had enough to eat and a meagre roof, and I cooked his food and kept his house and mended his clothes, and all I wanted was someone I could run with. Someone I could experience joy with. Someone who knew the stuff of my soul and I of his. I wanted someone to know me and love me like you did."

They stood so close together, fear and sadness and guilt wrapping around them, her hands gripped onto the front of his shirt as though she had grabbed it to make him pay attention. Gregoire's breath was erratic, and his eyes frightened again.

"I wanted someone to know me as Charlotte, not simply as wife. You have been a part of myself for as long as I have known myself. Is this not true for you?"

"God, Charlotte," Gregoire breathed and leaned his forehead against hers, eyes shut, his heart pounding so wildly Charlotte could feel it through the fabric. "Yes. You know my soul from the inside, because you helped shape it. I can never be myself without some part of me being you. But I can't ask you to take me on, with all my uncertainty. I have no prospects, no future. I have only a name that is synonymous with treason.

"You are much more than all of that. You are still you. Underneath all this bitterness and anger, there's still you, full of honor and honesty and misguided protectiveness," Charlotte replied softly. She was aware of how perilously close their lips were. Feeling his breath on her mouth, shivers ran down her spine.

"Honor? Honesty?" Gregoire repeated the words as

though they were foreign. "I have none of that. You don't know half of what I am. What I've done."

"You don't know all that I've done, either." Charlotte swallowed her guilt within her, but it wasn't hard. Gregoire in her arms made her forget the guilt. She was awash with giddy emotion. "You have more to offer me than when we were young. Now, at least, you could marry me if you chose, even if all you have to offer is yourself. Back then, for all your finery and titles and lands, you could not offer that." Charlotte blinked back tears. "Do you think I loved you for your nobility?"

"Of course not, but ... but is this enough?" Gregoire asked, gesturing at their surroundings. "Secrecy, lack of security, a small room, and my worthless words?"

CHAPTER 19

Gregoire's heart pounded as he waited for Charlotte's answer, aware how ridiculous his offer was. Secrecy and lack. No woman would settle for it.

"Yes," Charlotte replied softly, her eyes fixed on his. "You are enough."

His lips touched hers, and he felt as though the room were lit with a thousand suns, all warmth and light.

He felt as if he had jumped. Jumped off something terribly far up and discovered he could fly. Well, no, he could not fly. But with Charlotte in his arms, he could. For the first time since their fight the day he'd agreed to marry that noble girl of his mother's choosing, the day before his life had imploded and never recovered, for the first time since that day, Gregoire felt as though he had been set free.

Charlotte's unconditional trust and acceptance of him had set his soul free.

"But what will we do?" he asked, murmuring his insecurity against her, and she kissed him back, trying to draw it from his mouth and into herself where the suns that surrounded her would burn it out of existence.

"We will find a way," she replied.

"Would you take such a risk?"

"I will take any risk with you," she told him, her fingers running through his hair, his dark eyes locked on her. "Any risk, so long as you are there with me. Will you?"

"Yes," he replied, and this time when he kissed her, it was with purpose and abandon, passion and no reservation, pulling her body close against his. He had so long eschewed romantic assignation, but now his body was filled with a fire that was hungry to consume the winds that fanned it.

"Are you sure you want to do this?" Gregoire heard his traitor mouth speak, even as all of his body drew him toward her. "We can stop, and I can ... throw myself in the Seine to cool down."

"Don't you dare throw yourself anywhere," Charlotte replied fiercely, "except the bed over there."

"We have your maidenly virtue to think of—"

This gave Charlotte a moment's pause.

"That is long gone with a man who did not prize it," she replied after a silence. Gregoire felt foolish and blushed, but Charlotte smoothed his bearded cheeks with her hand. "No, you mean well and speak with the honor you profess not to have. I have been married and have no maidenly virtue to speak of. I only have my desire, which I offer to you, if you'll have me, a widow, out of wedlock."

"You're mad," he replied. "You are Charlotte, my Charlotte. I want nobody but you."

"Then do not doubt I want this." She kissed him again and again until they were both completely lost in passion. When Gregoire's hands found the lacing to her dress, she urged him on with encouraging kisses and whispers as he began to unlace it, pausing only to let her pull his shirt off him. Her functional but lovely outer dress came away piece by piece, leaving her breathless and wearing only her underdress.

Just like in his fantasy at the forger's, there stood Charlotte in a soft cotton chemise, the candlelight half illuminating, half hiding the body beneath the white fabric. She reached up to the neck drawstring and loosened the bow, allowing the ribbon to run through her fingers. As the neckline slacked, it slid down one shoulder, then the other, before puddling at her feet, and there was only the lightest bit of fabric around her middle obscuring the last of her from him.

As she stood there, all but naked in the candlelight, all curves and golden light, Gregoire was certain there was nothing in all of France, or even in all of God's creation, as wonderful as the woman before him. She looked at him almost challengingly, as if she wondered if he might run. He was not sure he could walk, let alone run. Kneeling on the bed, he pressed his lips against the skin of her stomach, drawing his kisses and his tongue up her body. He heard her sigh then moan as his lips traced the swell of one breast, then the other, and he could feel her trembling so much he feared she would fall.

He pulled her toward the bed, still exploring her skin with his mouth, his hands sliding down her back to cup her buttocks. Her hands roved with increasing intensity over his chest and slid lower and lower until they found his belt. Gregoire groaned in anticipation. His trousers were far too tight around him now; he wanted them off. Uncertainty had burned away, and every part of him now was wholly anticipating the moment her body and his would be completely intertwined. He wanted to hear her pleasure, what gasps and cries would be elicited by their merging heat. There was a soft clink as his belt was undone. Then her deft fingers unlacing the front of his trousers, his body straining at each new give in the fabric. At last he felt them slide down over his hips and Charlotte's hard breathing speed up, and as her fingers brushed down, down past his hips, and ran over his brands ...

Charlotte's hand paused uncertainly. Gregoire froze.

"What's wrong?" Charlotte asked, breathless. "Gregoire? What's wrong?"

Oh, merciful heaven, how had he forgotten? His dishonorable past was burned indelibly into his flesh, for fiends, judges, and lovers alike to look on and know the quality of his character. He struggled to sit up, and Charlotte moved aside, confused by the sudden cooling of their passion. How could he have forgotten?

"Gregoire, for God's sake, tell me what is the matter. Have you never before—"

"No, I have, I have. That isn't it."

"Are you worried about a baby?" Charlotte tried. "I have herbs I will take to prevent that." Gregoire only shook his head, his hand covering the brands. "Gregoire, if you wish to stop, we will stop, but please, talk to me. What did I do?"

"It isn't you. It is me. I told you, I am not a man of honor, and I forgot that I could not hide that without my clothes. You will not take me as I am."

"Let me be the judge of that," Charlotte said. "Only I can decide if I will have you." Gregoire looked at her, lying beside him, looking at him with a trust he could not accept that he deserved. "Let me see what it is."

He took her hand and placed it over the brand, ignoring the surge of heat as her hand passed so closely to his manhood. Charlotte's fingertips ran gently over the brands, tracing their outline and their shape.

"You are condemned," she said, sounding slightly shocked.

"I am."

"For murder?" she guessed.

"No."

"For kidnapping?"

"No."

"Not for rape, surely," she said.

"No."

"What then?"

"Theft."

"From the poor?"

"The rich. Rich young men. And assault on a noble, when I was caught." Gregoire could not look at her. "I've been a thief for several years. The other brand next to it is a thief's mark of the man I worked for. If you lie with me, you lie with a cowardly thief condemned to the noose."

"How did you escape?"

"I took this job."

Charlotte did not say anything for a long minute. They lay side by side in a state of arrested undress and simmering passion.

"Are you done making decisions for me about what I do and don't want?" Charlotte asked. "Shall I show you how little this matters to me? Will you let me?" She threw her leg across his and sat astride him, leaning forward to put her mouth on his chest, drawing down his body until her beloved lips lay against the harshness of his brands, and Gregoire felt lighter than air.

"Is there anything you would not forgive me?" Gregoire asked.

"There is nothing I believe you could do that I would not forgive," she told him, the words murmured against his greatest shame. "And I?" she asked tentatively.

"There is nothing, *nothing* I would not forgive you, no act under the sun," he told her.

All hesitation now vanished, and there was only the wondrous acts of giving their bodies to the other's hands and lips and demanding nethers. Each was driven into further fervor by the other's exclamations of pleasure, urgent hips, and thirst for contact, until they had nothing left to give and lay in a tangled embrace. Gregoire pulled Charlotte close, cradling her warmth against him.

"I love you," he whispered. Charlotte murmured her own love for him against his skin, and they drifted into peaceful sleep until the dawn, both feeling completely content, completely safe, and completely whole for the first time in many years.

CHAPTER 20

Gregoire was back in the stone chapel under the gaze of the gargoyles.

"The papers you and Madame Menard retrieved from the forger were revelatory of a few matters I am now pursuing, but I regret to let you know they were less than satisfying with regards to your original endeavor." Cardinal Richelieu leaned back in his seat, drumming his fingers on the papers in front of him, scrutinizing Gregoire by the light of dozens of candles. "We have discovered confirmation of what we suspected, that the forger was being smuggled exemplars of the queen's handwriting to create certain letters. We even discovered some information on what those letters were to say but not who is behind all this, nor when their trap is to spring."

"I suppose you want me to go back and get the information then," Gregoire said with a sigh. "Anything else?"

The cardinal hiked an eyebrow. "And how do you presume to do that, musketeer?"

"My first plan is to hit him until he tells me what I want to know, but I suppose you want me to confer with Charlotte and devise a sneakier plan."

"No, monsieur, I mean that the state you left him after your last reconnaissance mission is not one that has left him able to engage conversation. I'm aware that Madame Menard is the brains of this operation, but surely even a musketeer understands that dead men tell no tales?"

"Dead?" Gregoire repeated. He stared at the spymaster, trying to divine the meaning of his expression. "He's dead? Did the sickness kill him?"

"I am not aware of any illness that causes one's throat to be cut, are you?"

"That wasn't us. He was alive when we left. He was puking his guts out and worse besides, but Charlotte said he'd be fine, just have a rough day of it. Neither of us cut his throat."

"Interesting," the cardinal said, narrowing his eyes thoughtfully. "Well, perhaps the forger and his associates had a grief with someone else. Or perhaps the people we are looking for are more aware of us than we are of them. We will have to hurry this along."

"Good."

"I thought that might meet with your approval," the cardinal said with a wan smile. "You are dismissed. The next set of instructions will be delivered to Madame Menard tonight. Be sure to meet with her tomorrow morning. If I am correct, we will have a very narrow window of opportunity to make a play for the information we need."

"You sound like you're having fun," Gregoire told him.

"Oh, but I am," the cardinal answered calmly, his attention on the papers in front of him, Gregoire clearly no longer of importance.

"We are not toys to be meddled with."

"Are you not having any fun, musketeer? You're not living in the gutters. You are not worrying about your sister's money. You have friends who will not stab you for a half-full purse. And Madame Menard. Tell me you do not think she's having fun." Cardinal Richelieu looked up at him for the briefest of moments, sardonic humor dancing across his face. "It is a gross pity to waste such an intelligence on naught but needlework." He chuckled. "Go away now, Gregoire de Medici. Your sour banter will get you nowhere except make me perhaps less inclined to save you if you get yourself into trouble even the musketeers or the clever Charlotte cannot finagle you out of. *Au revoir.*"

Gregoire took half a step forward, but the look in the cardinal's eyes made him think better of it. He turned and left the church. As he walked through Paris, he thought about the days ahead. Guarding the king for a few hours. Drinking with Monnier after. Dawn training with Reynaud. Stolen kisses with Charlotte. Hearing her laughing, breathing in her scent. Aching for the opportunity to lose himself in her again.

He made himself remember the humiliation of being dragged away and imprisoned by musketeers, the implacable look in Treville's eyes, his mother's tears, and the snap of his father's neck in the noose.

But all it caused him to feel now was confusion. How could he be happy when they were dead? How could he be on the edge of contentment as part of the same system that caused their wrongful demise? And Charlotte ... his heart soared again but with a guilty twist. She did not know yet about his plans to go to England. He was sure she would join him, when she knew. They would be free.

He nodded to himself as he walked back toward the barracks. He could leave everything behind, even his parents' memory, as long as Charlotte was with him.

The day after her night with Gregoire, Charlotte returned to her duties with Lady Abigail. Even in her half-distracted state where her mind would simply not be shifted from remembering candlelit hours in Gregoire's arms, she noticed Lady Abigail was not herself. She too seemed distracted and slightly distressed, to the point of asking Charlotte to stop speaking to her.

Charlotte's senses were on high alert. She felt as though something had changed and new information was within her grasp. She was not quite sure, however, how to pry it from Lady Abigail.

She needn't have worried.

"I am supposed to tell absolutely no one," Lady Abigail said that night, leaning back into her cascade of pillows as Charlotte helped settle her into bed. "But I can't keep it to myself any longer. Charlotte, my dear, I am in love!"

“My lady, I am glad for you,” Charlotte said, handing Abigail her favorite hot drink.

"Will you not even ask who it is?" Abigail asked, looking at Charlotte, her face all expectation and fear.

"It's not my place, my lady," Charlotte said and smiled at the other woman. "But I am happy you are in love. I have noticed the lightness of your heart and wondered what was the cause. I assumed it was being closer to God by being in France."

Abigail frowned and looked mildly chagrined. "Oh, I suppose I am grateful to be closer to God. And I do not forget Him or my duties to Him. It's simply, I am in love, and it is more than I can bear at times. I feel I will simply explode from happiness. And I must keep it to myself. He has asked me not to tell anyone. I am not even allowed to confess it, can you imagine! That part grieves me, but I don't think it can be sinful, because he is a righteous Catholic man, and if I feel this good, it cannot be wrong. Can it?"

Charlotte bit her lip and decided against illuminating her on the nature of sin, that it was often tempting and felt good. That was probably best left for a priest. The revelation explained some of the behavior she had noticed about Lady Abigail before the anxiousness that overtook her today. There had been a gaiety about her that Charlotte had at first mistaken for a childish naivety or perhaps distraction by the novelty of being in Paris and free from supervision. Or at least, Charlotte mentally amended, free of supervision as far as she was aware.

"Is he quite respectable, my lady?" Charlotte asked carefully.

"Yes! Have no fear of that. He is the most respectable sort." She paused. "No, I cannot. He insists it be a secret, and I cannot betray it. I have so faithfully promised him." She sat up and put her hot drink aside, taking both of Charlotte's hands in her own. "Sit," she begged, and Charlotte found herself uncomfortably perched on the edge of the tall feather bed. "Now, do you solemnly swear that you will keep this between us and God?"

"I promise," Charlotte said with all the sincerity and sympathy she could muster. Abigail was entrusting her heart to her, and Charlotte knew she must give it over to the cardinal.

"We met in England. When the time came for me to come to France to follow the true church, I told him, and he made it possible. He loves me too, you see."

"Forgive me, my lady, but there is something I do not understand," Charlotte said delicately, her mind racing. "He is most respectable, as you say, and he is most Catholic, and he truly loves you."

"Yes, this is all the truth."

"I take my lady's word for it that it is," Charlotte said

before continuing. "I just do not understand why it must be so great a secret that not even your priest is to know of it."

Abigail heaved a great sigh. "I too ask him this often, and I confess my heart finds it difficult to accept his answer. But then, I am only a lady, and he is a great nobleman, and he knows more things of state than I do."

"I think my lady sells herself short. You have demonstrated to me a great grasp of social spheres, and your judiciousness in leaving England for warmer political climes is hardly whimsy or shortsighted."

"You are kind, Charlotte, but you are a maid. What can you hope to understand of politics?"

Charlotte tried not to feel hurt by this. After all, in her view, nobility were often irrational and motivated by feelings and petty pride, and she felt they possessed not a whit more intelligence in nature than did any other soul on God's earth. The luxury of being able to cloak one's capriciousness in mysterious dealings!

Luckily, Abigail did not seem to notice her hurt and carried on. "My beloved has explained to me that his position is precarious because he ... he has a special obligation to royalty that he must consider. He's expected to marry for the good of his country. He certainly cannot marry some nobody noble." She threw herself back on her pillows. "And the reason I cannot confess it to a priest is because of that cardinal. My beloved says he is very powerful and very sneaky and that surely all the priests report to him, and then he will have me sent away! Can you imagine a more dreadful abuse of office?"

"I am certain no earthly man wields such power. No cardinal can command the priests to break the vows on the confessional," Charlotte tried to soothe Abigail even as her thoughts traitorously jumped to the nuns.

"I don't believe it either." Abigail shrugged. "But I will

humor my beloved, because he feels persecuted, and I understand what that feels like. Oh, Charlotte, he loves me. My heart is filled with joy for his love. But I am to be patient. He says he will arrange things so that he renders some service to his king that will force him to let him marry me. And in the meantime, Charlotte, I need your help."

"My lady has but to command me," Charlotte said after the briefest of pauses. "But I cannot see what I can do to facilitate this marriage!"

Abigail laughed. "No, we leave that to my beloved. You must help me in meeting him. We have not been able to meet in private since we are both in France, and I miss him very much. It must be secret. I must ask you to lie. Will you do that for me, Charlotte? You are a good, honest woman, and I know it will sit ill with you, but for the sake of love, will you help?"

"I will, my lady. But now you must sleep. It will not do to be dozy in the company of the queen tomorrow."

"I enjoy sleep. In my dreams, I am with my love."

Leaving her mistress settled in her bed with the lamp blown out, Charlotte made her way to the main room of the apartment. By the light of a single candle, she turned all this new information over in her head. Lady Abigail was devoted to a powerful man, one who was deeply embroiled in politics. Charlotte was certain that this man was the one for whom Abigail was acting. She was besotted enough to do things for him without question, especially as she seemed to believe in the superior mental acuity of men of state. Charlotte must find out who the lover was, and it seemed all she must do was wait to be party to a clandestine meeting.

Yet something nagged her about the betrayal she was planning, and her stomach clenched with guilt. She had once been in a position not unlike Lady Abigail's. Would she exert the pressure on Lady Abigail that had been exerted on her, to similar results? Gregoire's face flashed into her mind. Would she be the destruction of another's love in the name of politics?

Unexpectedly, there were several light taps on the outer door. Charlotte recognized the sequence, a short code informing her that a messenger of the cardinal was awaiting entry. Opening the door, she found a stocky young woman from the palace laundry carrying a pile of fresh sheets, which she passed to Charlotte with murmured pleasantries.

Amidst the sheets, Charlotte found a coded letter, disguised as a harmless treatise on scripture. Translating it, she found instructions from the cardinal to break into and search the Duke of Buckingham's quarters the next day on the stroke of noon. The cardinal's final decoded words were, "Do not get caught," which seemed like sage advice given the duke's propensity to throw around threats of starting a war with England. The implication was clear. If she was caught, she was on her own. Or at least, in very big trouble.

CHARLOTTE AND GREGOIRE met near the Duke of Buckingham's quarters at midday, as arranged. As they strolled through the gardens, Charlotte hoped they did not look too tense. She prattled about needlework, and Gregoire gave her a pained look.

"If you think it sounds boring, try *doing* that much needlework," Charlotte hissed in an undertone, which at least made Gregoire laugh.

As the bell struck noon, the duke swept past them with a large group of servants and English courtiers. He was speaking to them in English, but Charlotte's lessons had come along well enough to understand that he was feeling outraged about the summons he had received. Then again, the duke wasn't trying particularly hard to disguise his tone, so perhaps it was not the English lessons.

As they vanished from sight around a corner, Charlotte and Gregoire climbed over the low wall from the garden and hurried down the corridor to the duke's apartments. Charlotte tested the handle; it was unlocked. The duke must have felt secure enough in his position to not worry about unwanted guests. Gregoire laid a hand on her arm.

"Be careful, Charlotte."

"Don't worry. I will not require you to start a war for me," she reassured him, but her joke did not melt the concern on his face. She slipped inside.

The duke's apartments were not small, nor were they what could be called tidy. Either his servants were extremely lacking or the Duke of Buckingham was such a whirlwind of chaos that he made more mess than the servants could keep up with. Perhaps it was a clever camouflage to genius.

Charlotte considered the latter to be rather unlikely.

The search took longer than Charlotte expected. She was looking for anything that looked like it would be the queen's handwriting or in Spanish or any letter that looked to her poor English skills that might be relevant. She rifled through his study first, finding not much more than letters from a multitude of women and a few letters from the king of England. Charlotte read them as best as she was able, but they seemed to be no more than general chatter between friends.

There were a few notes that she could make neither head nor tail of and were unsigned except for a familiar rose symbol. She was not surprised, after hearing from Gregoire who the woman worked for. Charlotte uneasily pocketed them. She hoped she would not meet "the Rose" here today. She had the feeling the other woman might be less sympathetic than she had been at their first introduction. The duke did not possess many books, and those he did were truly only books. There were no secret compartments in his desk or in his shelf or in his chair. It was maddening.

His sleeping chambers were as much of a fright as Charlotte anticipated. Either nobody had bothered to make the bed or he had only emerged from it moments after the summons. She was also grateful that his bed was empty, especially after she saw the multitudes of discarded parts of feminine wardrobe littered around. It seemed he never wanted for female company. But again, there was nothing secret, and the only papers were what appeared to be love poems and sketches of an inappropriate nature. She took the poems and left the sketches.

Panic was beginning to rise. She had been at this task for some time, and she didn't know how long the cardinal's diversion would work. She had found nothing of use. She was searching the main room one last time when she heard voices and footsteps approaching. Freezing, she looked around. Perhaps there was a hiding place she could take refuge in, or perhaps she could try and claim amorous interest, though the thought revolted her. Then she heard Gregoire's voice ring out.

"Halt! Duke of Buckingham!"

CHAPTER 21

The minutes stretched as Gregoire waited outside Buckingham's quarters. Charlotte was taking an age inside, and he was trying to remain calm. He reminded himself that surely the diversion the cardinal caused would take long enough. That Charlotte would be quick enough. That this would all be over soon. He hoped there would be large piles of papers with incriminating evidence left in an obvious place.

He began to pace. There was no sound from within. The chirping of the birds was too loud for Gregoire, who was utterly focused on listening for the return of Buckingham and trying to ignore his intense worry about Charlotte's safety.

Luckily, the duke had never been subtle in his life, and he had not picked that day to start.

The angry English duke's voice carried unmistakably, as did the footsteps of his entourage. Gregoire froze. He threw a panicked glance at the door, but Charlotte did not miraculously emerge. Could she even hear Buckingham? He rose to go after her, but it was too late. Buckingham was now striding down the corridor.

"Halt! Duke of Buckingham!" Gregoire shouted, leaping into the middle of the corridor. His mind raced.

Buckingham stopped and examined him before a large smile crossed his face.

"You," Buckingham drawled. "I remember you. You were the lippy musketeer from that dreadful dinner. I see you still have your cloak. What a pity. I was hoping I'd had you dismissed. Well," he said, spreading his arms in a mockery of a welcome, "what are you doing here, loitering at my chamber doors?"

Good question.

"I have thought over the events of that dinner," Gregoire bluffed. "And I have decided your behavior was ungentlemanly. Being an ambassador doesn't excuse you of good manners. It means you have a greater responsibility than most to uphold."

Buckingham stared. "And you want to what, explain to me what good manners are? I didn't take you for a governess, musketeer."

"I challenge you to a duel," Gregoire announced, surprising himself nearly as much as Buckingham. He pulled off a glove and threw it at Buckingham's feet.

Buckingham, his courtiers, and all his servants stared at Gregoire. Their faces made it clear they thought he was mad. Gregoire didn't disagree. It was a ridiculous idea, but it would definitely distract everyone.

"A duel," Buckingham repeated in disbelief.

"A duel. Have you heard that word in French, Your Grace?"

You are going to get executed, his brain informed him. *So be it,* some other part of him replied. *I've lived with the threat of execution all my life. I'll gladly die to save Charlotte.*

"Of course I have, you impertinent little upstart," Buckingham drawled. "I'm just surprised that you want to make it so easy for me to get you dismissed."

"Very well," Gregoire replied. "Let us go to an appropriate place."

"Oh no, lad, we're dueling right here, right now. Do you have a second?" Buckingham asked as he snapped his fingers for a servant to start unlacing his doublet.

"I ..." Gregoire paused. "We don't need seconds."

"Oh, but we do. Make your choice. My servant, John, he'll fetch your second when he fetches mine. For my second, I choose ... Captain Treville."

Gregoire's heart sank. The wolfish smile on Buckingham's face was all too clearly informing him that not only was he going to get his backside handed to him, it was going to be in front of his boss.

Not my problem, Gregoire reminded himself. That was going to be Cardinal Richelieu's headache to deal with.

"I choose Jean-Pierre Monnier," he said quickly. "Another musketeer. But I think it will take too long to find them."

"Oh, not at all. They are not far away. We just saw them." He nodded at his man John, who took off at a sprint. Gregoire fought the urge to look behind him at the doorway.

True to his word, the English servant returned a few minutes later with Monnier, but Reynaud instead of Captain Treville. Reynaud was already looking sour. Gregoire knew he would not be impressed at being summoned by the Duke of Buckingham's man, and when he saw Gregoire, a look of unhappy disbelief blossomed on his face. He turned to the duke.

"Your Grace, Captain Treville has sent me in his stead as he is not available to be your second in duels, which are, might I remind Your Grace and others"—he punctuated his words with a venomous look at Gregoire—"illegal."

"Oh yes, of course, dueling is illegal. Did you know that, musketeer? I am but a foreigner. I cannot know these things. Your French ways are so foreign to me."

"I meant only a test of arms, between gentlemen. It was Your Grace who started summoning seconds and the like," Gregoire said, his heart pounding. Monnier was making gesticulations that shutting up was a good course of action.

"Yes, and he just dropped his glove at my feet," Buckingham sneered, prodding the glove with a booted foot. "Perhaps I am confused. Perhaps this isn't a duel. Perhaps the musketeer is courting me. No matter," he said, adjusting his sleeves. "We will test his manhood either way."

Reynaud walked over to Gregoire and grabbed his shoulder, fingers digging in hard enough to hurt. "What," he hissed, "do you think you're doing?"

"I thought I would settle matters from that dinner."

Reynaud growled, obviously not impressed.

"Do you want me to back down?" Gregoire asked.

"No, not *now*. Can you beat him, Guillot?"

"I have God and my honor on my side."

"Yes, but he has skill and a *lack* of honor." Reynaud shook his head. "I'll stop him from killing you, should it come to that. Goddamnit, Guillot, you're so quiet, I forget you're a damned hothead just like the others." He released his shoulder and walked to stand between Gregoire and the duke.

"Gentlemen, since this is not an illegal duel, why don't we all make our way to the training rooms and witness this friendly training bout. Your Grace, if you and any of your people who are coming would accompany us." He bowed stiffly and gestured.

Buckingham smirked openly, and with a snap of his fingers, led the entirety of his entourage away toward the training rooms.

"Guillot, you're an idiot," Monnier whispered as they walked toward the sparring hall. "Buckingham isn't worth the fight."

"We'll know soon enough, won't we?" Gregoire replied, almost sagging in relief as the whole crowd moved away from the duke's quarters. Buckingham might not be worth the fight, but Charlotte was, a thousand times over.

CHARLOTTE ALMOST COLLAPSED in relief when she heard them leaving. Within a few minutes, there was complete silence outside, and she cautiously opened the door and slipped out. She felt as though she had run across the length of Paris. She had been so close to getting caught; only Gregoire's quick thinking and daring had saved her. She regretted the fact there wasn't better information to show for their efforts. She dashed up to her apartment and hid the material she did find, to go through later after Abigail was asleep. With her embroidery basket clutched in her hand, she took off at a sprint to see the duel.

As Charlotte walked through one of the many doors of the large training hall, she saw an audience had gathered. The crowd consisted largely of visiting English courtiers and their servants, as well as musketeers, palace guard, and French nobles who appeared to have been sparring in the hall before the interruption. Through the crowd, Charlotte could see Gregoire was bleeding from what looked like a stab wound in his shoulder, and he could barely hold his sword up. Buckingham was standing in perfect form, not a hair out of place, sword and flintlock pointed at Gregoire.

"Now, musketeer, you are going to surrender. Get down on your knees and apologize to me here, in public, for wasting my time." He arched a single eyebrow. "Get on with it then."

Gregoire stared at Buckingham mutinously and stayed on his feet. Buckingham smirked and lifted the flintlock.

"Oh, come now," he drawled.

"There's no need for guns, Your Grace," Reynaud began, stepping forward, when there was the deafening *bang* of a firearm in close confines and Gregoire crumpled to the ground.

CHAPTER 22

As Gregoire hit the floor, pandemonium exploded.

"The king will hear about this, you gutless worm," Reynaud was shouting, leading a wall of musketeers, forcing Buckingham up against a wall of his supporters. "And I will ensure your king hears about this too, even if I have to swim across the channel and tell him myself in your mongrel tongue. You are a dishonorable cheater and a disgrace to your nation!"

"I didn't shoot him, you cretinous frog!" There was no trace of humor in Buckingham's voice now. His gun was pointed up at the ceiling. "You were watching me the whole time! Check my flintlock yourself, unless you think I magically reloaded it in between firing and you bellowing in my face!"

Charlotte pushed her way through the crowd towards Gregoire. Fighting broke out all around her. There were sounds of steel on steel, of fists on flesh. More angry shouting as the fighters were separated. English guards, musketeers, palace guards, and even several of the cardinal's red guard had weapons out and were facing off against each other in various configurations: English against musketeers, palace guards against English, red guard against anyone.

"Gregoire!" She fell to her knees beside Gregoire's prone and bloody form on the ground. She felt cold all over. His shirt was covered in blood, and two musketeers were holding a wound closed with pressure. His face was white and slick with sweat. When he heard Charlotte's voice, he opened his eyes.

"Charlotte," he whispered. "You're here."

"I heard you were having a duel," she told him.

"I did. I won."

"You won? Then how is it you are lying in a puddle of blood while your opponent is engaged in verbal repartee with Monsieur Reynaud?"

"I consider it a moral victory when my opponent brings a flintlock to a rapier fight."

Charlotte looked down at his wounds. "Merciful heavens, Gregoire!" She looked over her shoulder at the musketeers milling around with their hands on their swords. "You, run to Baroness Abigail's apartments and demand my medicine basket, run. You, fetch strong alcohol—I don't care where from, fetch some. You and you, your shirts, now."

The musketeers obeyed without a murmur of dissent.

"It's time to do some needlework," she said out loud, thanking God she hadn't put down her embroidery basket. "I hope this will not be too boring for you, monsieur."

While two musketeers helped cut off Gregoire's shirt, Charlotte selected her finest silk thread, aware everything she touched in the basket with her bloody fingers was ruined. Taking deep, steadying breaths, she found her needle and began to thread it.

There was a calm place inside her she went while she was doing things that terrified her. The world became distant, less immediate, and her mind began to prioritize the things she needed to do with cold clarity. Later, she could give in to her emotions. But for now, her mental path was clear.

The musketeer she had sent for alcohol had arrived back. She doused all her instruments in alcohol.

"Give him some now," she said. She knew the next bit would be awful. She waited for the musketeer holding his head to feed him some alcohol, Gregoire tiredly lifting his head just enough to not choke on the liquid. Charlotte touched his face absentmindedly.

"I'm sorry for the next bit," she told him. Gregoire didn't respond. He lay back with his eyes shut and labored to breathe. Charlotte picked up her little long-nosed sewing scissors and reached into the bullet wound, feeling around as gently as she could until the scissors met metal resistance. Gregoire's body was tight with pain, but Charlotte had to blot that out as she focused on opening the scissors to encompass the shot's breadth and gently drew it out. He had been lucky. It had hit him on the upper thigh. Any higher, and it might have been buried in his guts, condemning him to a certain, ugly death.

"It's all right, *mon ami*. You see, she's got the shot. Now she's going to stitch you up, and you're going to stop bleeding all over your nice new cloak. You'll be just fine, Guillot," the musketeer holding his head said.

Her basket of herbs appeared beside her, and the musketeers holding Gregoire's limbs changed out. Reynaud and the duke were still arguing.

"I have never heard Reynaud tell it to Buckingham like that," a musketeer commented.

"That's because Buckingham has never almost killed a musketeer before," another replied.

Charlotte focused on the sewing. With each small stitch, she closed up first the rapier slash, then the bullet hole in Gregoire. One stitch, then another. Her hands trembled slightly when she remembered her fingers gliding over his chest the two nights before, when his sudden intake of breath at her touch was pleasure, not agony. That night their intimacy had been quiet and private. Now the world was pressing in around them with noise, anger, and danger.

After what seemed like an eternity, she was packing the wound site with herbs to fight against fever and infection, herbs for clean healing, and wrapping makeshift bandages around it. The stab to his shoulder was shallow; it barely needed attention. She sat back up and realized suddenly how thirsty she was and how much her shoulders and back ached. Gregoire was breathing steadily, his eyes shut.

"Take him somewhere clean and quiet where he can rest. He will need lots of clean water to drink, and I will make him some tea for sleep and to ward off fever." She tried to stand and then collapsed again straight to the ground; her legs had gone completely numb under her.

"My dear Charlotte," Abigail's voice came from behind her. Charlotte turned to see her employer standing back, looking at her in amazement. "I had no idea you were so skilled."

"It is nothing, my lady. Just steady hands and a cool head in a crisis. I am sorry for having abandoned you for most of the afternoon."

"Charlotte, you've been here no more than twenty minutes. It must have felt an age. We must get you cleaned up as soon as your patient is settled."

The musketeers were loading Gregoire onto the stretcher. They were making jokes as they did so, and there was a ghost of a smile on his face.

There was a commotion at the door as an unfamiliar man dressed in the practical finery of a rich man's servant led several guards and musketeers into the room, breathless and angry.

"We couldn't catch the villain. He fled too fast for us, but he dropped his weapon," the unfamiliar man said, presenting an ornate flintlock to Reynaud and the Duke of Buckingham. "It looks English made."

Charlotte, with her basket in hand, moved toward them.

"I have never seen it," Buckingham said after a moment's pause. "Now that you have satisfied yourself that it was not I that fired the shot in plain view of several dozen people, I hope you are not insinuating I took the trouble of arranging a villain to shoot the braggart musketeer."

"I would never presume to know the breadth of Your Grace's cunning," Reynaud replied. "Did you see anything else of him?" he asked the servant, never taking his eyes off the duke.

The manservant and the others shook their heads. "He knew the palace well, whoever he was."

"It was like chasing a ghost," an out of breath guard said.

"Finding a mystery assassin seems like a job for you fine idiots," Buckingham said, sneering at Reynaud. "That shot could have been meant for either of us, and frankly, I think it's far more likely they were aiming for me rather than that nobody. Get to work and flush the rat out rather than wasting your breath haranguing me."

"The king will hear about this," Reynaud said.

"From both of us, rest assured." With a final sneer, Buckingham and his people left the room.

The unfamiliar man's gaze alighted on Charlotte, and his eyes widened.

"Madame, are you hurt?" he asked. He was a man in his thirties and clearly a Frenchman.

"No, it is Monsieur Guillot's blood, not my own. You did not find the man who fired the shot?"

"Alas not, madame. He remains at large in the castle. I ran

after him the second I realized the shot came from the doorway."

"Good job," Reynaud said, finally unclenching his jaw. "Who are you?"

"Artus Daumont," the man said, with a short bow. "In service of the Duke of Orleans. I was passing when I heard of the duel and came in to watch, which is why I was near the door."

"Let's go over what happened. Madame Lefort, you should go with Monnier to tend to Guillot. He most likely owes his life to you. The lads can do all right with stitching up a stab wound, but we weren't prepared for a shot."

Charlotte briefly wished she could go with Reynaud and investigate the shooter, but not so much that she would forgo tending to Gregoire.

"I will listen for you, my dear Charlotte. I wish to know if the Duke of Buckingham has brought all his countrymen and women into disgrace, and I will tell you all I learn," Lady Abigail promised her. Reynaud did not look pleased but decided to not argue with a noble.

"Thank you all, Lady Abigail, Monsieur Reynaud, Monsieur Daumont," she said before letting herself be led away by the musketeer Monnier.

THE ROOM GREGOIRE had been settled in was clean and contained good stocks of medical supplies. It was part of the infirmary where injured guards and the like were cared for. Charlotte had been informed the musketeers' physician would attend shortly, but she had a few minutes alone with him.

"I am so sorry," Charlotte whispered, gripping his hand

after he finished the tea she prepared for him to aid with sleep and to ward off fever. "I should have been faster."

One of Gregoire's eyes opened a fraction.

"It's all right. At least now my debt to you is repaid from the other day. And you saved my life just now; I'm sure of it. That noxious prancing cad," he spat and coughed.

"Why aren't you asleep? That tea should have knocked you out by now," Charlotte fretted.

He smiled weakly. "I'm fighting it to be able to talk to you." He motioned for some more water, which Charlotte gladly gave him. "I thought I would die on the floor of the room after I was shot, and all I could think about was that I was leaving you behind, again."

"I'm sorry. It's my fault you're in this mess. It's my fault you had to fight him ..." Charlotte trailed off. "I'm here now. You're not leaving me behind. I'm right here with you." She gripped his hands, and he squeezed back faintly. She leaned in to kiss his forehead, savoring closeness, his breath and hers so intimate. She lifted her head and saw that his eyes were open and focused, looking at her the way a man dying of thirst gazes at water.

"Charlotte," he whispered, tilting his head back, lifting his mouth toward hers. Trembling slightly, she leaned her head down and pressed her lips, parched from work, to his lips which were still moist from the tea she had made him. She remembered the sweetness of their night together and tried to pull him closer, wishing her kisses were magic and could heal him. His muscles trembled, and she knew it was exhaustion, not desire.

"Oh, Charlotte," he whispered, slumping out of her arms and back onto the bed.

Charlotte drew back, her lips tingling. "Remember when I used to tease you about kissing girls?" she whispered.

"You were the only girl I wanted to kiss for so long," he

murmured, his eyes shutting and some of the tension starting to drain out of his face.

"I never was fancy enough for your maman," Charlotte laughed. "My dresses were too tatty—when I bothered wearing them."

"I'm going to miss you," he murmured, eyes still closed, on the verge of sleep.

"You're not going anywhere. You'll have to rest up a bit, but you'll be well soon enough."

"I'm going to miss you in England, when I go. When this is done."

Gregoire's kiss suddenly burned sour on her lips.

"Gregoire? What do you mean?" Charlotte demanded, but sleep had taken him and there was no answer but his steady breathing, in and out, his bandaged chest rising and falling with soothing regularity.

The woman in the gold dress had told her to think about this. To think about what Gregoire's prize in all this was. Charlotte hadn't given it much thought. All she could remember Gregoire wanting when they were children was to be a musketeer, and now he had that, he didn't particularly want it.

A new life in England. She had never guessed—never imagined. What could he possibly want to do that for? Why had he not told her?

How could he take her in his arms the other night, knowing he was planning on leaving?

"Madame? How is he? You look troubled," Monnier, who had waited outside, asked.

"He is as well as can be expected. I've given him tea for fever and sleep. I leave the rest for the physician to deal with. He will have to examine his bandages in the morning, change them for clean ones, and ensure infection isn't setting in."

"We will, madame. The musketeer physician will be here

shortly. And we will guard his door lest His Grace, or the mystery shooter, has any bright ideas." Monnier's face was like a storm cloud.

"It was good of you all to ... help him."

"He is our brother. He is a musketeer. Buckingham strikes one of us, he has struck all of us. Make no mistake, Captain Treville will be seeing the king about this."

Charlotte had her own ideas about whom to see.

CHAPTER 23

"Madame Menard, I had not expected us to meet. Indeed, as much as I enjoy your company, you know how loath I am to leave my spiritual pursuits for these conversations," Cardinal Richelieu said with a faintly amused smile.

"I don't have any clever replies, Your Eminence. I too would prefer not to have this conversation, but with Monsieur ... Guillot indisposed, there seemed little recourse but to burden you with my presence."

He inclined his head, his smile growing slightly wider.

"Were all that professed a lack of cleverness as witty as you, madame. But speak on. We only have a little time before we are noticed."

Charlotte reached into her dress and pulled out the papers she had stolen from Buckingham's quarters. "That's all. I could find nothing concealed. Two letters signed with a rose and what look like ill-composed love poems but I am hoping are a cipher. That man had nothing useful, or at least nothing I could find. Nothing that was worth Gregoire getting nearly killed over."

The cardinal looked up from the papers. "That was indeed unexpected and unfortunate. I was there when Monsieur Reynaud debriefed with His Majesty. Dueling the duke was rash, but it fit his persona well enough. I don't believe it should have caused a concern." He tapped his fingers as he looked over the papers again, his lip curling slightly at one of the love poems. "Oh my, this is enough to make me blush."

He rose from his seat and walked over to the window. "How long until our musketeer is fit for duty again?"

"A week until it's safe for him to be out of bed. If he is healing well, he should be almost returned to normal within the fortnight."

"The shooting was rather unexpected. I am not yet certain if it was Buckingham's orders. It is more petulant than I would have guessed, even for him. If it was not him, then it begs the question whether the shot was meant for him, and thus he has been discovered by those we are chasing, or if it was intended for Buckingham." He didn't turn from the window. "How very odd. I will shake my web and see what falls out."

"Your Eminence, I have a question, if I may."

"Make it quick," he said, sounding bored.

"Gregoire said something about a new life in England. Is that true? Is that what you're giving him in return for his help?"

Charlotte saw the reflection of the cardinal's face in the window glass grow more considering. "A more intriguing question than I thought I would get. I assumed more coyness over lock picking or spying. I am pleased we are past that. Well, madame, that will take some time to answer. Or rather, I am prepared to trade you the answer in exchange for your answer to my own question."

He swept back to his seat and arranged himself, the deep vermillion robes falling in elegant drapes and columns around him. His hand beckoned to her. "Sit, madame. It seems we are to be engaged in a baring of souls."

"I don't think I want to bare my soul, or anything, to Your Eminence. I thought it was a simple question."

"A question about another operative is always complicated. Sit, madame."

Charlotte covered the distance to the chair in a few hurried steps and sat down before she changed her mind.

"So, you want to know if I am sending him to England, or —I see you about to interrupt—if I know anything about him going to England at all. Very well." He looked at her, his dark eyes piercing through her. "Tell me, Madame Menard, about the night musketeers came to Gregoire Medici and his parents' home. To your home."

"No," Charlotte said before she could even think. "I don't want to talk about that night."

Cardinal Richelieu raised his eyebrows, and his hand delicately flicked toward the door. "Well, then."

Charlotte half rose and then paused. "You know already. You must. I'm certain it was no coincidence you put us together."

"Or perhaps I've since looked into your histories and educated myself on my new employees. And if I do know, what harm could it do to tell me again?"

"I might say something that you don't know yet. I might ... give something away."

"Give something away about a situation that is eight years gone? Gregoire's parents already paid the price for their treachery. And as far as I am aware, young Gregoire and his sister had no part in it. But come, Madame Menard, let me show you what a world of comfort I am to a confession. It must be burning you up inside. Have you told a single soul about that night?"

He knows. Every fiber of Charlotte's body was certain that the cardinal already knew her darkest secret.

"Why do you want to make me say it?"

"The human memory is a fascinating thing. No one, not even one who was there and reports it minutes afterward, will have a true recollection of the event. Our minds constantly embellish and rewrite based on our feelings, our natures, and what we want to be true. It has been my life's work collecting people's versions of events, and it never fails to fascinate me how people constantly rewrite the world, even when they don't intend to. So, in answer, I may know of the version of events I heard from Captain Treville, of the attending musketeers, and even Monsieur and Madame de Medici themselves, God rest their souls, but I have not had Charlotte Menard's story. And in return, I will tell you everything I know about our musketeer Gregoire and his planned trip to England." He tilted his head. "Unless there's something you're desperate not to reveal? Perhaps about Gregoire? Or his sister?"

"No. They are innocent. They were young."

"Gregoire had come of age by then. He was taking his first steps in the world as a man. His sister, I grant you, was a child."

"All right," Charlotte whispered. "If you do not tell him what I have said. It's not ... relevant to anything."

"Madame, though we are not on sacred ground, you may consider this as sanctified as the confessional box itself, albeit more comfortable and not at all dark and pokey. You can skip the 'forgive me, Father, for I have sinned' bit. I have heard it unto death."

"It was coming up for dinner time when all the musketeers came over the hill," she hesitantly began. "Everyone got worried, though the master, Gregoire's father, told us all there was nothing to worry about. I was out playing, but my mother dragged me back inside. All of us servants were put into the kitchen to wait. They even barred the doors.

"We weren't sure what was going on. Everyone was scared. We'd heard about musketeers, everyone had, but it seemed strange to see them in person. Everyone was wondering what they would be doing there. Why they were locking us up in the kitchen."

Charlotte looked down at her hands. She remembered the hours they waited in the kitchen very clearly. Her mother's anxious foot tapping, the cook and her kitchen girls keeping busy by cooking food, people whispering to each other about suspicion and fears.

"Then some musketeers came. They started splitting us up, taking us away one by one. No one was coming back. I thought something terrible must be happening."

"Did you have reason to fear?" the cardinal asked, but his voice seemed far away and intrusive to the story.

"Yes," Charlotte all but whispered. "They took my maman. I started shouting and crying and tried to cling to her, but the musketeer pulled me off and threw me back into the kitchen. I remember him being unkind. I don't think they know what to do with screaming servant's children, musketeers. I think they only know how to fight and shoot and be nice to the king."

"Not a bad assessment. Go on."

"They took me upstairs next. It wasn't as bad as I feared. Captain Treville was waiting in one of the drawing rooms. I remember he was kind. He told me that everyone they talked to was just waiting in another room. He apologized for scaring me. He asked me to sit."

She stopped.

"Go on," the cardinal said softly.

Charlotte took a deep breath. "He asked if I knew who he was, if I knew who the musketeers were. He asked if I knew about the king. Of course I did. He told me they kept the king safe from enemies. They kept France safe from enemies. He told me that the king's mother had done something bad. They were looking for traitors, people plotting against the king."

"And did you know any?"

Charlotte looked up. She could feel tears on her face. "You know I did." The cardinal's face remained impassive. "I thought I was good at lying. But maybe Captain Treville is good at spotting liars. I told him I didn't. He asked if I was sure. He told me that it would be very bad for me to lie, that a lot of people would get hurt if the king wasn't protected." She sighed. "I wasn't very good at following rules as a girl, Your Eminence. Almost anyone will tell you, I was dreadful at being a proper girl. But I had heard all the stories of the king and the musketeers, and I wanted to do the right thing. So I told Captain Treville what I had overheard."

She remembered the musty smell of the largely disused drawing room. She lay flat on the wooden floor underneath a sofa, covered in dust. She didn't sneeze. She didn't want to get caught. She knew it would be bad. Even as she lay down and listened, she knew it was bad.

"Charlotte, what did you overhear?"

"I heard Madame de Medici and Monsieur de Medici saying they were to have an important talk there, with an important guest. I thought it was about Gregoire's marriage. He told me that morning that he was getting married to a fancy girl with a fancy name. I was so angry. We had a big fight. I was stupid, Your Eminence, I didn't understand that noble boys married noble girls and that was that. We were friends, and I knew if he married, we wouldn't be able to climb trees and talk to each other anymore. I thought the guest was his bride. I wanted to know what was happening, and I knew Gregoire wouldn't tell me." She took a deep breath. "But it wasn't a girl. It was a man. It was Gregoire's uncle. I had seen him a half dozen times before. He and Gregoire's parents were talking about a rebellion. The king's mother was having a coup. I didn't even know the word. And Gregoire's uncle talked them into supporting it. They were so reluctant. It took hours. I heard them agree that the king was not fit to rule and it was better to stand with family. I heard the plans they made."

She still remembered trembling on the cold wooden floor in the darkness after they left. She knew she heard something terrible she shouldn't have. She lay awake all night wondering if she should tell anyone. If she should even betray the trust of her family's employers. If anyone would even believe her.

"Was Gregoire there?" the cardinal asked.

"No," Charlotte said firmly. "They even said they would keep it from their children. I swear it. On my soul." She looked at the, her dark eyes squarely meeting his, and did not flinch beneath his gaze. Satisfied, the cardinal merely waved his hand again.

"And this is what you told Treville?"

"Yes," she replied. "I told him what I heard. What they said. What plans they made. I told him how hard they were to convince. As I talked, I saw his face ..." She shivered. "I knew this was what he'd been looking for. He sent me back to my maman. She asked why it had taken so long. Why I was crying. I asked her what happened to traitors, and she didn't answer. We both cried, and she held me." Charlotte drew a ragged breath. "The next day, Gregoire and his family were locked in a cart and taken back to Paris. I asked Captain Treville if they would kill him. He said it was up to the king, but he would argue against it. He told me to not feel guilty. I had done a good thing. But I didn't. I killed my best friend's parents. Sometimes I worried I killed him too."

A minute of silence followed. Charlotte wondered what was going through the cardinal's head, whether he was weighing the honesty of her words or simply undertaking whatever mental exercise he did to commit what she had said to memory.

"You were quite correct. I had the bulk of this from Treville's report on the matter, but it is always refreshing to hear it from the source. You were placed in a difficult situation, and I commend your honesty at the time. There was some debate over whether the elusive third de Medici existed. He was not found when the musketeers arrived, and there was speculation whether the young witness, yourself, simply invented him to cover up the presence of her friend, but it was argued that it was too sophisticated a device for a thirteen-year-old girl and that it did not adequately explain the information from the capital that was introduced into the conversation. So the boy, Gregoire, was acquitted. Am I to gather he does not know who revealed his parents' involvement in the treason?"

"No. You cannot tell him. Please."

"He will not have it from me. Madame, be assured you did the right thing."

"I don't think Gregoire would see it that way."

"It is unlikely that he would, yes. The correct course of action when it comes to one's conflicting duties is often difficult. King or kin? Of course, in Gregoire's instance, the king is also kin. Madame, it will be difficult for Gregoire to understand and let go of his anger and bitterness. Mostly, because to do so, he'll have to acknowledge fault with his deceased parents. Can you imagine how damaging that would be for the soul?" He leaned across the desk. "Madame, hear me. Your actions prevented more deaths than you know. It prevented the country from plunging into civil war. There is no absolution to grant because there is no trespass, but if it eases your soul, I grant you absolution anyway."

"With all due respect, Your Eminence," Charlotte whispered, holding back tears, "it is not your forgiveness, nor the Lord's, that I worry about."

A few moments of silence passed. The cardinal spoke, and his voice was businesslike again. "Very well, you've given me the information I asked for; therefore, I can confirm that Gregoire de Medici's requested that his payment for his work be in the form of a good marriage for his sister as well as her schooling being paid for and the papers and funds for him to begin a new life in England. I will of course be providing this as soon as the tasks I require are completed."

"I see," Charlotte said quietly. "And does Your Eminence know why he wishes to leave for England?"

"He has not opened his feelings to me. I suspect it rather has something to do with the legacy of his family being hard to shake in France."

"But he can take a new name. He can stay here ..." Charlotte trailed off. She looked at Cardinal Richelieu beseechingly, but the man simply shrugged.

"I rather suspect it also has something to do with his resentment of the king and the nation that killed his parents. At a guess. We have not discussed it, but his distaste is not as well disguised as he might like to think."

"I see. Thank you."

"I see this news is quite a wrench for you, madame," Richelieu offered solicitously.

"No, I am not upset about Gregoire. I merely feel ... his rewards exceed mine. You simply gave me this job with the assurance that once Lady Abigail's works were discovered and stopped, I'd be free to go. There was no reward offered."

"I confess myself surprised that you only noticed now. You

normally have much finer attention to people's words and their omissions. The reason is simple enough and does not, no matter what you may feel, involve trying to swindle you. Monsieur de Medici is a man who knows what he wants. He wants his sister to have a life befitting her birth, and he wants to escape his family. You, on the other hand, don't know what you want."

"That is ... that is simply not true, Your Eminence," Charlotte protested.

"At the time, your most pressing need was shelter and employment, so I organized that, with the hope that in the wake of the tragedies you would find your purpose. I am delighted to hear you have been successful. Please, madame, tell me what reward I can render to you that you feel you want that is comparable to Monsieur de Medici's."

Charlotte opened her mouth and found no words to say. What did she want to do?

"I can arrange a good marriage for you, to a man of appropriate breeding, with good resources, who is kind. I can arrange a genuine lady's maid position for you, for you to help dress a noble woman and do her needlework until you are called to the Lord. I can arrange for you to come into resources and open your own shop. You can take vows with the abbess. Please, madame, what is it you wish to do with your life?" He propped his chin up and leaned forward with the smug expression on his face of someone who knew they were right.

How did this man know more about her than she did?

"Your Eminence is very wise to give me so much time to consider my future. It is not a gift afforded many women of my station. I will take it into careful consideration and my prayers. I've delayed you long enough. I better be going."

She rose, curtsied, and turned to leave.

"Do not feel pressured by time, madame. If by the end of

this assignment you do not know, I am happy to give you another one to buy you time."

"That is ... that is definitely not necessary."

The cardinal smiled warmly. "I'll start looking for a marriageable option then."

"I can find my own husband, if I need one," she snapped, without bothering with politeness. She was certain she heard him laugh as the door shut.

The man is the devil, she thought as she stomped through the corridors. She hated to admit he was right. What did she want with her future? Especially now that Gregoire was secretly planning to leave her again?

CHAPTER 24

Charlotte could not sit by Gregoire's bedside and wait to ambush him with questions about his planned departure. Lady Abigail demanded her attention, now that Charlotte was to play assistant in clandestine meetings with Abigail's secret sweetheart. The day after Gregoire's dramatic duel, Abigail informed her that that afternoon they would be taking a walk in the palace gardens and that Charlotte had a very particular role to play.

They strolled in the largest of the palace gardens. Abigail wore a meticulously chosen dress, her hair artfully arranged. She was resplendent in jewels, paints, and perfumes. As the bell struck the hour of three, Charlotte dutifully stumbled and fell to the ground, clutching her ankle.

"Oh, my dear maid! You've hurt yourself! Why don't you rest here on this bench, and I will see if I can find some aid."

Abigail concluded her brief fuss before nearly skipping off into the twisting paths that took her from view. Charlotte smiled with unfeigned fondness, waiting for her to have just enough of a head start before attempting to follow her.

"Good afternoon, madame," a familiar male voice said.

Charlotte looked up. Approaching her was Artus Daumont, who had followed Gregoire's shooter the previous day.

"Monsieur Daumont." She glanced in the direction Abigail had gone. She would be getting further from her with each passing second of delay. "Thank you again for trying to catch the villain that shot Monsieur Guillot. Did anything come of the investigations?"

"No, unfortunately. The Duke of Buckingham insists the bullet was almost certainly meant for him and that the man missed, striking the musketeer by mistake. The musketeers believe it was a servant of the duke instructed to deal with the upstart musketeer, should he look in danger of winning the duel. His Majesty the king is unhappy about the whole affair, especially if Buckingham was meant to be the one to take the bullet and the shooter missed." Artus Daumont smiled. "He makes no secret of his dislike of the English duke. May I join you, madame?" He gestured at the space on the bench beside Charlotte.

"Please, do not feel as though you must provide me with company. I have injured my ankle, and I am waiting for my lady to return with aid. I am quite content with my needle-work." Charlotte smiled, but inside she was frustrated that he lingered. She wasn't sure she'd be able to tail Abigail now and find out who her mysterious suitor was. And there was something about the manservant that was bothering her. He seemed familiar to her somehow, but she could not place it. His face, but especially his voice, reminded her of something, or someone, and skirted the edge of her memory.

"I fear your lady will be some time in returning with aid. She is taking a turnabout in the gardens with my master. They have been apart for so long I suspect it will not be a short meeting." At Charlotte's surprised face, Artus Daumont smiled widely. "I too am left on my own in the name of young love. My lord of Orleans was most anxious to see the lady. We are both relieved that she has found a lady's maid that can be trusted with her greatest secret."

"Orleans? Not the Duke of Orleans?" Charlotte stared, amazed. "The king's younger brother?" She tried to recall what she knew of the younger de Bourbon, but it wasn't much apart from the fact he existed. That certainly shed light on why Daumont was walking here, and why he was so well dressed for a servant. And as the servant of the prince, he must be confident of his master's support if he was capable of standing against Buckingham as he did the previous day.

"The very one." He gestured again at the seat beside her, and Charlotte this time gave him leave to sit. It seemed following Abigail was no longer an immediate priority, and since Daumont would not leave, she would use the opportunity to get information from him.

"I am pleased for my mistress, that she has someone whom she loves so well and who loves her in return," she said as Daumont sat down at the far end of the bench, leaning back comfortably and tilting his face up to the sun. He was older than he had looked initially. "I fear the secrecy will not be easy for her. Young women often feel the need to shout their love from the rooftops."

"Young women?" Artus looked at her with a raised eyebrow. "Why, madame, what advanced years have you reached that you can set yourself apart thus? Your face does not wear the ravages of years, but your voice bears a note of—"

"Healthy cynicism in the affairs of love," Charlotte finished his sentence for him. She tilted her head as she examined his face. He looked unexceptional—dark haired, of no particular age between young and old, dark eyes, and an easy smile. "Forgive me for staring, monsieur. You look somewhat familiar. Have we met before? Before yesterday, I mean."

Daumont looked closely at Charlotte's face in turn. "I cannot recall, madame. You do not look familiar to me, forgive me. I do not believe I even know your surname; Lady Abigail only calls you Charlotte."

Charlotte mentally chided herself to do better in remembering her courtly manners. "Of course. I plain forgot my manners yesterday when we met. My name is Charlotte Lefort."

The man shook his head. "I do not know anyone from a Lefort family. Perhaps we have seen each other around the palace or Paris. Or perhaps I just have one of those faces. Common." He grinned self-deprecatingly.

“I do not think so at all. Certainly, yesterday you were a welcome sight. I am glad of your quick thinking in chasing the shooter. Will you not get in trouble with your lord for getting muddled in the whole thing?"

"My master has no love for Buckingham, nor any fear. They quarreled at a diplomatic dinner several weeks ago. A loathing for Buckingham is one of the few things he has in common with his brother."

"The dinner," Charlotte said suddenly. "That is where we must have seen each other, in the servants' quarters."

"Indeed!"

"Your lord is a powerful man, Monsieur Daumont," Charlotte said after a moment's careful consideration. "And Lady Abigail is just a girl. I hope he is not trifling with her heart." She watched Artus's reaction.

"It is commendable that you take such care of your mistress," he said with a sigh. "But in truth, even genuine affection doesn't make this a more workable situation. My lord of Orleans is not as powerful as he might seem. He is the brother to the king, yes, but he will spend all his life with the limited choices of a king and none of the power. He is not so old himself; he is scarcely in his majority. I do not think he has accepted that he will have to marry for the state. No, he does not toy with the lady's heart, no more than he toys with his own."

"Your answer has not reassured me."

"Good," Artus Daumont said with a sad smile. "The Duke of Orleans is as much a subject to the king as we are, and without any of our freedom. My lord's future is a strategic marriage to someone of his family's choosing, for the betterment of France. He will not get to marry one he loves. Perhaps it is worse for him in the long run, to have this taste of what he can never have. But who am I to tell him? I'm just his servant." He sighed and looked at Charlotte. "I help him get his joy from this. He is a sullen man otherwise, and I fear that should we try to prevent them, it will become more attractive. At least now I have someone I can talk with about it, rather than let it all sit in my head and worry."

Charlotte felt herself smile. Artus Daumont's manner was kind and easy. It was hard not to instinctively trust him. "I am also looking forward to ... making more of your acquaintance."

What Daumont said about the Duke of Orleans's future reminded Charlotte of what Gregoire had said about how he felt as a young man, when he had nightly wished away his heritage and his prospects so he could be with her. The vice that Orleans was trapped in seemed to be the same one: a privilege unasked for that restricted as much as it gave.

"Oh good, Charlotte, you found a friend!" Abigail was emerging from the paths. Her cheeks were pink and her eyes were bright.

Artus Daumont rose. "It was a pleasure to meet you, Madame Lefort." With a small bow to Charlotte and a deeper bow to Abigail, he walked off in the direction Abigail had just come from.

Abigail squealed. "How marvelous! Would it not be

wonderful if you fell in love with my beloved's manservant? What a happy pair of couples we would be! He is much more respectable than that musketeer you fancy, and so much less likely to get shot!"

"Please, my lady, let my poor heart be. It cannot take any more excitement. I am content to simply enjoy your happiness." Charlotte smiled weakly at Abigail, but she had already changed the topic and was chattering away. Charlotte had a headache coming on. There was simply so much information to sift, and she could not shake the feeling she was missing something important.

She knew she should go and tell Cardinal Richelieu immediately what she had learned about Lady Abigail and her lover. It had to be significant that the brother of the king was now involved. But Artus Daumont was convinced it was a harmless dalliance before having to face his responsibilities, and he knew his master better than anyone. The Duke of Buckingham still seemed muddled into all of this somehow too.

In an instant, Charlotte made her decision. She would wait for more information. If she revealed this, it would immediately be destroyed, whether it was harmful or not. She would wait and see, watch for whose advantage Abigail was playing for. Perhaps her love was harmless and she was blackmailed by the Duke of Buckingham to act against France? Truly, Charlotte could not bring herself to turn Abigail's affection over to the hands of the spymaster. Not yet. Not until she was sure Abigail meant harm by it.

CHAPTER 25

Gregoire was returned to the musketeer barracks to complete his recovery as soon he was able to make the trip. Reynaud and the other musketeers thought the sooner he was out of the palace the better. The mysterious shooter was still at large, and the musketeers wanted to make it difficult for him to try another strike on Gregoire. The first few days, Gregoire spent mostly asleep. He had confused dreams about the duel, of Charlotte, and unhappy muddles of the two where it was Charlotte who shot him, and those dreams always woke him with a dull throbbing pain where the bullet had hit him.

When his head cleared and he spent more time awake than asleep, he asked his musketeer friends for news of Charlotte. Monnier reported that she was busy with Lady Abigail and could not come to visit but sent her best wishes. Gregoire wondered about the meaning of that. Was there a development in their spying endeavor that she was caught up in? Or was she loath for some reason to come to the barracks? She certainly could not be afraid to; Charlotte was fearless. He simply had to hurry his recovery so that he could go to her and aid her in their mission.

Being up and about around the barracks put him in much better humor, which lasted until all of a week after the duel, when Captain Treville gathered the whole company of musketeers in the courtyard after dawn duties were completed. The rugged captain stood in front of them, his well-worn cloak stirring behind him in a light breeze. He looked almost as tired as Gregoire felt.

"Lads," he opened solemnly, and all chatter amongst the men died at once. "I know we don't deal in spy craft, and we don't much like it when there's no clear and present enemy to confront, but in this case we've been called on to help find a potential deadly threat to the crown." Gregoire exchanged looks with Monnier, who looked as confused as Gregoire felt. Whispers broke out briefly before Treville continued. "There is reason to believe that there is a dangerous agitator from the de Medici family lying low in Paris at the moment."

A dangerous de Medici agitator. Gregoire felt like he'd been shot all over again, and it was all he could do to keep himself standing up.

"It is suspected that the agitator is part of the French branch of the de Medici family, which in plain speech means a reasonably close relative of the Queen Mother. Not much else to go on, lads. This fellow has been engaged in clandestine operations around Paris in the last several weeks or months, and we've been asked to keep our eyes out."

Gregoire forced himself to breathe slowly as the muttering around him took on an angry hum, like a hive of bees being stirred up. He felt as though his family name were branded on his forehead and any second the musketeers would look around and realize that the de Medici they were looking for was standing amongst them right now.

"How are we meant to keep an eye out for someone

when we don't know what he looks like, let alone if he exists?" one of the musketeers across the courtyard complained.

"I wish I had better information for you all, but you'll just have to trust your gut and use your wits," Treville replied with a shrug.

"Use our wits? Half of us don't have any, Captain, you know that," another musketeer shouted out.

"Didn't they hang all the de Medicis they caught?"

"Not all of them. Some of them got away, and others they let off," Etienne said. "My father was there for the trials, such as they were."

"Why would they let traitors off?" thundered the musketeer with the Scottish accent.

"They didn't let any of the traitors off. They let some of the de Medici children go."

"You don't let children of traitors get away. They just grow up to try for revenge," one tall musketeer growled. "My brother was killed in the rebellion. Let me at this agitator when we find him! You'll see he's some discontented son grown up with a chip on his shoulder."

"Enough of that, Mercier!" Treville barked. "We do not execute people for being the children of traitors, do you hear me?"

From the sound of discontented rumblings around Mercier, it sounded to Gregoire that plenty of musketeers agreed with the notion of hanging all members of a traitor family from the highest branches. Gregoire felt like he was about to be sick. Perspiration broke out over his body, and black spots swam in front of his eyes. These people whom he had thought of as his friends would hang him if they found out the truth about him.

"Guillot, are you all right?" Monnier asked, and Gregoire realized his friend was staring at him.

"Fine," Gregoire managed. "I think my fever's come back is all."

"Well, get back to bed then, and we'll get the doctor to come look at you again. Don't fall over here in the courtyard. I'm not carrying you back up to your bed." Monnier grinned, but his smile faded as Gregoire didn't return it.

"What do you make of this news?" Gregoire asked, not moving from where he was standing. "Reckon there's really a de Medici in Paris?"

"We're not high on the list of people they give reconnaissance to, so if they're roping us in, it's fairly likely," Monnier said.

"Wouldn't put it past old Marie to be fomenting rebellion from whatever nunnery they banished her to," Etienne muttered darkly. "Or for one of her brood to be out to elevate the family again."

"That whole family is a nest of snakes," Mercier sneered, overhearing their conversation. "A poisoned gift from Florence is what that marriage was. Marie wasn't fit to replace the previous queen."

"That is the mother of the king you're talking about there, Mercier," Reynaud commented mildly.

Mercier shrugged. "A mother who tried to oust her own son."

"Since you're so fired up, Mercier, why don't you and your lads take guard duty on His Majesty's morning at the tailor?" Treville said, appearing beside them. "You can make sure no de Medicis are hiding in bolts of cloth or disguised as mannequins."

As Mercier moved off, grumbling all the while, Reynaud turned to Captain Treville.

"Orders, Captain?"

"Take your lads down to where the thieves' guild congregates. See if you can find anything about a Medici who might be using lower Paris to hide himself." Treville spread his hands. "It's chasing ghosts, but while information is scant, I think the information credible."

Reynaud nodded. "As you say, Captain."

"God's mercy, Guillot, what are you doing up and about?" Captain Treville had caught sight of Gregoire. "You're white as a sheet. You're not to be out of your barracks until the doctor has cleared you, is that clear? Monnier, make sure he does as he's told."

"I don't see why I'm stuck babysitting Guillot," Monnier grumbled good-naturedly. "Come on, Guillot, you heard the captain."

Back in the barracks, Gregoire lay in his bed. He felt as helpless as the day his family had fallen. Once again, people whom he thought were his friends hated him. Or at least, they would when they knew whom he truly was. He was cut off from Charlotte. He was still too infirm to make his way to safety. He had to wait here amongst those who were out hunting for him and do his best not to be caught.

It was more imperative than ever that he finish this job and head for England. He had fooled himself briefly that his camaraderie with the musketeers was real, especially when they had rallied around him after he was shot. But it was Guillot they held in such regard, not Gregoire de Medici.

Gregoire de Medici was a traitor, who they thought should have been hung, and they would be only too glad to administer the punishment now if they caught him.

There was nothing for him in Paris, and he must never forget it again.

CHAPTER 26

Charlotte stayed busy during the two weeks that Gregoire was recovering from his injury, so that she would not be tempted to give in and see him. She knew he must be confused about her absence, and every time she felt as though her resolve would weaken, she found another thing to do. She stayed closer than ever to Lady Abigail, through daily outings to church, long hours with the queen's ladies, and endless walks in the garden. There were clandestine meetings with her lover too, that she supervised as best she could while keeping Artus Daumont company.

During the nights, she went and learned from Madame Sabine. She enlarged her repertoire of herbs and poisons, practiced lock picking, and learned all manner of unexpected tricks that might one day be useful. She enjoyed Madame Sabine's company immensely. When she had confided in her teacher about her romantic woes, Madame Sabine did not have a high opinion of Gregoire's secrecy and urged Charlotte to stay independent. In one lesson, Madame Sabine gave Charlotte a gift from "the Rose"—a hook with a rope ladder attached, small enough for hiding under one's skirts. It was the same sort she had escaped with on their first meeting. Charlotte was delighted.

But all through her occupation, Gregoire was never far from her thoughts. She treasured the time they had spent together, but knew a reckoning was coming, where she would confront him about England and he would undoubtedly do something stupid in the name of protectiveness. She did not look forward to it. She loved him, she was sure of it, but love couldn't be enough. Not if he wasn't honest. Not if he would not let her be herself.

Instead, she chose to avoid him. Two weeks to the day from the duel, she was on another long walk with Lady Abigail, her beloved, and Artus Daumont.

"How did you come to serve the Duke of Orleans?" Charlotte asked Daumont as they strolled along a number of steps behind Abigail and the prince of France. The weather was mercifully overcast, no bright sunshine. She was walking in the private gardens of the Duke of Orleans and conversing with the amiable Artus Daumont. She hid her resentment.

"It was some combination of hard work and good luck, madame," Artus replied. "My family has been in service for many years to high ranking nobility; we have a good reputation. Unfortunately, one of our mistresses moved abroad to Spain some years ago for marriage, and her brother went with her, and seeing as I was serving him, I followed. Spain was an interesting country to live in, but in my heart I am a Frenchman. When the Duke of Orleans came to visit the Spanish court, one of his roaming adventures, his manservant fell in love with a Spanish girl and married, leaving the duke short of help. My master loaned me to him for a few weeks until the end of his journey. We got along very well, and at the end of the trip, he offered to hire me. Well, I was heartily sick of Spain, and the opportunity to serve royalty does not come along often, so I said *adieu* to my former master and travelled back here with my lord of Orleans." He chuckled. "Not that I've spent a lot of time in France, after all. My lord travels a fair bit."

"Is he an adventurous type or the restless type?" Charlotte inquired. Artus seemed to enjoy talking, and the more he talked, the less Charlotte would have to. She felt she ought to be trying to eavesdrop on the conversation between Lady Abigail and her lover, but her heart was not in the mood for spy craft this afternoon.

"He is the type who is not often in favor with his brother the king," Artus said diplomatically. "My lord and his brother are both young men, and siblings often have friction between them as they grow up. It is entirely normal, of course, particularly between brothers. Particularly between powerful brothers. My lord loves his brother and so travels to be out of his way." He paused for a few moments. "Of course, His Majesty also cares for his brother. Sometimes it is best for siblings to spend little time together, until these growing pains are resolved. When they are both mature men, they will be a force to be reckoned with."

"Of course. I've seen siblings with far lesser inheritance become aggrieved with one another," Charlotte said.

Artus fixed her with a sudden look. "There is no matter of the inheritance. My master is quite happy with his estates. He has no further designs." Charlotte blushed, but Artus continued, kindly. "In fact I think he enjoys the vast freedoms denied to his brother. The greater dispute is, of course, whom my lord of Orleans will marry."

"I believe it is safe to say whom his heart belongs to, but whom is he promised to?"

"His majesty and his advisors are looking for a strong political match. I believe they are looking at Marie de

Bourbon, the daughter of the Duke of Montpensier, as the frontrunner, but there are some others, including some from Spain. England, I believe, is not a consideration, as his sister Henriette Marie is in negotiations to marry Prince Charles."

They regarded the couple ahead of them and contemplated what this meant.

"Is my lord of Orleans likely to prevail upon his brother?" Charlotte asked, feeling sad for her lady.

"I think he would, if it were only his brother to convince. Louis—His Majesty—is a romantic, and I believe he wants to keep his brother happy. Unfortunately, it is not just the king to convince; there is the matter of the queen, who is insisting on a Spanish bride, and then there is the first minister. His religious affiliations make him think poorly of England, of course, and I believe he has some other reasons for wanting to keep my lord from, in his own words, being too reliant on the good humor of his brother."

Charlotte pondered this new piece of information. The cardinal was against an English marriage. She wondered whether he knew something of this liaison after all and the true purpose of her assignment was to put a stop to it. She wondered if he knew that she had been keeping this information back. And not for the first time, she wondered if this was all as innocent as it seemed. There was some uneasy niggle at the bottom of her stomach, some gut instinct that gnawed at her, a hint of disquiet.

"Madame, you have gone quiet. Are you worried for your position should your mistress succeed in her marriage?"

"As servants we must think about these things," Charlotte lied. She wondered what would happen to her if Abigail were to marry or the assignment were to come to an end. She bit her lip slightly. She could ask the cardinal for another job. He had made it clear he would be only too happy to oblige her.

There was no other option in her future. She would not stay with Gregoire if he moved to England.

"I am something of a foundling, monsieur," she told Daumont. "I had fallen on some very hard times, and the good sisters at the Port Royal-des-Champs took me in for their charity and trained me as a lady's maid in their finishing school. My lady Abigail is such a sweet Catholic soul that she chose me to serve her. But I have no illusions about my prospects. I am competent, but if she marries your lord ... well, I am not fit to serve one married to a prince."

"Your relationship with Lady Abigail is strong, madame. I do not think she will get rid of you so easily."

"If she were to, I would not fault her, nor would I pose an impediment to her marriage for my own selfish purposes."

"I didn't wish to suggest that," Artus replied, sounding frustrated. "Madame, I mean only ... I hope this is not an impertinent observation, but it seems you are without a husband," he said carefully.

"I am a widow," Charlotte told him. The conversation suddenly felt as though it were on thin ice. Dear sweet, merciful Lord above, he wasn't about to propose, was he?

"I see. You have my condolences for your loss." They walked in silence for a short span, leaving Charlotte's imagination wild with possibilities. He at last continued. "Madame, you are a well-spoken, kind, and honest woman. I enjoy your company very much, and there has been no flaw in your service to your mistress. There is some measure of security marriage can provide, and I hope such a union would provide a more pleasing alternative than falling on charity or destitution. I am not proposing. I know we have met only a handful of times, but"—Artus spread his hands—"I am not a great romantic. But I have found myself very fond of you, madame, and I think we would work well together. Think on it. Even if we were to lose our present employers, I think the pair of us would not be out of work."

The offer he made was not terrible, from a purely pragmatic standpoint. If they married, it would be a great incentive for their masters to keep them if they also wed, regardless of Charlotte's apparent lack of service pedigree. And if they were dismissed, he would certainly be able to get work, and her safety was assured.

It was good and sensible, and she could almost hear her mother's voice in her head telling her to think like a practical woman for once.

But, of course, that was how she'd ended up married to her first husband. She had had one marriage of convenience, and it had been terrible. And how could she even think of accepting a proposal from a man she barely knew, when Gregoire ...

"You do me great kindness with such an offer," Charlotte said slowly. "And you speak so sensibly."

"I am not a romantic, but I am sensible, it is true," Artus readily agreed, with his charming smile.

"It is too soon for me to think about marriage yet, as ... as excellent as your offer is. I am still newly with my mistress, and there are many impediments between them and their wedding bells. I will pray for her and the duke to prevail in their wishes, but for the moment, let us continue as we are, with no rancor or enmity?" She looked hopefully at him.

He smiled easily. "Madame, I assure you, I expected no other answer. Simply, I wanted you to know I am interested, if ever your attention turns to such things. I believe in being open, Madame Lefort. Romances seldom develop when one party expects the other to divine the truth of things from a glance, no matter what the poets say." He paused in his walking and took Charlotte's hand. His eyes on hers, he laid a soft kiss on the back of her hand. "If your prospects are ever bleak, it would be my honor to help you, Madame Lefort. I would be lucky to have such a partner as you."

"Thank you for your honesty," Charlotte said at last. She meant to say something further, but her words caught and died in her throat, as over Daumont's shoulder, she caught sight of Gregoire arriving in the garden.

CHAPTER 27

"Excuse me," Charlotte said to her companion, and rushed past him towards Gregoire. Her heart beat rapidly, from love and dread at the same time. She had been able to will herself to stay away from him, but seeing him in person destroyed all her resolve, and she all but ran to him.

"You are looking so much better," she said.

Gregoire smiled at that. His eyes seemed to drink her in, and his thumb brushed over her cheek. "Lottie." His eyes flashed with adoration for a second. "You saved my life."

"The musketeer surgeon could have done the job; I was just there first."

"But it was you. Your hands. Your skill. Thank you." He leaned forward to kiss her, but Charlotte stepped back.

"Not here, there are too many people," she said softly. "I am here with the man who chased whoever shot you. You must meet him." She turned to look where she had left Daumont, but the manservant was nowhere to be seen. "He must have returned to keeping his master company."

Gregoire leaned forward again, and this time Charlotte

met his lips. She savored their softness and comfort before pulling away. She had to ask now, before she lost her nerve.

"Gregoire," Charlotte asked, her voice quiet and calm, "when were you going to tell me about England?"

Gregoire startled, and she could see his fingers flexing. He looked at her, uncomfortable and wounded.

"Who told you about England?" he asked. Anger kindled in his face. "Was it *him*?"

"You did. When you were half asleep and recovering from being shot. You sighed that you would miss me in England. *He* only confirmed it when I asked directly."

"How dare he tell you." His outrage fueled her own.

"How dare you not tell me!" Charlotte lowered her voice to almost a hiss. "How dare you ... kiss me, take me to bed, tell me you love me, all the while knowing that you don't plan to stay around and make anything of this at all?"

"I wasn't going to leave you behind!" Gregoire took her hands gently in his, as if afraid she would slip away. "I wanted you to come with me."

"But when were you going to tell me? Was I supposed to guess that our future was going to be in England? Were you planning to knock me out and take me on the boat, and then I'd just wake up in England, saving you the trouble of having to take into consideration what I want with my life?"

"Goddammit, it wasn't going to be like that. It wasn't set in stone." Gregoire drew a breath. "When I asked for that, there was nothing for me here, not once my sister's future was assured. Nothing but ignominy. Then I found you." His face softened. "I never expected what happened between us. I didn't have a chance to think about it, between what happened and the duel. I didn't know you loved me. I'm not even sure I knew I loved you until I heard myself say it."

"You have changed your mind then?" Charlotte's hopes

dashed as Gregoire looked away at the question. "Gregoire, are you still going to England?"

"I was changing my mind. I was starting to think maybe it wouldn't be so bad to stay here." He shook his head. "But now they're looking for me, Charlotte."

"Who is?" Fear chilled her heart.

"The musketeers. They've heard there's a Medici in town, and they're hunting him."

The fear on Gregoire's face made Charlotte's stomach clench. It was a fear she had seen only once before, when she watched him be taken away with his family. It was a raw, primal fear, and it made Charlotte briefly forget her anger and take him in her arms.

"Gregoire, it would be different if they knew it was you and that you meant no harm."

"Would it?" There was so much hurt in his voice. Charlotte held him tighter, but he did not relax. "Charlotte, you didn't hear them. They were baying for blood. One of them even said we should have been hanged as children, to prevent us growing up and seeking vengeance." He wrenched himself away from her, leaving her standing with empty arms. "Hanged as *children*."

Charlotte felt the gulf of pain between them. She knew she could not comprehend his ordeal as a young man. She felt only the guilt knowing she had caused him to suffer it. If he was angry and frightened, it was understandable, as were his wishes to flee France. She looked at his eyes. They were staring at some point in the middle distance and looking at memories only he could see. She felt a sharp pang. If France was hostile to him, it was because she had made it so.

"He's not going to get a chance. You're not a child anymore. You can protect yourself. I can help protect you, if you would let me. Oh," she said, catching the look on his face, "it's all right for you to harp endlessly on about protecting me, but when I offer the same, you take offence?"

"That's not what I meant."

"Is it because I'm a woman?" Charlotte demanded. She had no right to get angry at him, but her guilt was overbearing, and being angry was easier than staying silent and letting it gnaw at her. "Because I'm a commoner? Gregoire, I want a partner, not a protector. You are the only person who understood when we were children. You were the only person I could have adventures with."

"Charlotte, stop, stop." He smiled at her, a gentle warm smile that broke through his pain like the first sun of spring through ice. "I know. I've learned my lesson after the forger. Having you at my back is better than the entire company of musketeers. I am never safer than when I am with you." He paused for a moment, then continued, a little uncertain. "I brought you a present. The others said you might prefer flowers, but I had a different idea."

He presented a narrow leather sheath, then drew the slight dagger it contained. It was short, no longer than from her wrist to the end of her longest finger, and it gleamed in the sun.

"You're giving me a dagger?" Charlotte asked, looking from the weapon to his face and back again.

"Yes. It fits inside your boot. I'm certain Madame Sabine has at least half a dozen other clever hiding places for something like this." Charlotte was aware he was watching her carefully. "Do you like it?"

"It's perfect," she said, stepping into the circle of his arms and kissing him, wanting the warmth of his thoughtfulness to drown the burning guilt. Her secret weighed on her more than ever. She kissed him harder, burying the guilt. *We love each other. That has to be enough.*

"Monnier and Etienne thought I was going to get stabbed

with it. They said you'd want flowers." He rolled his eyes. "No woman wants a knife, they said. That's because they haven't met you." He held her tightly. Charlotte buried her face in his shoulder, drawing in his scent, then pulled back so she could kiss him.

Gregoire's kiss had the power to make her forget everything else except him. The fervent pressure of his lips made her feel in a way she hadn't since her childhood: as though all were right in the world. As though she were loved, and safe, and whole. She had professed to not want any protection, but she had lied: this was one safety she craved above anything else. His kiss made her feel protected from everything. She poured into her kiss all the love she had for him, and all her sorrow for his pain. The dagger must have been discarded, since his hands gliding over her back. They lingered where her dress swelled over her hips for a few seconds before he pulled himself away with a gasp.

"A pity we are in the garden," he said, struggling to compose himself. Charlotte felt the same, and distracted herself by picking up her new dagger and sheath from the grass where it had fallen.

"Gregoire," she said as she straightened up. "I'm scared of going to England with you because I never want to be dependent on a man—on a husband—again. I never want to be dependent on anyone again."

"You would not be dependent on me. For one thing, you're the only one out of the two of us who speaks English." He smiled. "But I cannot stay here. Everything in my life comes back to losing my family. I was betrayed by my country, God, and everything I held dear. I cannot forget about it. And, it seems, there are many others who haven't forgotten it."

I cannot forget either, Charlotte thought. Her secret burned inside her.

"I'm not asking you to." She took a deep breath. This would have been easier had he continued to be patronizing and overprotective. "I'll think about it. We will find a way. We have time until the assignment is over. But now I must get back to my lady."

She accepted his farewell kiss, lingering and drawing it out. Running away to England to escape his betrayal might be a fine solution for him. Unfortunately for Charlotte, wherever she ran, her betrayal would always follow.

CHAPTER 28

"With Madame Menard's continued pilfering of confessional hat letters, we've established that there is going to be a surprise attack tomorrow by several companies of Spanish mercenaries wearing the livery of the Spanish army," Cardinal Richelieu informed Gregoire under the gazes of gargoyles. "It would be a crude false flag attack, easily disputed, if it were not for the letters in the queen's handwriting arranging it all." A muscle twitched in the cardinal's face; Gregoire took it to be an indication of irritation. "Captain Treville has been briefed on the nature of the attack. Try to look surprised when you hear about this later tonight. You will be assigned to the unit ambushing the group that has the leader attached. Captain Treville has been informed that this is a false flag, and he will be on the lookout for the letters in possession of the leader, but you are there as a fallback option. Get the letters before anyone else does, so we can prevent all damage to the queen and the alliance with Spain—Monsieur de Medici, is something I'm saying boring to you?"

"No," Gregoire replied, trying to focus on the Cardinal, rather than think about Charlotte.

"Then try to look like you're paying attention."

"Are we done? After tomorrow? After we've got these letters and we've stopped these Spaniards?"

"We are done when we have traced this back to its architect," Cardinal Richelieu told him. "Are you in such a hurry to leave us? What about fair Madame Menard?" Gregoire scowled. The cardinal quirked an eyebrow. "Trouble in paradise? Am I in danger of losing my wager?"

It took Gregoire a second to remember what wager the cardinal was talking about.

"You are. Have you heard the musketeers are looking for a de Medici in Paris?" Gregoire watched the cardinal's reaction. He was rewarded with nothing but a slight raise of one eyebrow. "Did you tell them that?"

"Not I. Captain Treville doesn't trust me nearly as much as he ought to and has sources other than myself for information. I assume you're worried that they're looking for you?"

"Who else would they be looking for?"

"Young man, you are far from the only branch of that tree left. It would do you well to remember the world does not revolve around you."

"Don't you dare lecture me, Cardinal." Gregoire was suddenly so angry he could hardly bear it. "I am the one trapped night and day in the company of trained soldiers who are looking for me to murder me. I am the one who was shot two weeks ago."

"The bullet was almost certainly meant for the Duke of Buckingham, and you were unlucky."

Gregoire ignored the interruption.

"And you have Charlotte half convinced she's got some kind of career as a spy."

"She could, if she wanted it. Why, did you want her doing needlework forever? Or," the cardinal said, leaning forward, "did you think she would simply trail after you to England, become your wife, keep your house, mend your shirts, and never use that brilliant brain of hers ever again? Ahhh, you did, didn't you? Well, I assume she disabused you of that notion with her acid wit, and perhaps that's why you are in such a foul temper. When will you learn that she's not for you to coddle and keep?"

"Don't tell me—" Gregoire started, but the cardinal cut him off.

"Take it from me, Monsieur de Medici, if you truly do love your Charlotte, then let her make up her own mind about her future and be supportive. You should know very well that no one likes their decisions being taken from them."

"I'm not going to take advice on relationships from a priest. After all, what would you know?"

"What would I know indeed. It is well known that I was born from my mother straight into priesthood and did not spend my youth in the army." Richelieu rolled his eyes. "I thought you were a smarter man this, de Medici. Not much smarter, but smarter." He sighed and shook his head. "I don't know why I bother. Well, you have your orders. Don't let those letters fall into the wrong hands. And I promise, as soon as I have the head of whoever is orchestrating all this, you'll be on the first boat to England. In the meantime, why don't you see this as an opportunity to try to ... work things out with your beloved Madame Menard?"

"It's none of your business what goes on between myself and Charlotte. Why does it matter to you so much?" Gregoire demanded.

"I consider it part of my charitable works. Be gone with you."

The cardinal did not wait for him to leave this time. He

rose and vanished through a barely perceptible door in the stonework behind him, leaving Gregoire alone in the ominous chapel. The only sound in the room was the soft crackle of candles and the grinding of Gregoire's teeth.

Infuriating, meddling man. He was never going to let Gregoire go; he would keep him dancing on a string for as long as he could, and then, likely as not, hang him.

But Gregoire would stay in Paris even now. And the cardinal knew that. There was his sister to think of. And Charlotte. He would not leave until he could convince her to travel with him.

He left the church and strode angrily back toward the barracks, frustrated and confused. Lost in his thoughts, he almost didn't hear the voice calling his name. He stopped, and a man emerged from the shadows of an alleyway. It took Gregoire a moment to recognize him.

"Hello, Gregoire," the man said with an easy smile. "My favorite nephew. I am ever so pleased to see you. It's been a long time."

CHAPTER 29

"Uncle," Gregoire said. Uncle Alessandro, his father's brother, his favorite uncle while growing up. "I was afraid you were dead. Where have you been all these years?"

"I feared the same about you, my boy." His uncle stepped in, grabbed his shoulders firmly, and looked at him, shaking his head. "*Mon dieu,* how you've grown. You're a man now, aren't you?"

"I've been a man since ... you know when." Gregoire looked around the street, feeling uncomfortably exposed. "I can't talk about it here."

"Of course." His uncle nodded genially. "You know what it takes to survive in Paris, don't you? Come inside. I have a room." He slung an arm around Gregoire and steered him into the inn across from the barracks, leading him upstairs to a private room. The same room Gregoire and Charlotte had made love in two weeks ago. It was surreal to be sitting here with his uncle.

Ordering food and drink, his uncle clapped him on the back.

"I can't tell you how pleased I am to see you. Though I have to admit some surprise at your occupation. I never thought I'd see that cloak on any of our family." Gregoire looked away, uncomfortable. His uncle leaned in knowingly. "Let me guess. They don't know who you are."

"There's false pretenses involved, yes."

"I don't blame you, not at all, for leaving the family behind. It's hard not to feel like the king and his boys are going to shoot someone just for being a Medici, isn't it?" He popped some grapes in his mouth and leaned back in his chair. "I have to ask how you stomach working for the folk who killed your family though. Hard to swallow, isn't it? Or are you past all that? Forgotten about your father and mother?"

"Don't you dare," Gregoire snapped. "Don't you dare accuse me of forgetting about them for a second. This"—he gestured at his cloak—"is temporary. I'm doing it to provide for my sister, that's all. She doesn't deserve to suffer as the rest of us have. And when it's taken care of, I'll throw this in the Seine and leave this city behind for good."

He glared at his uncle, fists clenched, daring him to argue. His uncle, however, seemed mollified by his answer.

"I'm sorry, Gregoire, I didn't realize." He sighed and rubbed his hands over his face. "I still haven't forgiven the insipid king, his blue-cloaked bully boys, or that skulking cardinal for how they gutted our family. I won't ever forgive." Bile and anger dripped off his words. He poured them both a drink, pushed a tankard toward Gregoire, and stoppered the bottle. "So, how do you feel about revenge?"

"Against who?"

His uncle blinked slightly.

"Well, the people who reduced our family to being too afraid to utter our name in public, banished Marie, executed our brothers, sisters, mothers, fathers. Revenge on the whole festering lot of them."

Gregoire's insides burned. The memory of his parents' execution was as raw as the day it happened. He remembered the anger of the musketeers as they hunted for the de Medici agitator for the last week. He wanted revenge on those who ruined his family, yet ...

Marie was wrong to try to overthrow her son. And those who supported her were wrong too. The musketeers had been doing their job stopping traitors.

He was only angry that his own family was lumped in with them.

Gregoire looked at his uncle's face. Behind the genial smile, there was an iron will and the spark of vengeance burning in his eyes. His uncle clearly didn't think the Queen Mother was in the wrong.

"All I know is," Gregoire said at last, choosing his words carefully, "my parents were good people, and they were never mixed up in treason. They didn't deserve to die."

"Yes, my brother and his wife were loyal when it mattered." His uncle stood up and leaned against the window frame, looking down at the street below. "Gregoire, tell me honestly. Don't you want our family to be great again? Don't you want to be able to speak your name proudly? To have the respect that befits our heritage? You can't tell me you've lived the life you were meant to."

Gregoire drank from his tankard while he considered what his uncle said.

"I would like it if our family name was restored. What are you asking, Uncle?"

"There are those of blood who would sit on the throne and who would not forget who raised them there. Our family would be the right hand of the monarchy again." His uncle smiled. "If you assisted me with this, your sister would be one of the most eligible girls at court. You could be the captain of the musketeers if you so wished. I know how badly you desired it as a boy."

Something cold crept through Gregoire's veins. "You talk of treason," he said at last.

"I talk of setting right the wrongs of the past," his uncle snapped, then started smiling again. "Come now, Gregoire. Is your loyalty truly to that purloined cloak and that idiot king?"

Was it?

The question struck Gregoire right in his heart. When he first put on that cloak, the answer would have been no, a resounding no, with all the same bile that his uncle harbored. No, he would have borne no loyalty to the musketeers. No, he would have borne no loyalty to the king that commanded them. He would have given anything to see them all punished and his family restored.

But now, having served with the musketeers, having known the king, Gregoire was not so sure. The death of his parents for treachery they were not part of still weighed on him, as did his life lived in the gutters for the actions of others.

But what his uncle was asking ...

His uncle was watching him, his face imploring. "Come, my boy. We can rise to greatness again. Your father would be proud."

Gregoire stood and faced his uncle. For the first time, they were the same height. Gregoire had grown. His uncle, it seemed, had not.

"For a long time, I let the past weigh me down. I thought that night would forever define me. But I've realized," Gregoire said slowly, "I get to define who I am. And I won't be weighed down by this. I can't pursue a vendetta forever. To betray the king would shame my father. I'm sorry, Uncle, I won't help you plot revenge. I beg you to let the past go. Letting it go and living honorably is the greatest way to honor the death of my father, your brother."

For a long moment, his uncle simply looked at him with eyes that seemed dead. A hardened anger filled his face, and Gregoire thought he might attack. Then the look vanished and his uncle laughed.

"Ah, my boy, maybe I was wrong. Maybe you're not quite a man yet." He strolled over to Gregoire and gripped his shoulder. "Never mind. You have a good heart, you know that? Too good for this world. Anyway," he said, "you best get going. I hear the musketeers are skittish if one of their own misses curfew. If you're going to report me, at least do the decent thing and warn me, right? We are family."

"I won't report you," Gregoire said after a moment. "But they already know one of us is in Paris."

"I appreciate the warning, my boy. You won't need to worry about me getting up to anything. All this is temporary. I won't be your concern after tomorrow."

"Moving on?" Gregoire asked as he paused by the door.

"That's me," Alessandro said, still leaning by the window, the sunset throwing his face into grotesque shadow. His teeth glinted. "Always moving on. Oh, by the by." He smiled, and Gregoire felt uneasy. "If you could find out why your parents were implicated in treason, would you want to know? Why they were killed?"

"Of course I would," Gregoire said. "What do you know? Why did you not start with that?"

"I wouldn't want to be compromising your morals and loyalties, would I? Well, look for my messenger tomorrow morning. One last gift before I move on. See how you feel after you get my present. Maybe it will change things." His smile was wide and easy, except for the hard eyes. "*Adieu*, my nephew."

Gregoire turned and walked down the stairs and out of the inn. He glanced up at the window from the street, but either his uncle was gone or the shadows too deep for him to be seen. The meeting rattled him. For the first time in eight years, he had family other than his sister. Was his uncle merely talking from the bitterness in his heart or did he have nefarious plans in motion?

Was he right to promise to not say anything? He wasn't sure. Kin or king? The question felt heavier on his shoulders than the cloak did.

CHAPTER 30

Everyone was on edge as the next day dawned. A grim cloud of tension hung over the musketeers barracks despite the blue skies and sunshine. Treville's office had been broken into during the night, and two of the musketeers on watch were dead. It was not clear what had been taken from the office. It was the first time in memory that Treville's office had been violated and musketeers killed on watch at their own barracks.

Gregoire, despite his growing distance from his supposed brothers-in-arms, was horrified and angry. Everyone was eager for some action. Terrible potential hung in the air, as before a storm, and the brilliant morning seemed incongruous with the events. The men were tense, both because of the coming action that day against the "Spanish" and because of the strike so close to home. Gregoire was at breakfast in the barracks when a runner arrived with a parcel of papers wrapped in oiled leather. "To musketeer Guillot" it read, and as Gregoire peeled off the outer layer of leather, there was a note:

Read this alone, else you risk your secret. The reason for your parents' death is enclosed. Do with it what you will.

Abandoning his breakfast, he stalked out into the yard, where in a private spot, he unwrapped the next layer and found an aged sheaf of papers in Captain Treville's hand. As he read the first few lines, his blood chilled. It was a report on a mission from eight years ago.

It was about his family.

Gregoire realized this must be what was stolen from Treville's office during the break-in that night and that it was a breach of trust to read it. The right thing to do would be to hand it back in. But the boiling rage of the sixteen-year-old Gregoire, the one he thought he had left behind, reared its head again. And it wanted to know what had condemned his family. Standing here, so close to the information, Gregoire could not persuade himself to abandon it.

He read feverishly, his eyes racing over the pages, how they had arrived, their actions, the interviews with the servants, until there it was:

A young girl on the staff of the family reported being concealed in the room where Monsieur and Madame de Medici and a third unknown male member of the Medici family discussed the actions that Her Grace the Queen Mother and her supporters planned in Paris and around the country. She recounted that, after some convincing, Monsieur and Madame de Medici agreed to support the coup and agreed to the following actions requested by Her Grace the Queen Mother ... The servant girl, one Charlotte Menard, did not recognize the third member of the family present but is confident it was not their son, Gregoire de Medici, nor his sister, Eloise de Medici.

The world felt like it vanished from around him. The noise of the training yard vanished into a high-pitched whine, and Gregoire saw his hand was shaking. Charlotte? Charlotte had betrayed his family? Charlotte told them this odious lie that his mother and father had a meeting where they were convinced to betray the king?

It seemed he had desperately underestimated her cunning. How much of what she had said since those lies fell out of her mouth were calculated to get what she wanted? Was any of it true? Any affection for him? Any sympathy for his condition? Perhaps she was the cardinal's creature through and through, and they were playing some twisted game with him.

He hastily wrapped the papers in their coverings and strode toward the gate.

"Guillot! Hey, Guillot!" Etienne grabbed him by the shoulder. Gregoire pushed him away with force, causing him to stumble, and his friend's eyes widened with surprise. "What's the matter with you? Where are you going?"

"I have business," he snapped and turned to walk away.

"Guillot! You can't have business. You're needed here! Guillot!"

Gregoire ignored him and vanished into the busy morning streets of Paris. He approached the palace at a stride nearer a run. He had to know the truth. He had to hear it from Charlotte.

ABIGAIL WAS NOT WELL that morning, and for the first time since Charlotte had been her lady's maid, Abigail declined to attend church that morning.

"It is no great matter. I simply feel it would be disrespectful for me to vomit inside the confessional," Abigail said with the ghost of a smile. Charlotte examined her gently but could not conclude more than a fever, lethargy, and stomach pains.

"It's some passing ill. You'll be better for some rest, my

lady," Charlotte reassured her, handing her a tea for the reduction of fever. Internally, she was more worried and was doing a mental stock of all that she knew her lady had eaten and drunk in the past day. She could not shake the feeling she was possibly being poisoned.

If she is, they're being slow with the doses to make it look like an illness. I'll have to watch what she eats and drinks today.

"Thank you, dear Charlotte. I think I will sleep. If I am better in the afternoon, we will go to church then." She handed the tea back and settled into bed. "You are a treasure."

Charlotte shut the door softly to Abigail's bedroom and reached for her basket of needlework when there was a hammering at the outer door. She wrenched it open to find Gregoire standing on the doorstep, his body radiating anger.

"For goodness sake, softly. My lady isn't well," she told him in a hiss. "What is the matter, Gregoire? Has there been some terrible news?"

"In a manner of speaking, yes," he said stiffly, each word forced past his gritted teeth. "Come this way. We will not discuss it here."

Glancing back at Abigail's shut door, Charlotte slipped out of the apartment and followed Gregoire to a secluded space in the nearest garden. He refused to say a word and strode ahead without a care if she kept up. Charlotte's heart hammered with fear. She could see the swathe of papers in his hand. Whatever they contained, it could not be good.

"Here, it is enough, Gregoire. Tell me what happened," Charlotte demanded. "You are frightening me."

"You already know what happened," he said, stopping so suddenly Charlotte almost barged into him. He shoved the papers at her. "It's simply now that I know too."

Charlotte unwrapped the papers. As she cast her eyes over the pages, the words refused to make sense. After a moment, she said, "Gregoire, this is a report by Captain Treville."

It couldn't be the one she feared, could it?

"Yes. About my family." His eyes met hers. "And what you did."

And suddenly Gregoire's implacable fury made sense. It seemed to Charlotte the world tilted and did not right itself, for it was alien that Gregoire would look at her with such naked hatred. It seemed he was barely staying his hands from violence; his whole being quivered with unexpressed anger.

"Gregoire—"

"Were you ever going to tell me, Charlotte?" he demanded. "Were you simply going to keep this secret between us forever?" Charlotte started to answer, but he kept pressing. "Do you truly love me, Charlotte, that you could do this, that you could destroy my family, reduce me to a thief and brand us all as traitors until the end of memory?"

"Please, let me explain," Charlotte tried, but in the face of Gregoire's fury and hurt, she knew there would be no words that could calm him, nor make amends.

"Explain what? Explain how you've manipulated me this whole time? Do you even care, Charlotte, or is this part of some game? Has the cardinal put you up to this, to some strange end that I cannot see because I am a plain-spoken man, and you and he are masters of lies and manipulation?"

"I am not manipulating you."

"How can I trust anything you ever say again, Charlotte? Ever? How can I ever hold you? Look at you? Think of you? Knowing that you said the words that sent my parents to their death? I heard their necks snap, Charlotte!"

Charlotte wished he would strike her. Perhaps some of the awful tension in him would ease and she would feel something instead of the awful cold and horror that had swallowed her. She felt as though she had been turned to stone. She was the lowest of the low, and there would be a place in Hell reserved for people like her. How could she have ever believed Captain Treville and the cardinal's assertions that she had done the right thing?

"I need to tell you the full story, so you know what happened. There was a visitor, and it was the day you told me you were marrying—"

Gregoire suddenly laughed, an awful laugh that was dragged out of somewhere deep inside him and sounded more like the shattering of a window than an expression of mirth.

"And you thought if my family were in disgrace I'd be able to marry you instead?" There were tears in his eyes now.

Charlotte saw black spots in her vision, and her chest had a vice around it. She felt as though she could not breathe.

"Never," she told him. "I wasn't thinking of me. I thought I was doing the right thing."

"You destroyed my family," he shouted. Charlotte shook. "How could you possibly think you were doing the right thing?"

"I'm so sorry," she whispered, but he didn't seem to hear.

"We're done. Forever. Tell the cardinal whatever you like. I never want to see you or hear your voice ever again." He started to walk off then turned. He seemed to be taking in Charlotte in her entirety, his face writ large with pain, sorrow, and betrayal. "I hope you burn in Hell," he said finally and vanished, his blue cloak snapping behind him from the force of his turn.

Charlotte sank onto the grass, her whole body shaking, and started to sob.

GREGOIRE BARELY SAW where he was heading as he stormed through the palace. He had the vague plan of returning to the barracks to retrieve his things and finding some way to vanish. He had some money, and he'd have to go and get his sister. It was time for them both to leave France. There was nothing for them here but false friends and treachery.

He didn't notice the musketeers until they had surrounded him.

He looked at the circle of his friends, Etienne, Monnier, Reynaud, and others he had lived and worked alongside for two months. They had their rapiers raised against him and were watching him warily.

"What is this?" Gregoire demanded.

Reynaud stepped forward. "Are you Gregoire Guillot, the sixth son of the Comte de Guillot?" he asked, his voice hard.

"Yes," Gregoire said, though even he had to admit it sounded unconvincing.

Reynaud sighed. He looked disappointed. "Are you sure, Gregoire de Medici?"

"What are you all doing?" Gregoire demanded, turning this way and that. The circle of rapiers closed in ever so slightly. His friends were poised to kill him. It was his worst fears made real.

"We received information this morning that the man we knew as Gregoire Guillot was in fact the de Medici we have been searching for. You are implicated in a plan to frame the queen for colluding with Spanish rebels and to assassinate the king." Reynaud looked pained as he spoke. "Is that true?"

"Of course not! Reynaud, I would never harm the king. I couldn't frame the queen even if I wanted to! I wouldn't know how."

"Sir, he's got papers in his hand," one of the musketeers Gregoire did not know well pointed out. Reynaud reached out, and Gregoire let him pull the papers from his grip. Wordlessly, Reynaud flipped through the pages.

"It's an old report from the captain. I think we know who broke into his office and murdered the two musketeers on guard. It's about the night the musketeers seized Gregoire de Medici's family." He passed it to a musketeer behind him and set his jaw. "This doesn't look good for you, *friend*."

Gregoire felt as though he were in a nightmare. Everything stable in his life was gone. Everyone he cared about was gone. Everything good was turning to ash. Charlotte, the woman he had loved since before he knew what that meant, had destroyed his family. Now, once again, he was surrounded by angry musketeers accusing him of wanting to murder the king.

Except this time the musketeers had been his friends.

Now, again, he would be sent to jail for treachery he was not responsible for. Only this time it would be his neck snapping in the noose, and it would be the last thing he heard.

"I'm not behind the treachery," Gregoire said, ashamed to hear the desperation in his voice. "It isn't me."

"The information is consistent. There's a de Medici agitator, and you're the only Medici left."

Suddenly, his uncle's talk of restoring family glory sprang into his head and Gregoire felt horror wash over him.

"There is another. I saw him last night at an inn. He told me he was just travelling through." It sounded implausible even to him. "I can show you," he said and started forward, but Reynaud seized him, and the musketeers tightened around him.

"Gregoire de Medici, you are charged with high treason against His Majesty the King of France and Her Majesty the Queen of France and for conspiring with a foreign power."

Gregoire sagged in defeat. Musketeers plucked his weapons off him. Someone cut the ties on his cloak, and it was pulled off him, stripping him of the brotherhood. As they half dragged him down the corridors toward the cells beneath the palace, they regarded him with mingled looks of betrayal, anger, and disgust. Gregoire didn't bother trying to protest his innocence. It had not worked for his parents; it would not work for him. He too was betrayed. Perhaps by Charlotte. Perhaps by Richelieu. Always by France, and always by the musketeers.

As they threw him into a filthy room, with the slimmest of barred windows letting some dregs of daylight in, he looked up to see Monnier look at him with utter heartbreak.

"I don't believe it," he told him. "Tell me this isn't true. You were our brother."

Gregoire turned his back to him. "I'm Gregoire de Medici. As for everything else, none of it is true. But it doesn't matter what I say. You won't believe me."

There were no more words. The door slammed, and Gregoire was left betrayed in darkness once again.

CHAPTER 31

"Madame Lefort?" Charlotte heard a male voice over the sound of her sobs. "Madame, what is wrong?" She looked up, wiping at her cheeks, and saw Artus leaning down toward her, his face concerned. "Are you ill? Can I fetch some aid?"

"No, I am only heartbroken. Everything I have ever wanted was in my reach for one shining moment, and now it is gone, and it is my fault."

"Madame, I scarcely know what to say. Please, let me assist." Charlotte took Artus's offered hand and let him pull her to her feet.

"I did something a long time ago I regret, and I do not think I will ever be forgiven."

Artus gripped her hand. "There is always forgiveness from the Lord," he soothed her.

"I don't care. He is not the one I am worried about. My maman always told me I was too much of a dreamer. Too many ideas for my own good. I get into where I don't belong. I see and hear things I shouldn't. That I want too much. Well, she was right." She swiped angrily at her face with her free hand. Did she really believe she and Gregoire would ever be able to be together and be happy? That she'd be more than a woman who dressed others and did needlepoint and existed to serve? "I'm done. I'm ready to be an adult."

"Madame, I am sorry you have been hurt. Is there anything I can do?"

Charlotte took a deep breath. "You offered, once, that we might marry."

Artus inclined his head. "I did, and I stand by that. Are you considering it?"

"I'd like to accept."

"I am honored, but I do worry that this is a reaction to whatever injury you have just suffered. I think we will make a fine pair, do not misunderstand me." He reached out and gently touched her cheek. His eyes were lit. "Why don't you go and talk it over with your mistress? And if you are still sure, come find me at His Grace's apartments."

Charlotte nodded. She wondered if Abigail was awake and feeling better. Was it selfish to burden her with this?

Artus lifted Charlotte's hand to his mouth and kissed the back of it. "I will see you soon, *cherie,* and I hope I can give you the future you deserve."

Charlotte turned the key and quietly entered the apartment. As she stood in the doorway, even in her distress, the hairs on the back of her neck stood up.

Something was amiss.

"My lady?" she called softly, walking through the main room and turning into the antechamber that served as her own room. She saw Abigail's room door was ajar. "My lady?" she tried again, but there was no answer. She tiptoed across her room and nudged the door open entirely.

The first thing she saw was the blood. Blood all over the bed, the wall, pooling on the floor. There was no movement from the bed. Charlotte ran across the room and cried out as she saw Abigail's slight form, somehow even smaller in death than in life, lying contorted on the bed. There had been a struggle, but even so, the attack was savage. Abigail's eyes were still open. The cornflower blue orbs stared sightless at Charlotte, who stood rooted to the floor in horror.

Who had done this? Who had killed Abigail?

"My lady, my lady," Charlotte murmured, tears falling down her cheeks again. She reached across the bed to pull Abigail's form forward, tidying her limbs and settling her into bed. "My poor lady, you did not even get to go to church this morning."

This is too much grief for one heart to bear, Charlotte thought as she laid her mistress to bed mechanically. *First Gregoire, now Abigail.* Poor Abigail. Whatever she had been involved in, it had got the best of her. It was too hard, too evil, and she had been killed.

Something clattered as it fell out of bed, and Charlotte picked it up. It was a knife, and it was slick with Abigail's blood.

Think, think, think! Charlotte's brain screamed. Someone killed her. Think! Why?

It wasn't Richelieu. So it wasn't the people trying to stop Abigail. Which meant it must be her cohorts. They were done with her.

Which meant whatever they were doing, it was happening soon. Today. Maybe even now.

Charlotte looked one last time at Abigail, whispered a prayer in her heart, and turned to leave. Coming through the doorway at the same time were two musketeers.

"*Mon dieu*!" one cried, and Charlotte recognized Gregoire's friend Etienne. The other simply drew a sword and pointed it at Charlotte.

"Madame, drop the knife, and we will need you to come with us."

Charlotte realized how it must seem, with her holding a bloodied knife, with blood on her clothes, standing over the dead body of her employer. She couldn't even fault the musketeers for the conclusion they came to.

"No! This isn't what it seems. Someone has murdered her!" She dropped the knife, letting it fall on the bed. The musketeers advanced.

"Is this part of whatever you and Guillot—or Medici or, whatever his name is—are planning?" Etienne asked. "We have locked him up already. If you are in league with him, confess it, and you may be spared."

Charlotte rocked back. Gregoire, arrested, locked up? It had been a scant half hour since they parted. What had happened?

Charlotte, there is no time, the calm and rational part of her mind whispered. *There is trouble, and you might be one of the only people who can stop it.*

Charlotte allowed herself to sag to the floor, as if in defeat. "I do not understand what is happening, but I will go with you, gentlemen. I did not kill her. Not for Gregoire. Not for anyone." She looked at the floor, trying to heave her shoulders in wracking sobs while reaching under her skirt, to the dagger hidden in her boot. Her gift from Gregoire.

She saw the boots of the musketeers approach.

"Madame, if you will let us—"

Charlotte surged forward, just as the lady of the night had taught her to, stabbing the first musketeer in the side of the thigh, while she slammed the heel of her other palm into the nose of the second musketeer.

Both yelped in pain and surprise. Charlotte was out of the apartment before they realized what had happened, slamming the outer door of the rooms and turning the key. Then she ran. The woman in the gold dress's words of advice echoed in her head. Run faster than any man would expect you to. She pelted through the corridors, conscious of the blood staining her hands and her dress.

Where was safe? Not with Gregoire; he hated her, and God only knew what predicament he was in. Where was Richelieu? There was only one person she felt she could trust. She ran toward the Duke of Orleans's apartment and hammered on his outer door.

Artus Daumont answered the door almost immediately. He looked immensely taken aback at the state of her.

"Madame! What is happening?"

"The musketeers are after me. They think I have murdered my lady."

Artus pulled her into the room and shut the door.

"Madame, this is most unexpected. Please sit down and tell me everything."

Inside the apartments, Artus gave Charlotte water to wash her hands and face with, to wash away Lady Abigail's life blood. There was nothing to be done about her clothes, but Charlotte felt a little better with clean hands.

Well, she amended mentally, *a little better doesn't go far given how terrible everything is.* Gregoire despising her. Abigail dead. Her wanted for the murder. And whatever was happening, it was obviously happening today.

"I'm boiling some water for the tea. Tell me what happened," Artus said, drawing her to a seat.

Charlotte gratefully took the seat and considered what to say. "I need to see the abbess," she said finally. She couldn't compromise herself by revealing her involvement with Richelieu. But the abbess would be able to get in touch with him. "She will protect me. She knows me well."

"I will send a message immediately. But won't you tell me what is going on? Madame, you can trust me." Charlotte looked at his face, the picture of earnest pleading and concern. He had her hands in his. "You were prepared to marry me not an hour ago. Surely I am worthy of your trust?"

"Yes, of course," Charlotte said, something inside her still uneasy, and she was unaccountably wary of telling him the truth. "I feel something terrible is afoot. Someone murdered my lady, and I don't understand how. I was only gone half an hour. Somebody must have been watching. We would normally be at church."

"Perhaps a thief was surprised by your lady being home. She would not have been able to fight back, as unwell as she was," Artus told her gently.

"How did you know she was not feeling well?" Charlotte asked.

"I assumed as much, given she is so regular in her devotions. She must be unwell if she didn't go to church," Artus answered after the slightest pause, and he laughed softly. "You have nothing to worry from me, madame, you know that?"

"Of course. I am all out of sorts."

Artus squeezed her hand. "Let me fetch some tea." He left the room, leaving Charlotte alone with her thoughts, which were loud and chaotic inside her head. She felt she was missing something obvious, that she was missing something vital. She had so many pieces, and no matter how she turned them, they refused to fit together. She tried to think over Abigail's murder. She had not been gone for long. She would not have left if not for Gregoire needing to speak with her. Had Gregoire drawn her away?

No. She shook her head. His hatred and grief were too raw to be falsified.

But someone had given him that report. Someone who knew he would come straight to her. Who knew? Charlotte racked her brains. Captain Treville knew. Charlotte hoped he wasn't the traitor; that would make life terribly difficult.

Cardinal Richelieu knew. Was he the one acting against the crown and using her and Gregoire to measure how much people knew about the plan? Possible, but very convoluted, even for the red spider.

"You look like you're thinking very hard, madame." Artus's voice startled her. He had returned and was placing a fresh cup of hot tea in front of her. Charlotte drew in a long breath. Even the scent of it was relaxing. She wrapped her hands around it to warm herself. "Have the tea. It will soothe you."

"I don't particularly want to be soothed. I want to know what is going on. I think I need to find Gregoire. No matter how angry he is, I think he will want to know."

"Madame, I do not want to be the bearer of more bad news, but ..." Artus trailed off. Cold seized Charlotte's heart.

"Is he hurt?"

"No, madame, he is alive. He was arrested just earlier. I came across the commotion after I left you. The musketeers were arresting him. It seems he was involved in some treachery against His Majesty's life."

"This is madness! That is simply not true! He would never do that!" Charlotte all but shouted. How could things have gone this wrong?

"I overheard he was actually a Medici. I have heard from my lord that there was one of them back in Paris, center of some web." Artus leaned back, his face going oddly stony. "I'm sure they will be quite glad to have caught him."

"Gregoire could never betray the king," Charlotte contested. "There is another. There must be another."

"You do not know that. His parents were perfectly capable of it, why not the son? Drink your tea, madame, it will help."

"Stop telling me about the tea!" Charlotte cried. She didn't want to drink the tea. There was something wrong with it, her instincts were screaming. She wasn't safe. "I know how to drink tea. And you don't know Gregoire. He might be a Medici, but he isn't like his parents. And his parents would never have betrayed the king if it weren't for his treacherous uncle."

They never found the uncle.

There is a Medici in Paris who is not Gregoire.

The tea is poison.

Artus Daumont has looked familiar since the day I met him.

These thoughts hit Charlotte all at once, and she lifted her eyes up to Artus's face. His face was that mask of easy-going joviality.

"I know this is poison," Charlotte whispered.

Artus's smile spread wider, but it was no longer friendly or easy-going. It was now all teeth and cold glee. She knew who he was now, and he knew that she knew.

"Drink the tea, Charlotte," he said. "You're all worked up. Come now, that is a ridiculous notion. You think too much; that's your problem. You always go sticking your nose where it doesn't belong. Eavesdropping on conversations you shouldn't. I'd quite like to offer you the opportunity to work with me, but to be honest, I don't trust you to do as you say, and ever since I've found out who ruined everything eight years ago, I've been promising myself a decent revenge. You're not as smart as you think, Charlotte Menard."

It was obvious that whatever Artus Daumont—or rather, Alessandro de Medici—had in mind for her was going to be far from pleasant.

"Is the Duke of Orleans in on this?" Charlotte asked, her mind racing through the options she had. He'd locked the door. She'd never get the key off him in time. On the other hand, behind her was a window. If she could just get some more information or, failing that, catch him off guard. "Or is he just a happy benefactor of your plotting and scheming?"

"Yes, the duke—or, as of this afternoon, we'll be calling

him His Majesty—is in on it. It's why he hired me in the first place. He had been sent abroad for peeving his brother, and I was in hiding because of you. We were natural allies. I'm not so much his servant as his co-conspirator."

"And Abigail was your ... what?"

"I believe the term is patsy. Alas, dear Abigail and the queen will bear the blame for all of this, and perhaps my nephew. I will give him a chance to throw in with me, I think. He is young, and he is family. But if he won't"—Alessandro shrugged—"he'll merely be a rotten conspirator, just like his parents."

He leaned forward. "Drink the tea, Charlotte, else I'll have to cudgel you into unconsciousness. I don't have all day. I have to get going to kill the king while all the musketeers are chasing phantom Spaniards."

Definitely time to go. Charlotte lifted the tea toward her mouth and paused. "I have only one question. Do you remember, two weeks ago ...?" And then she threw her scalding tea in his face.

Artus howled and clapped his hands over his eyes, and Charlotte grabbed the teapot on the table and dumped it in his lap, making sure she caught his flintlock. *Can't have him shooting after me,* she thought as she turned and ran for the window behind her. She threw open the shutters and looked down. Third floor. Her stomach wobbled for a second, but from behind her she heard Artus coming for her.

Come on, Charlotte, you climbed higher than this when you were a girl! She reached under her dress. The collapsible grappling hook the Rose had gifted her was everything she needed. Up and over. The hook bit into the window ledge, and she was letting herself down on the knots as fast as she could. The rope burned. She tried not to look down. Her boots found easy purchase on the stone walls of the castle.

"I'm still going to kill you," Artus told her with an odd

calm from above her. She spared a glance a up. He had his knife out and was sawing away at the top of her rope. Her stomach tightened, and she rappelled down faster, even as it got more difficult, the rope swaying backward and forward as he sawed away at it.

Please God, she prayed as she looked down. So close.

A grunt of triumph from above her and the weightless feeling of the beginning of a freefall, and the ground came rushing up at Charlotte.

CHAPTER 32

Gregoire didn't spend any time wondering what was going to happen to him next. He knew that already from his childhood. Instead he thought about where things had gone wrong. How he had let himself fall in love with Charlotte, and how he had not realized what a conniving snake she was.

It seemed unreal that she would concoct a lie like that. But then, it had happened.

He had always seen Charlotte as fearless and resourceful. She let nothing daunt her. She never let anyone tell her she couldn't do anything. It had bothered him so much as a young man that her mother was forcing her into the mold of the dutiful servant. It bothered him seeing her as Lady Abigail's servant, her head bowed, quiet, an arm full of needlework. That wasn't his Charlotte. His Charlotte was the one with the lockpicks, ciphers, and the quick wit. The one climbing things she wasn't meant to and being in places she wasn't meant to. His Charlotte had the steady hands that pulled a pistol ball out of his gut and sewed him shut.

He had never imagined her to be vicious or duplicitous. She was always just unexpected. Had she overreached herself as a child, told a lie and not realized where it would end up? Was it her malice or her stupidity that had cost his parents their lives and ruined his and his sister's?

He wished he'd listened to her this morning. Now he'd be dead before he saw her again.

There was a scrabbling noise at the door. Gregoire looked up. He couldn't see a face at the window in the door. He frowned. The soft scrabbling noise continued, confusing Gregoire more by the minute. There were rats, yes, but not in the locks!

THE DOOR OPENED INWARD SUDDENLY, and Charlotte Menard slipped in, closing it behind her with a finger to her lips.

"You!" Gregoire exclaimed, part anger, part surprise, and an unexpected swelling of affection even her horrendous actions hadn't been able to quash.

"Shhh," Charlotte hissed. She looked him in the eyes. "I understand you hate me. I do. I deserve all of your ire and my own, and God's on top of that too. I cannot undo what I did back then. I cannot ask you to forgive me. All I ask is that you let me save your life. Let me help clear your name. They are trying to make it seem like you are at the center of this web, and we both know you are not."

Gregoire felt a war within himself. How could he trust her words and her motivations ever again?

"I cannot possibly end up any more betrayed or condemned than I am now," Gregoire said. "So I'm going to believe that this isn't some nefarious ploy to get me right where you want." The hurt in her face was raw. It almost shamed him. "Tell me one thing. Why did you tell Captain Treville that lie about my parents?"

"Lie?" Charlotte repeated, looking dumbfounded. "You think I made up a lie? No, Gregoire, no. I said it because it was what I overheard. I swear it. I thought they were meeting someone about your marriage. I hid, and I listened, and he was there, your Uncle Alessandro, and listen, he's here now too. He's been acting as the king's brother's manservant, and it's all him." Charlotte stared at him. "Do you hear me, Gregoire? He made your parents take the fall for it," Charlotte told him. Her voice was insistent and clear and empty of all guile. "And now he's going to make you into his strawman for this mad scheme. We have to stop him. He's already killed Abigail. He'll be going for the king next. We have to go."

Gregoire remembered his uncle's cryptic comments the previous night in the inn. He didn't know why he had not taken them more seriously. He was so certain his family were innocent, he never considered his uncle's impassioned ravings to be more than words, to be a plan. To be the very plan they were looking for.

"My parents were innocent, Charlotte. I don't care what you think you heard, they were not traitors." His words came out so harsh, Charlotte took a step back. He took a breath to master himself. "All right. I will trust you this last time. After this is over, I never want to see you again."

Charlotte nodded and turned away. He thought he saw her blue eyes bright with tears. But he couldn't think about that.

They made it out of the dungeons without being caught, and as they made their way to the cardinal's ostentatious offices, Charlotte hurriedly explained everything that had happened to her since he'd left her in the garden—the bloody murder scene, her conversation with his uncle, her narrow escape after she landed on the grass and played dead.

"Nobody ever thinks of the women," she explained. "So I went to the palace laundry to change my bloodied clothes. I told them I'd done surgery on another injured musketeer."

Gregoire found himself laughing at her ingenuity.

They reached the doors of Richelieu's palace office, and two heavily armed Red Guard were blocking the door.

"We need to see His Eminence. We have information on the Spanish attack," Gregoire demanded.

"He said the two of you might be turning up in a state," the guard said. "If you have any last words, leave them with me. And whatever you're about to tell him, it better be damn good."

"YOUR EMINENCE, WE HAVE IT," Charlotte all but shouted as she and Gregoire ran down the length of the long ornate room in which they had first been reunited. At the end of it, Cardinal Richelieu rose to his full height, shrouded in his opulent red, his face like a thundercloud.

"You have what, apart from assorted murder and treason charges?" he demanded. "That was some interesting news to have with my breakfast this morning, that Madame Lefort had murdered Lady Abigail and escaped, and that Monsieur Guillot was in prison for plotting against the king. Do explain; I am certain this is going to be an entertaining comedy of life-or-death errors."

"There is almost no time, Your Eminence," Charlotte told him. "Even now Alessandro de Medici is going to go kill the king!"

The cardinal's face froze slightly. This was clearly new information. "Elaborate, quickly. How did he get into Paris?"

"What do you mean, how? He's the Duke of Orleans's manservant and has been for months. He's been in the palace the whole time!" Despite the desperation of the situation, Charlotte took a moment to savor the look of acute horror that briefly flashed across the cardinal's face. It seemed he too was human and with limits to his knowledge, and Charlotte had brought him information he had truly not anticipated. "Abigail had been used by the Duke of Orleans as little but an errand girl in the plot, stupid and in love with the duke. The duke and Alessandro de Medici are planning to kill the king today, while the musketeers chase, in his words, 'phantom Spaniards.'"

The cardinal swore in a manner that made Charlotte blush.

"The king is in the gardens. He is meeting his brother by the Gracious Muse fountain. The palace is under lockdown, and the musketeers are all away." The cardinal looked at Gregoire. Gregoire nodded. "All but one."

"I will go at once. But I will need a sword."

The cardinal went to the back wall of the room and unlocked what looked like part of the wall but turned out to be a cabinet. He brought over a large wooden box. The clasps released with a satisfying clicking sound, and he lifted the lid to reveal an old, ornate rapier.

Charlotte saw a look of sadness and wonder come over Gregoire's face.

"Your father's sword came into my possession in the last few weeks. I held onto it, as I felt, should things go well, you would enjoy it being returned to you. This feels as fitting a moment as any could be. Take it and go."

Gregoire lifted the sword out.

"It was always too big for me," he murmured, hefting it.

"Yes, yes, isn't it wonderful. You are a man now, but you are going to be quite dead if you don't save the king, so I suggest hurrying."

"Do you not worry about my loyalty?" Gregoire asked.

The cardinal actually rolled his eyes. "Terribly worried. That is why I armed you and sent you to the king's unaccompanied side. Stop talking and go."

As Gregoire turned to leave, his eyes lingered on Charlotte's face for a moment, and he looked on the verge of saying something, but then he lowered his face and took off at a dead sprint.

"Not even a goodbye, let alone a kiss," the cardinal remarked.

Charlotte didn't bother inquiring how he knew about their relationship. "He found out I told Treville about his parents. He believes I lied out of jealousy. He does not believe his parents were truly traitors."

Cardinal Richelieu shook his head as he bent over a piece of parchment, writing orders. "And that is why I trusted him to go. He's stupidly straightforward and honorable. He cannot fathom treachery because it isn't in him. Even now, after all this time, after so many reasons to hate the king, he still raced to defend him. Remarkable. Absolutely remarkable."

He stamped his seal into a patch of wet wax and handed Charlotte the paper. "Urgent summons to the musketeers. Hand it to my guard on your way out."

"What am I to do, Your Eminence?" Charlotte asked. "Do not leave me idle during a crisis!"

"I thought it was perfectly obvious what you are to do. You must get evidence on Alessandro and the Duke of Orleans." He smiled at her as he handed her a key. "This will save time with the lockpicks. Come now, you do not believe I'd have anyone useful wait idly, least of all you, who wouldn't listen anyway?"

Charlotte found herself smiling widely. "Yes, Your Eminence," she said, and she too left at a run. Adrenaline sang through her. Despite the desperation of the situation, the horror, and the danger, she felt as though she had purpose. She was not wasting time or sitting by. Whatever resolution this grim day would have, she would have done her absolute best to make it come out in favor of the people she cared about.

CHAPTER 33

Gregoire sprinted through the palace gardens, heart hammering, looking for the appointed place. It was a secluded, private spot. He turned the corner, the white pebbles from the path going flying, and the king leapt up, startled.

"Guillot!" he exclaimed. "Good heavens, man. You look as though you're running from the devil. What's the matter?"

"Your Majesty, you are in grave danger," Gregoire said. "You've been lured here under false pretenses."

"Oh, you don't mean all that nonsense about Spain, do you? Armand and Treville have it in hand. Say, why aren't you with them?"

"They've been deceived. It's not your brother coming to see you. It's an assassin."

King Louis's eyes widened. He looked around nervously and then back to Gregoire.

"And why should I trust you, when you come barreling in here, and you're the only person that's armed? You don't mean to say my brother means me ill?"

"No," Gregoire lied, his heart twisting slightly when he

contemplated the enormity of the betrayal that Gaston of Orleans was undertaking. "I think his correspondence has been intercepted. Your Majesty. I have known you for several months now. You have talked to me of what you go through as king. I want to lay my life on the line for you. Not in the abstract. Right here, right now, I will shield your life with mine, because no matter what people may say about you as king, you are France's rightful leader, and I will die sooner than let someone depose you." He drew his rapier and dropped to his knees, offering the king the sword.

"Yes, yes, that's all well and good, but we don't have time for theatrics if someone is coming to kill me!" Louis said with a note of genuine panic in his voice. "Get up, Guillot. We'll save the theatrics for when we tell the poets after we survive this. Besides, if you meant to kill me, you would have done it by now. I'm told by Armand that most assassins don't usually stop for chitchat or to explain their elaborate plans. What shall we do?"

Gregoire rose. "I'm going to need your doublet and hat."

"If this is a jest, it is a very poor one and I will have you executed," Louis grumbled, but his shaking hands were already undoing the buttons on his doublet.

"And then I need you to obscure yourself in the bushes."

"We definitely will not be telling the poets about this part," the king said. He handed Gregoire his doublet, as Gregoire pulled off his own shirt and pulled on the king's doublet. "With the hat and the doublet, someone from the back might believe you're me, but we're going to have to talk about your hair just as soon as we're done surviving here."

Gregoire jammed the king's hat on his own head. Louis stepped back into the bushes. His whole body was shaking. Gregoire knew the fear. Louis's whole life was in Gregoire's hands, and he knew it. For a moment, he realized how subject the king of France was to others' whims. He had to trust that his advisors were loyal and correct. He had to trust the people who served him. One mistake, and he was finished.

"I will die before I let him harm you, Majesty," Gregoire told him. "But if I do die, stay hidden. Cardinal Richelieu is finding reinforcements."

Louis gave one last frightened nod before he vanished into the rich foliage of the maze. Gregoire took a deep breath and began to stride around the enclosed circle, wildly swinging his sword in the manner of the king. And he prayed he was right.

He heard the subtle approach of footsteps only minutes later. He struggled to not whirl around immediately and instead let the would-be assassin get closer.

"Your Majesty," he heard a voice say. "Your brother has been delayed and will not be able to join you. Is there a message I can deliver back to him?"

"No," Gregoire said, trying to make his voice sound like the king's. "But you and I can talk."

"Certainly, Your Majesty," the arrival replied after a moment's hesitation. He took a few steps closer. Gregoire turned and brought his rapier up into a guard position. He had his back toward the other part of the garden, so no one should be able to take him from the back, and now the assailant had his back to the king and shouldn't be able to see him.

And he came face-to-face with his uncle for the second time in two days. He looked so much like Gregoire's father that Gregoire's heart twisted. Alessandro wore expensive clothes, he was well groomed, and he had rapier and a flintlock in his hand.

"Uncle Alessandro, what a surprise," Gregoire said, keeping his rapier steady.

The older man looked taken aback to see Gregoire. "I heard you were locked in the dungeons."

"Framed and out of the way?"

"Safe, nephew. Safely out of harm's way until all this is over, and you and I can start rebuilding the fortunes of our family." His uncle smiled, the same wide, friendly smile that Gregoire remembered from his childhood, when Alessandro was only a rakish young uncle whom he'd looked up to. "You're about some of the only family I have left, since the brat king had our family purged from the realm after the coup. I am overjoyed to be reunited."

"I will not help you, Uncle. My father was steadfast in his loyalty, and so am I. I owe nothing to the Queen Mother."

Alessandro de Medici laughed. "And neither do I; the old biddy failed utterly, even with me helping her. I support a much worthier candidate now. Everything is in place. All you have to do is tell me where you've put the king and walk away. You won't even have to see me do the deed."

"No," Gregoire said. "If you surrender now, I will plead for clemency and have you only imprisoned for your life instead of killed."

Alessandro's smile got more wolfish.

"Come now, nephew, come. It's what your father wanted. He too saw the weakness of Louis and pledged to back Marie. It's what he gave his life for. Do not dishonor him by being petulant."

"My father was not a traitor. He was framed. He was innocent," Gregoire insisted.

Alessandro shook his head. "Your father and mother both agreed. I was there with them. Your father was no traitor, on that score we can agree, because it is not treachery to depose that worthless, simpering worm who can't see his strings being pulled by that parasite cardinal. Your father saw the truth. Your father supported his family. Are you going to be a greater coward than that? When I run you through and you face him in the hereafter, will you tell him you betrayed his death?"

It is not treachery to depose that worthless ... will you tell him you betrayed his death?

The words rang in Gregoire's ears, and for a moment he was only sixteen again watching the musketeers drag his family out of the house and rob them of their dignity and their freedom. For a moment he was only sixteen, locked in a cold stone room, listening to the crimes being read out, holding his sister close to him and hearing the gasp of the crowd as the hangman pulled the lever.

"My father—he wasn't! He didn't!" Gregoire shouted, his hand wobbling. "He was a good, loyal man. We were belied!"

"He would have succeeded too, if it wasn't for the stupid servant girl getting into things she oughtn't," Alessandro spat. "I killed her too, did you know? She leaped out the window rather than drink poison. She never was that bright."

Charlotte hadn't lied.

The knowledge crashed through Gregoire like a tidal wave. She had told the truth. Charlotte had not made up a vindictive lie that got his family killed. If Alessandro was telling the truth, Charlotte was innocent.

But if Charlotte is innocent, then my father is guilty.

All his life, Gregoire had believed that core truth: his family was innocent. His mother and father had instilled in him the loyalties he held, even after some of the darkest times of his life. For a while, after his parents were executed, he believed that there was no point following the king or being loyal to France, because it didn't get you anywhere. His parents were loyal. Look what happened.

What if he had been wrong? What if his father had betrayed the king and sided with the Queen Mother, his grandmother?

Alessandro was watching his face closely. "Ah, now you realize. Louis's line is a waste of time. He has no heirs. The alliance with Spain has outlived its usefulness. We can be done with Anne. Gaston of Orleans will make a fine king, and you and I will put him there. Our line will be strong again, and you can use your true name again instead of skulking about in the identity of a sixth son of some nobody."

Gregoire took a deep breath.

"You're right. Family should stick together." Alessandro grinned, but Gregoire continued. "But you forget, Louis is the son of Marie de Medici. He's our cousin. And if I do not stick with him because he is my king, I will stick with him because he is my family too, and family should not turn on family. Stand down, Uncle, I will not give him over to you. I will die first."

"Then you will die," Alessandro said simply, and before he even finished the words, he fired his flintlock.

They were both surprised, as instead of the resounding crack and the wet noise of the ball burying itself in Gregoire's flesh, there was only a slight thud and weak smell of smoke. They both looked at the gun.

"Someone wet your powder, Uncle?" Gregoire laughed.

"That goddamned *witch*," Alessandro snarled, and he lunged forward. Gregoire had been prepared to block, and he deflected the rapier, steel singing as it struck and then whisked back through the air. Alessandro was a fine fighter, and Gregoire only a mediocre one, and the difference in their skill showed. Alessandro pressed Gregoire hard, not letting him pause between thrusts, not letting him do much more than defend. Gregoire fought back, sweat pouring from him, his limbs already aching from the trials of the day, and as he defended, he led Alessandro backward, away from the king, trying to draw him away from where Louis was hidden in the trees.

Gregoire felt trickles of sweat coming down his brow, and he knew he had only seconds before he was blinded and it was all over. *Maybe I should side with him,* a part of him asked. *After all, my father had.*

But Gregoire remembered the somber regret and sadness on his father's face after their arrest. Gregoire had wondered why his father had not protested his innocence more, and now he knew why. The gray sadness of his final days was not of being betrayed by king and country, but of his own betrayal and the downfall and death he had brought to his family.

What would my father do? he wondered in the split second as the sweat dripped into his eyes and he was blinded. He fell to his knees to dodge Alessandro's strike, but he was not fast enough, and hot pain lanced through his left arm.

He saw his mother and father before their execution. He remembered kissing them farewell. He remembered their grief.

He remembered their regret. At once, he felt as though his maman and papa were standing with him as he kneeled bleeding on the ground, and the agent of their foolish treachery poised his rapier over his heart. He knew what they would want.

"Last chance, nephew," Alessandro said. "Give up the king and join me, or join your mother and father in the hereafter."

Gregoire thought for a second of Charlotte. *Charlotte, forgive me for how I wronged you.*

"I have made my peace with death. I will not betray the king." Gregoire's gaze did not waver from his uncle's face.

His uncle shrugged. "Give my brother my regards," he said, and the tip of his rapier pierced Gregoire's flesh.

Gregoire's vision distorted with pain. First he thought it was only the hallucinations of death that saw Alessandro's face contort with surprise and the blood that burst forth from his chest, dripping onto him.

Alessandro dropped his sword, looked down, and whispered, "How?" before he sank to his knees before Gregoire.

"I think we've had quite enough out of you," King Louis said, pulling his sword out of Alessandro and kicking aside the would-be assassin's dropped sword well out of his reach. He looked down at Gregoire. "Guillot, are you alive? Was I too late?"

Gregoire took mental stock and realized with elation he was indeed alive. Alessandro had barely stabbed him before the king struck, and the blade had not reached anywhere vital.

"No, Your Majesty's timing was impeccable. I am alive."

"Except I suppose you're not Guillot at all, are you? You've been pretending all this time," Louis noted.

Gregoire made no move to rise. He lowered his head. "I beg Your Majesty's forgiveness."

"Don't be stupid Guill—whatever your name is. You quite clearly saved my life just now. You were prepared to die for me. And we're family, you said." Gregoire didn't look up, but he could almost hear the gears turning in the king's head. *He's always a little slower,* Gregoire thought with a small smile. *He gets there though.* "Enough of this, Medici, enough of this. I will be discussing this with Treville and Armand, make no mistake. But you don't need to kneel there like that."

"But, Your Majesty, my family were traitors. This man was a traitor. I am not fit to be forgiven."

"Medici," the king said with uncharacteristic sharpness. "Look at me, and that's an order."

Gregoire looked up. Behind and around them he could hear boot steps hurrying toward them.

"Medici, you say your family are traitors? And thus you're not fit to be forgiven?" A sad smile with a touch of bitterness crept across the young king's face. "I will not be so insulted. It would do you well to remember my mother too was a traitor." The king reached down and gripped Gregoire's shoulder. "We are not just our families, my friend. You were loyal, even when it would have been a thousand times easier to betray me. It doesn't matter to me what your—what *our* family has done. I have seen what *you* do."

"Get back, Your Majesty! The man is a traitor!" A dozen musketeers, led by Reynaud, appeared in the garden, armed to the teeth with their guns and swords. Horror blossomed on their faces when they beheld the scene in the royal gardens, the blood on both Gregoire and the king, the bleeding servant, the discarded weapons, the king's hold on the suspected traitor's shoulder.

"Stand down, all of you!" the king snapped. "Anyone who shoots him will be shot himself. Am I understood?"

"Your majesty, he is a Medici!"

"And so am I! Will you shoot me too, Reynaud?" the slight king bellowed back. "This man saved my life. He was prepared to die for me. He wouldn't back down. Even with his dying moments, he led the killer away from me. He will be fully exonerated of whatever he has done and given the reward of his choice, are we clear?"

Reynaud looked between the king and Gregoire and motioned for the rest of the musketeers to lower their weapons.

"Your Majesty, we will not harm him, but His Eminence has asked us to retrieve him and bring him to him."

"Oh, right, well, if Armand wants him." The king shrugged and looked at Gregoire. "You haven't annoyed the cardinal, have you? That won't go well for you. Well, tell him you're to be forgiven and bandaged up. You're to join me for supper tonight." He paused. "Perhaps tomorrow. Musketeers, with me."

Gregoire allowed himself to be hauled up by his erstwhile colleagues, all of whom were giving him a look of deep suspicion.

"I don't care what it looks like," he told them. "I did the right thing. I protected the king."

"Come along, Guillot—Medici—whoever the hell you are," Reynaud snapped. "If you're as innocent as you say, and you're cleared by the cardinal and the king, then you are buying us all several rounds and explaining every step of this mess, is that clear?"

"Several rounds of *good* stuff," Monnier added.

Gregoire grinned, almost lightheaded from the relief of saving the king. "Is Charlotte safe?" he asked.

The musketeers exchanged glances, before Reynaud spoke. "We don't know anything about where she is."

"She went to—there's another assassin. We have to help her!" Gregoire tried to pull away from Reynaud and Monnier's grip. "No! I'm not losing her!"

"We have orders! Settle down!" Reynaud barked. "I'm sure she's fine. She'll have hidden herself somewhere safe."

"You don't know her at all. The last place she'll be is somewhere safe." Gregoire's eyes blurred with tears.

Reynaud stared into Gregoire's eyes for a long moment. "We'll get you to the cardinal. He'll probably know where she is. On your feet. Let's go."

"If we end up having to execute him, can we find out when he fell in love with Madame Lefort?" Monnier asked. "I really want to know who won the bet."

CHAPTER 34

Charlotte cautiously slid the key into the lock on the prince's door. It was hard to believe she had fallen in through these doors with such relief less than an hour ago. The day was so rapidly turning from one thing to another. By sundown she felt she might not recognize the world she lived in at all—*if* she lived.

Quietly turning the key, she held her breath as she slowly pushed the door inward, waiting for some reaction. Nothing greeted her but silence. Not much had changed in the front room since her previous visit. Her discarded teacup and teapot lay where she had thrown them. The divan was damp from where she had doused the nefarious Medici with his own narcotic tea. Her grappling hook was gone. She'd have to look for it later; it had saved her life once, it may yet again.

She slid into the apartment and was about to begin her search when a harsh voice called out.

"Who is that? Alessandro, are you returned so quick? Is it done?" Gaston, Duke of Orleans, the younger brother to the king, walked into the room.

Charlotte dropped into a curtsy, her heart pounding. "Pardon me, Your Highness."

"Who are you?" Gaston demanded.

Charlotte tried to hide her surprise. She had been Abigail's maid for months, and he didn't recognize her, not even now when she lifted her face to look at his. "Your Highness, I am Lady Abigail's lady's maid," she told him.

"Are you?" He examined her face for a long moment then shrugged. "If you say so. I can't tell any of you servant girls apart. Why has Abigail sent you skulking to my rooms? How did you get in?"

"Monsieur Daumont sent me, Your Highness," Charlotte told him, inventing fast. "He gave me a key. He bid me to ask Your Highness to destroy all the papers relating to what he called the matters of today. He bid me tell you it will soon be complete and you can rest easy."

Gaston set his mouth in a straight line and nodded.

"Wretched business, today. Still, once it is over, Abigail and I will be married, and we will have to think no more on it." Gaston flicked a coin at Charlotte. "Tell Daumont not to fret about the papers. If he succeeds, there won't be any reason for us to worry." He began to turn away.

"If Your Highness and my lady marry?" Charlotte replied. The Duke of Orleans paused and looked at her.

"It is none of your business, I assure you. Begone."

"It's only ... Do you not know, Monsieur Daumont killed my lady today? I happened in on the scene, and Monsieur Daumont beat me and threatened my life if I did not do as he told me for the rest of the day." Charlotte angled herself to show off the blossoming bruises down her side from her freefall earlier. She took a deep shuddering breath and willed herself to cry. It was not terribly difficult; she pictured Abigail's broken and bloody form in the bed she ought to have felt completely safe in. Tears rushed down her cheeks.

"Abigail is dead?" the Duke of Orleans repeated, his face paling. His mouth moved wordlessly for a few moments. Then he strode forward and seized her by the arms. "Are you lying, wench?"

"No, Your Highness! Monsieur Daumont murdered her in her bed, and I happened in, and he said she was a liability. He said he was protecting you."

He released her roughly, sending her stumbling back a few steps. "How could he?" The duke was obviously overcome. His gray pallor was rapidly being replaced by a rising red.

Charlotte fell to the floor in abject subservience. "My lord, I begged him, but it was too late. I thought it had been done on your orders."

"Never! I loved Abigail. She was my own heart." He grabbed an expensive divan by the arm and threw it onto its back, bellowing in inarticulate rage. "He will answer for this! What purpose is there to any of this if not to marry her? Villain!" He upended a chair, which landed with a violent clatter, and Charlotte pressed herself to the floor, visibly shaking with fear and grief. Inside, she was not as out of control as she seemed, and she thought about what this might mean. The duke truly loved Abigail and had no idea of the murder. Perhaps it was true what Artus Daumont had said a few weeks ago, that the duke sought to marry but his brother stood in the way.

Gregoire had told her, in the candlelit room as they embraced each other, how he had wished for all his responsibility to vanish simply so he could marry her. Could the duke, bitter at being kept from his love, have been persuaded to act against his own brother?

"Your Highness, she loved you," Charlotte whispered as the duke tried to catch his breath, even as rage clearly throttled him. "Her dying words were whispering your name."

"Damn him, damn him, damn him." The duke seemed to be in physical agony. "You, woman, where did you say he was now?"

"He said he was headed to the garden. If it please Your Highness, he said he was completing the matter. He seemed ... happy."

The duke's lips went pale as he pressed them together. One hand lingered on his sword, and he looked toward the door. It seemed to Charlotte that an internal struggle took place, where he considered stopping the whole thing and saving his brother, but in the end, he sat down in one of the remaining chairs.

"Very well. We have come this far," he murmured and lowered his head into his hands.

For a moment, Charlotte had thought his better nature would prevail. That he would fly off after the villain Alessandro and stop him from murdering his brother now that he no longer stood to gain his love. But with the kingdom within his grasp, it seemed he was not willing to relinquish that. No mercy, then.

Charlotte rose to her knees. "Forgive me, Your Highness, you are unwell. May I fetch you some tea to soothe you?"

The duke looked up, as if he had already forgotten she existed. "Oh, very well. Then I suppose you might as well clean up and wait for Daumont to get back here. He'll know how to deal with you. I suppose you'll want some compensation for loss of employment." He sighed.

"No, Your Highness, I only want to see you cared for. My lady loved you so well; it is the best testament to her memory to give you comfort."

The duke waved his hand to dismiss her.

Charlotte took refuge in the servant quarters with shaking legs and hooked a small cauldron of water over the fire to heat. She looked through Alessandro's collection of tea; she knew he had the one she needed. It was the one he almost got her with today.

It was easily found. He kept his collection of drugs and poisons tidy. There were no labels, but Charlotte knew these things by smell. She brewed the duke's tea strong, and then as she served it, she added a dash of alcohol to hide the taste. She arranged everything on a tea service and carried it in. *I hope I don't kill him,* she thought, but only because she didn't want to be facing charges of killing a prince. This man might have loved Abigail, but he was willing to condemn his brother to die.

She put the tea in front of him. The duke sniffed it as she poured it out, and for a heart-stopping moment, she thought he recognized it and prepared her lies about finding it in the kitchen. The words sat on the tip of her tongue waiting, but the duke merely said, "Brandy?"

"Yes, Your Highness. My maman always said a dash of brandy for grief." Her mother had said no such thing. It sounded like the plausible, humble wisdom of the servants, and clearly the duke thought so too because he drank one cup straightaway and motioned for another.

"Perhaps I ought to have gone for brandy by itself," he murmured, sipping his second tea. He leaned back in his chair and shut his eyes. "You don't know what it's like, servant, to be one such as I. Whatever you hear about the rest of today, know this. I loved Abigail, and I was not going to let my brother who has everything stand in my way. Why should I spend my life waiting? I am nothing but an adjunct, a spare. I have all the limitations of a king and none of the power, and my brother can't stand the sight of me." He took a deep breath. "Get gone, servant."

"Yes, Your Highness." Charlotte didn't move. He didn't open his eyes, and his breathing slowed and became regular, and the teacup tumbled from his hand.

All that power, Charlotte thought as she tiptoed into Alessandro's quarters to begin her search, *and still powerless.* She tried to focus her whole mind on the search and not think of the terrible danger Gregoire was in, going to face off with his uncle. His uncle, who was an excellent swordsman and in fine health, and with so much on the line he could not lose. Gregoire would have sympathy for his kinsman. He was still recovering from when the Duke of Buckingham tried to kill him, and he did not have enough dueling experience. She prayed as she worked. *Please, God, do not let him die. I have so much unresolved with him. Spare him.*

She wondered if there was much point to her prayers. Abigail had been as pious as a nun, and she was slaughtered in her bed this morning. Well, pious, except for being party to this treachery.

Alessandro's belongings yielded nothing to Charlotte. She could find nothing hidden in either likely or unlikely places. All the papers she did find were for the most mundane of things. She pocketed them regardless, in case the cardinal's codebreakers could get anything from them, but deep down she knew they were pointless.

It was time for the prince's room.

The room was as spartan as a guest room. There was nothing in it by which to identify it as having an owner. Even Alessandro's chamber had more personality. There were a few slim volumes on the largely empty bookshelf and a Bible. It was hard to search a cluttered room, but Charlotte didn't even know how to start with one that looked like it had never been touched. She chose the chest at the foot of the bed.

As she lifted the lid, she found something of the duke. Sheet music. Gloves that must now be too small for him. Some trinkets, such as brushes that had obviously belonged to a woman but Charlotte had never seen with Abigail. She turned the jeweled comb in her hand. She recognized the crest of the Medici family and could guess what the initials M.d.M. stood for. There were letters, many letters, mostly from his family. Some recent ones from his banished mother. Some older letters from the king. She scanned them. They were all arguments.

Toward the bottom of the chest she found a box, ornate and engraved. Even as she pulled it out, she recognized the smell of it. It smelled of Lady Abigail's perfume. Opening it, she found letters from her, at least a hundred, and little tokens. Charlotte searched the letters looking for the dates she suspected treachery to occur on and found Abigail questioning instructions, clarifying things, and assuring him that she would do the things exactly as he asked. Charlotte shut the box and laid it aside. She contemplated the chest before her and ran her fingers over the marking. The chest didn't seem deep enough. She suspected a front panel. There was a rewarding click as she probed one of the carvings and the front of the chest leaned forward on hinges, and she found instructions from Alessandro to Gaston.

Evidence. As she turned to lay it with the rest, she saw the Duke of Orleans staggering toward her with a large dagger in his hand.

"You witch," he gasped. "You drugged me, you impudent witch. You're working with him, aren't you? Daumont put you up to this. Wretched treachery!"

His movements were ungainly, as he was still under the effect of the drug. Charlotte marveled he'd fought it off as much as he did.

"Your Grace, you mistake me. I used only the herbs from the kitchen!" she tried, kicking the papers under the bed.

"Lying strumpet, you're looking through my papers!" he bellowed and leaped forward. Charlotte grabbed his wrist and tried to force the knife away from them. He was bigger, but he was drugged, and Charlotte was terrified. *I can't die yet,* she thought. *I have to get the papers out of here.*

The duke suddenly released her, and she fell to the floor unexpectedly. Dazed, she looked up to see him come down with the knife, and she rolled to the side, aiming a kick to the side of his knee, knocking it from under him, sending him sprawling too. Charlotte leapt forward to stand on his wrist.

"Release the knife, Your Grace. No one need die," she begged him. The duke only shouted in response and surged up, sending her staggering back. Her foot hit the wooden box. Ducking, she avoided his swing and swept the box up in her hand. With both hands firmly on the box, she hit him over the head with it. For a second he staggered, gazing in disbelief. Then, with a faint moan, he crumpled to the ground.

Charlotte stood frozen, the box in her hand, poised over the prone duke's head. For a wild moment, as she looked at him, she was overwhelmed by the thoughts of the treachery he had committed to. Love is a noble purpose, but not when it breeds fratricide and regicide in one. Because of him, Abigail was dead, and the king and Gregoire were possibly dead.

"Charlotte," came a familiar and commanding woman's voice. "Don't do it. It isn't worth your life."

Charlotte looked up. At the door to the prince's room was an elderly woman in an enormous gown with well-coiffed hair and an abundance of face makeup. Wealth was resplendent on every part of her. The woman walked toward her. There was something familiar about her eyes ...

"Did you get the papers?" the woman asked. Charlotte did not reply. The woman smiled. "You have grown unexpected, my girl. It suits you."

It was the abbess.

"I have it," Charlotte told her faintly. She reached under

the bed to pull out the letters from Alessandro, while the abbess kicked the front panel of the chest back into place. From outside, they heard commotion.

"Under my skirt, quick," the abbess-turned-noble-lady told her, and Charlotte found herself crawling under the enormous hoop skirt. Hiding under a nun's skirt was probably still not even in the top five unexpected things today.

"Musketeers! Foul villainy! My godson has been assaulted!" The abbess's voice rang out. "Quickly, quickly, there are villains afoot!"

Boots thundered into the room. "The assailant was long gone when I arrived. Quickly, my godson must be taken to safety."

"We believe the culprits are all apprehended, your ladyship. The king was attacked by an assassin in the garden, a Medici. One Guillot saved him."

"I care not a whit for who did what, only that His Majesty and His Highness, my godsons, are safe. To it!" The abbess's tone was imperial and commanding. She hadn't budged an inch.

It seemed an age before the musketeers carried the unconscious duke to some other, better safety, and the abbess lift her skirt for Charlotte to crawl out.

"Come, my child," the abbess said with a warm smile, pulling a shaking Charlotte into her warm embrace. "Come now. It is over."

CHAPTER 35

It was late afternoon of the same long day when Gregoire received a letter from the convent informing him that Madame Lefort was receiving treatment and rest under their care, and she would welcome his visit. He felt a profound sense of relief. He had heard from Richelieu she was not dead, but now at last he could lay eyes on her and tell her all the things he thought of when he thought he might die.

While not, strictly speaking, under arrest, he was accompanied by Reynaud everywhere. Gregoire did not have the energy to mind. He simply rose and informed the other man they were going to the convent. Reynaud's manner toward him was cool. Gregoire did not blame him.

When they arrived outside the convent gates and Gregoire thought for a moment of all the things he had to say to Charlotte, his feet would no longer move, and instead, he stared at the gate, frozen as though he were a statue.

"Come on, Medici. Are we going to stand out here all night or do you have business?" Reynaud demanded.

"I don't know how to apologize for being an ass," Gregoire answered.

"It's a good idea to practice. You owe that apology to quite a few people," Reynaud said, then relented with a sigh. "Just be honest. Don't get too clever or complicated. Don't try to excuse yourself." Then, as an afterthought, he added, "Remind her you saved the king's life this afternoon and that you're a national hero."

"I love her, Reynaud, and today I thought she was the most awful person imaginable. I'm not sure I forgive myself. How can she forgive me?"

"It might be hard. It might take a while. But she most certainly won't forgive you if you do not make your apologies. Let's go, Medici. This can't be the most frightening thing that's happened to you today."

"Oh, but it can," Gregoire muttered, bringing a laugh from Reynaud. With more reluctance than he'd shown heading to the dungeons, he walked up the stairs to the nunnery.

A sister showed him inside, where Charlotte was resting in a comfortable room. There was a roaring fire, and she was lying on a tall, soft mattress piled high with warm blankets. Her injuries were bandaged. She was chatting tiredly with the abbess, who caught Gregoire's eye and rose to depart. Reynaud gripped his shoulder for a moment, an unexpected show of friendship, and then stood by the door pretending to be deaf.

"I did not think you would come to my letter," Charlotte told him. "They told me you had survived and saved the king. Is it true? Is Alessandro captured?"

"Yes," Gregoire told her. "He is being interrogated by Cardinal Richelieu himself."

Charlotte nodded.

"Gregoire," she said, looking at him with her blue eyes earnest. Gregoire no longer saw the child Charlotte in them but the vulnerability and depth of the adult woman who had grown through heartache and danger. "I know you can never forgive me for what I did all those years ago. I respect your wishes that we shall never see each other again. But I wanted to tell you how truly sorry I am, and I will make what amends I can in the care of your sister."

"No, no, this is all backward." Gregoire strode forward and knelt beside her bed, taking her hand. "Charlotte, I came to ask you for *your* forgiveness. I assumed the worst of you, and that is unforgivable. Alessandro told me how he had convinced my parents. He told me they were a part of his plot." Gregoire still felt a wrench as he admitted that. He did not know how he would ever reconcile his image of his parents with the actions that had undone their family. But that was not Charlotte's work to do. "You did what any of us should have done. You did a hard thing. My parents made a mistake. And I will have to find a way to live with what they committed to doing. I will have to find a way to live with my family name. But what they did, that was not on you, Charlotte. I beg your forgiveness for assuming you had lied to your own advantage."

"I forgive you," Charlotte told him simply. "Do not look so surprised. I will not say I was not hurt that you thought that. But I forgive you with my whole heart." She yawned widely. "Before I forget, the cardinal wishes to interrogate us both tomorrow after the king makes his announcements about your reward. I must sleep now, Gregoire. But I am glad we have forgiven each other. It makes it easier in my heart to contemplate your future in England."

Her eyes drooped shut. Gregoire held her hand until her steady breathing showed she was asleep, and then he turned away.

England.

What he had wanted for so long now seemed utterly alien

to him. Tomorrow at noon the king was going to grant him his reward.

"England?" Reynaud asked, falling into step beside him as they made their way back to the palace. "Is that what you will be asking the king for, passage to England?"

"Perhaps," Gregoire replied shortly. "I cannot imagine I am welcome in Paris any longer. Now that I have deceived all my friends, it seems wise to leave."

Reynaud was silent for a few moments. "Once you are a musketeer, it is as if you are our brother. And certainly, it might have turned out you're a cuckoo, but brothers are also about being annoying prats that make bad decisions." They stopped outside a tavern, and Reynaud shoved him toward the door. "Can't let you out of my sight. And Captain Treville and I are mighty thirsty and hankering for a story."

Gregoire hesitated and looked at Reynaud's face. "Come," Reynaud said more gently than he had spoken to Gregoire all day. "You cannot get forgiveness if you do not ask."

Gregoire smiled at him with gratitude. "Thank you, brother."

AT NOON THE FOLLOWING DAY, Gregoire found himself once again in front of a whispering crowd, inside the king's throne room, with the entirety of the resplendently attired court at his back. At his direct back, however, were Captain Treville, Reynaud, Monnier, Etienne, and a dozen other musketeers. On the raised royal dais, King Louis and Queen Anne sat in their large thrones, various loyal servants and attendants framing them. Looming behind the king was the unmistakable and ever-present figure in red.

"Yesterday my life came under threat from a treacherous and despicable man, Alessandro de Medici, a nephew to my mother whose actions we all remember from years ago. His manipulation was thus that he'd managed to position himself in my court, of all places. But luckily, his disgraced kinsman, Gregoire de Medici, volunteered to work with Captain Treville and my first minister Cardinal Richelieu to draw him out, and he excellently detected his treachery, and despite being falsely accused of the very crimes he was trying to prevent, Monsieur de Medici—the good one that is, not the wicked one—came to my aid heroically and laid his life on the line to defend me from his kinsman."

Gregoire glanced sideways at Captain Treville who, to all appearances, seemed to hear this as established fact. Gregoire wondered how much of this he truly knew from the outset or whether he was playing along with this doctored version of events to save face. Treville and Richelieu were unlikely and uneasy allies, but their reluctant ongoing truce was for the benefit of France and the king.

"Therefore," the king said, winding up his speech, "Gregoire de Medici is hereby pardoned of any and all crimes he may have committed in bringing this treachery to light. Or any crime at all, really. He has the thanks of France and of myself and Her Majesty the Queen, and of all of you."

Applause and murmuring burst out behind him. Gregoire bowed to the king.

"You may go ahead and name your reward. I suppose you'll want your parents' estate and titles restored, and what have you?"

Gregoire, for a fleeting instant, thought about saying yes and taking back everything that was rightfully his family's. But his deeds could not undo the last eight years. He could not go back to being who he was then.

"Your Majesty, I thank you for your generosity. It was my duty and my honor to serve you yesterday, and I would happily do it again. There are two things I would ask."

"Two? Well, we'll see. I suppose you did save my life, and I'm very fond of my life. Go on."

"I would not have my family's whole estate restored. Rather, I would like some modest estate and living for my sister to have as a dowry and a place for her here at court."

"That's hardly anything. Consider it done. And the second?"

"I would like to continue to serve France and Your Majesties. I would like a commission to the musketeers of my own."

There was a stirring behind him. None of the nobles had expected him to ask for that. The musketeers made no move. King Louis, however, lit up.

"Truly?" he asked joyfully, then looked to Treville. "What say you, Captain, surely you can afford him the room? He's already all set up, and everyone will have to learn another name, but as you can see, he's very good."

Treville cleared his throat. "Certainly, Your Majesty. Monsieur de Medici is well liked by the men, and though his duplicity is not a favored method amongst the musketeers, his actions speak louder than words. It would be an honor to continue to have him serve us."

"Done!" the king announced. "Step forward, de Medici."

Gregoire walked up onto the dais and knelt down on the highest step. The king rose and stood before him.

"Gregoire de Medici, I hereby offer you a commission in my musketeers."

"Your Majesty," Gregoire said, "it would be my honor and highest desire to serve Your Majesty, to protect Your Majesty from harm, to lay down my life for the kingdom."

It was the second time he'd uttered those words in that place before the king. The first time, he was an imposter, his heart filled with hatred toward the king. Today, he was nearly overcome with pride.

"You may rise," said the king, and Gregoire did so. The king still stood there, and he took him by the forearm, gripping him in comradery. "Thank you, cousin," Louis told him quietly, a look of genuine affection and gratitude on his face. "You have done our family proud."

Gregoire inclined his head.

"Thank you for my husband's life," Queen Anne told him, as she too came up to him.

Gregoire didn't even notice the crowd as he half stumbled off the dais back to the musketeers, who surrounded him.

"Thank you for giving me another chance, Captain," Gregoire told the leader of the musketeers.

"If you do as well at your second chance as your first, Medici, I will keep giving you chances," he replied. One day, Gregoire planned to ask him about his family and what he knew of all this, but now was not that time.

"I am loath to interrupt your business, but I need to speak with your newly minted musketeer," Cardinal Richelieu said, appearing next to them. "It is relating to his kinsman."

The musketeers groaned in disappointment.

"Very well, but he will need to be back at the barracks shortly," Captain Treville told him. "If he vanishes, I'll know whose dungeons to search, Armand."

"Vanish? He, a national hero? Hardly. I thought you trusted me, Pierre." Richelieu smiled widely, with teeth, and Captain Treville repaid him with a wintery, closed-lip smile of his own. "By the by, it might interest you all to know that Alessandro de Medici confessed to being the one who shot Gregoire during his duel with the Duke of Buckingham. Please do not continue trying to provoke a war with England over that misunderstanding." The musketeers all groaned. "Don't be petulant," the cardinal said indulgently. "I'm sure you'll find another reason to hate the ambassador soon enough."

"Thank you for that, Armand," Treville said, managing to sound almost entirely professional.

"Medici, before you go. Monnier is fit to explode; he wants to settle the bet once and for all," Reynaud interrupted. "Tell us, honestly, when did you fall in love with Madame Lefort?"

Gregoire looked at his musketeer friends and his captain, and he felt the comforting weight of his own blue cloak around his shoulders. As of this moment, he had achieved half of everything he'd ever wanted. It was time to deal with the other half.

"I have loved her since we were children," he told them, and Monnier cursed in agony.

Etienne smiled widely and nodded in acknowledgement as Reynaud handed him the purse. Gregoire turned to follow the cardinal, and hopefully, complete the second of his great goals.

To marry Charlotte.

CHAPTER 36

"Monsieur Medici, Madame Menard, I suppose then here we are at the end of a job ... I'm not sure I'd call it well-executed, but in truth, it turned out to be a great deal higher stakes than I had first anticipated," the cardinal told them from behind his voluminous desk. He still looked pleased—most likely with himself, rather than them, Charlotte thought. "We have managed to eliminate the last of the serious Medici threats, and we have confirmed that the Duke of Orleans is still a threat to the king."

"Will he be punished?" Gregoire asked.

"Not publicly, no. Peace, monsieur." The cardinal held up his hand as Gregoire started. "He is the king's brother. His Majesty hopes that he will grow out of his peevish rebellions. He is being sent abroad with a complement of guards, once again. Madame Menard's excellent information and incapacitation of the duke was invaluable in this."

"Thank you," she said, though like Gregoire she was rankled by the fact that Gaston de Bourbon would not be punished at all for his treachery. Though she was a traitor, the death of Abigail still caused her hurt. At least her lady would not be known for her treacherous plans. That too was suppressed, to cover up the duke's involvement. Her remains were to be returned to her family by the Duke of Buckingham.

"All that remains, then, is to talk of the future," the cardinal said brightly. There was something anticipatory in his smile. He looked first at Gregoire. "I see you have asked your reward of the king already. It seems have I won our little wager, then."

Charlotte saw Gregoire's movements still and the color drain from his face.

"As you have accepted a commission with the musketeers, I presume that means your emigration to England has fallen by the wayside, is that correct?"

Gregoire opened his mouth and then shut it. "I had forgotten," he said at last.

"But nevertheless I am correct, you no longer want to leave for England." The cardinal looked immensely smug. "Therefore I win."

"You have been granted a commission on the musketeers, Gregoire?" Charlotte exclaimed. "I am so happy for you." And she truly was. She knew how much he had coveted that cloak his whole life, and now he had it under his own name, earned by his own actions. She did not understand why he looked so crestfallen.

"I have changed my mind," Gregoire told the cardinal. "I will tell the king I must leave."

"Why? What was the wager?" Charlotte asked.

"The wager was simply that he would no longer feel like leaving for England by the time this assignment was finished. If I was right, he would owe me a favor. If I was wrong, I would grant you your freedom from any further obligation to me and a comfortable living of any manner you chose," the cardinal explained.

"Charlotte, you need not worry. I will not see you stuck working for him. I will resign and depart," Gregoire told her, all the while glaring furiously at the cardinal, his fingers struggling to untie the cloak.

Charlotte laughed. The sound made Gregoire pause in his fumbling with the cloak and look at her in bewilderment.

"Stay, Gregoire. I would not have you leave, no matter what reward was promised."

"I don't understand," Gregoire said, frowning. After a moment, something like clarity began to dawn. "You don't want to stop working for him, do you?"

Charlotte shook her head.

It would have seemed like madness to her the first time she sat in this room, to not want to escape the life of a spy.

For so long she had heard her mother's voice in her ear, chiding her to be a more proper woman, to leave her wild, childish fancies and to settle: to marry, to serve, to be dull and unquestioning, to be meek and unremarkable. And how badly it had all gone!

Charlotte and Gregoire stood facing one another. Gregoire took her hands in his.

"Of course," Gregoire said and smiled at her. "It suits you well. You are too clever and prone to adventure to leave it off."

"Are you angry?" Charlotte asked.

"Would you care if I was?" Gregoire asked. He sighed. "Charlotte, some part of me will always want to protect you and shield you from dangers. But I know to stop you would make you not only hate me, rightly, it would destroy you to not pursue this. There is danger everywhere. Let us embrace it and make a mockery of it."

Charlotte's relief was profound. "I would not be stopped by you, but my love for you would have decreased if you could not understand this."

"I am pleased," interrupted Cardinal Richelieu, whom they had managed to both forget, "that the happy couple have come to such an understanding. Let us then continue to settle our accounts. I do have a prisoner to deal with today. Monsieur de Medici, you no longer require passage to England. With your sister having a good estate and a healthy dowry, and with the restoration of the family name, she will hardly be needing my assistance in finding a good marriage, though I will provide one if you like. What reward can I render you for your service?"

"I cannot think of anything. All my desires are provided for," Gregoire replied.

"Really?" the cardinal said wryly. "All but one, surely."

Gregoire knelt down before Charlotte. "His ever-perceptive Eminence is quite correct. All but one. Charlotte Menard, you are the only woman I have ever loved. I have loved you since we were children. I love all of you, even the dangerous and irrationally daring bits. Would you be my wife?"

Charlotte looked at her suitor. For so long she had wanted this and never imagined that Gregoire would be thus enamored or in a position to freely offer her his marriage. Sensing her hesitation, Gregoire ploughed on.

"You need not keep my house or mend my clothes, and you will not need to bake my bread or quit your employ. I'd like it very much if we could have children, but I will be equally happy if it is only you and I and the defense of the state through sword and subterfuge until our untimely deaths in the service of France when we are called to the Lord."

Charlotte burst out laughing. "Any sane woman would run screaming from this proposal."

"You are no sane woman, no ordinary woman," Gregoire replied. "You are clever and daring and slightly mad. I would have no one else, not for all the housekeeping and bread and mending and children in all of Christendom."

"Such wonderful epithets," she said. "And I'll have no other but you, who constantly strives to keep up with me rather than stop me."

"Keep up! I mean to overtake," he said, but he was all smiles as he leaned in, and then it was all kisses.

"Please, Madame Menard, tell him your answer and take your kisses elsewhere. I am very busy man, and you are both making me blush," the cardinal interrupted, though his amusement was too obvious for it to be a threat.

"Yes, Gregoire, let us marry as soon as possible," Charlotte told him. "And then onto the next adventure. I never imagined Your Eminence to be such a capable matchmaker."

"The heathen idol cupid has rendered unto me his bow, and God has given me His blessing for this." He rose and inclined his head slightly toward Gregoire. "Well done, Monsieur de Medici. And you, Madame Menard, we'll discuss your next assignment a week hence. *Adieu,* to marriage with the both of you."

Charlotte and Gregoire left the cavernous, imposing chamber, hands held fast. As they emerged into the brilliant Paris summer sunshine, Gregoire turned to her and said, "All I ever dreamed of as a boy was to become a musketeer and to marry you. For so long I thought what happened to my family was my fault for my hubris. Now I realize it was nothing of the sort. If anything, it was a test to see if I was good enough for either."

Charlotte touched his cheek. "It was the actions of others, Gregoire, that caused your family's fall. And it was your actions that saved it."

"And yours. Though no one will know it."

"It is how I want it. There is only one thing I want people to know, and that is we are married."

Charlotte threw her arms around him and kissed him joyfully. It was a kiss like their first kiss, a kiss that felt like home. It was all the sweeter for knowing from that moment on, Gregoire would always be her home, and his kisses her safety.

"To the church, then," Gregoire said, when at last they breathlessly parted.

"I'll race you," Charlotte replied and took off at speed, her heart soaring as she heard Gregoire's footsteps unfaltering behind her.

THANK YOU FOR READING

Thanks for reading *The Lady Is A Spy*. I hope you enjoyed it!

To make sure you never miss a happily ever after, join my mailing list and stay up to date with new releases, specials and other fun stuff.

And while I have you here, it'd be awesome if you would take a few minutes to review the book on Amazon or Goodreads, to share your thoughts with other readers!

You can find all those links in one place:

https://linktr.ee/AnnaKleinAuthor

ABOUT THE AUTHOR

Anna Klein is a literary nerd, general geek and a big fan of cats. She has a Masters degree in horror fiction, and in addition to writing novels, she writes and runs live action role-playing (LARP) events. Anna lives in Aotearoa New Zealand with her husband.

She is also the author of two sweet contemporary romance books about geeky people falling in love. Flip the page to find out more!

ALSO BY ANNA KLEIN - THE MODERN WOMAN'S GUIDE TO FINDING A KNIGHT

All's faire in love and war...

Connie leads a double life. During the week, she is an up–and–coming designer and dressmaker, creating sleek, elegant gowns for the wealthy elite. But come the weekend, Connie becomes Lady Constance, a member of the House Felicitous at the local Renaissance Faire, creating beautiful historical garments for herself and her friends and teaching dancing to fair attendees. Fearing loss of business should her stylish clientèle discover her extracurricular activities, Connie keeps her professional life and her faire life carefully separate. However, everything changes when she's saved from certain death by Sir Justin: a rising star in the joust and an actual knight in shining armour.

Behind his mask as Sir Justin, Dominic is confident and charismatic, but out of his armour, his courage fails him, and to his own horror he finds himself accidentally pretending to be his own best friend. Suddenly, he is in Connie's life as two different men: the elusive Sir Justin who courts her over the internet and from behind a suit of armour and Justin's 'best friend' Dominic who hangs out at her apartment and helps her move. The lie only grows bigger and Sir

Justin finds himself faced with the most frightening challenge he can imagine: extricating himself from his lie and winning Connie's heart as his true self.

But there's something rotten afoot at the Faire, something that threatens its future, the community that has grown there, and even Sir Justin's life. Will Lady Constance find the courage to step up and risk everything to defend her friends, save the Faire, and rescue her knight?

https://linktr.ee/AnnaKleinAuthor

ALSO BY ANNA KLEIN - AS SWEET AS HONEY

Three dates to prove they don't belong together..

Chelsea Lambert is an unhappy receptionist, working for Honey, a glitzy dating website that she thinks is more than a bit sleazy. But she's got bills to pay, especially if she wants to avoid her manipulative aunt's clutches. She didn't plan on spilling her views on Honey to the handsome stranger who rescued her from being late for work - and she certainly didn't plan on him being the gold-plated sleazebag she was mocking - yet here she was, ready for the earth to swallow her up.

Neil O'Connell, a Californian businessman, thought New Zealand would be an idyllic escape. The perfect place to get some space, avoid his past and definitely to avoid complicated attachments. When he is the unwitting target of Chelsea's vitriolic diatribe, he unexpectedly finds himself having complicated feelings, the exact kind he needs to avoid.

When Chelsea's aunt puts pressure on her to find a rich husband for her cousin, Chelsea sees an opportunity. She proposes a deal to Neil: three dates with her glamorous cousin, who is the perfect match for him. And three date with her. Three dates to show she can't be dazzled with dollars. Three dates to prove they don't belong together.

It's just three dates. What could go wrong?

https://linktr.ee/AnnaKleinAuthor

ALSO BY ANNA KLEIN - HEART AND HEARTH

Addie didn't expect to inherit a ramshackle bed and breakfast in a tiny town - let alone a magical one!

She's sure a mistake has been made - her whole life, she's been taught to avoid her witch heritage. Her arrival has stirred something in the old town and Addie finds herself wrapped up in a decades old mystery.

Spring is just arriving, bringing with it new growth: for the plants, for Addie, and for the nearly-forgotten town.

A novella length book set in Aotearoa New Zealand, part of the Witchy Fiction project.

https://linktr.ee/AnnaKleinAuthor

www.ingramcontent.com/pod-product-compliance
Lightning Source LLC
LaVergne TN
LVHW091112080826
845145LV00008B/1884

* 9 7 8 0 4 7 3 6 2 3 6 1 6 *